CAGED

MACKENZIE GREY: ORIGINS #2

KARINA ESPINOSA

To all the strong women in the world.

Yes we can.

Dear Reader,

As a precaution, I want to inform you in regards to the book you are about to read. Please be aware the writing entails some sensitive trigger worthy material along the lines of sexual abuse (Chapter 16). I ask you to use your own judgment should you decide to read further.

Thank you,

Karina

PROLOGUE

No. Way.

No FREAKIN' way!

This had to be some kind of cosmic joke from the universe—not that I should've been surprised, since Lucian had a way of making you do uncomfortable things, but still. I crossed my arms over my chest and tapped my foot in annoyance. With a sturdy duffle bag slung over my shoulder, I oozed bad attitude. I was cranky and hungry. The bus ride to Los Angeles didn't make enough pit stops for a girl with a wolf inside her. Where was the justice in that?

"Are you just going to stand there or are you going to get in?" said the vampire who was my appointed tour guide since arriving in L.A.

He wore head-to-toe black with messy, dirty blond hair and hazel-colored, puppy dog eyes. Lord Jesus, help me. I focused on his paleness to divert my lingering eyes and reminded myself that the individual before me was a FREAKIN' VAMPIRE.

"I'm not getting in that death trap you call a vehicle. I enjoy being *alive*," I smirked.

"As if I hadn't heard *that* one," he chuckled. "But in all seriousness, are you going to get in the bloody Jeep, or am I going to have to carry you in myself? I'm not opposed to either option."

"Touch me and you die—again."

The vampire put his hands at his hips and sighed. "Two to zero; you're a real Ace, there."

I shrugged. "I try."

"Well, try some more inside the car. We're late."

"Late for what?"

"It's a secret." He grinned. His pearly whites shone in the city night and I caught a glimpse at his fangs. Gross.

"I don't like surprises," I growled.

"Someone's cranky." He laughed and took a step toward me. "Easy way or the hard way, Ace, your choice."

I scanned the busy parking lot of the Greyhound station in downtown Los Angeles. It was crowded at this time of night, full of flashing lights and yelling people. It would be impossible for me to make a run for it.

"Don't even think about it," he said, and I rolled my eyes.

"Fine," I relented. "At least tell me your name." I bypassed the vampire, tossed my duffle into the back of his Jeep, and climbed in with a huff.

"Roman." He dug around in his pockets for the car keys to an old Jeep Wrangler, its paint peeled and the body rusted. It squeaked when he sat in the driver seat.

I snorted. "Are you serious? Talk about a cliché."

"Excuse me?" He gave me a sideways glance as he turned the ignition and pulled out of the parking lot.

"Dude, you have such a vampire name. Did your folks know you'd turn into a blood sucker?"

"Ha-ha. Very funny," he deadpanned. "So what's your name? I was only told to look for the wolf with bright gray eyes."

I dug into my back pocket and pulled out my new driver's license, curtesy of Lucian Young—the Head Vampire of New York. "Well, according to my new ID, my name's Hillary Clinton." I wrinkled my nose. "Any way I can get this changed?"

Roman laughed. "Yeah, I know a guy."

I nodded. "Does this mean you're going to be my tour guide? What are your tour rates like—a pint of blood a day?" I smirked.

"Ouch." He crossed a hand over his heart. "Who leaked my rates to you?"

"Probably the same one who dressed you," I muttered as I gazed out the unzipped window. His laugh was background noise as I took in the quiet streets of L.A. at 3 A.M. I was used to the city that never slept and felt out of place in this strange new world. My human best friend, Amy, wouldn't like it out here. She needed 24-hour pizza joints and Gray's Papaya.

"Penny for your thoughts?" Roman asked.

I sighed. "I would tell you to mind your own business, but I'm curious about where we're headed."

"Has anyone ever told you how ... *demanding* you can be?"

"All the time, but you still haven't answered my question."

"That's because I can't. Not until we're closer to our destination." He turned on the radio and the calming guitar strains of U2 played against the harsh gusts of wind passing through the vehicle. "Just sit back, relax, and welcome to Los Angeles." When he winked, I nearly blew a gasket.

THE WORST PART about this two-and-a-half-hour car ride: how easy it was for my thoughts to drift. I thought about everything—where we were going, where I would be sleeping, if I was safe ... All these questions and more raced across my mind until my thoughts wandered back to a few days ago during the last full moon.

My time spent with Sebastian and Jonah was something I would never forget. Leaving them was hard, but if given the option again, I wouldn't change a thing. I needed to free myself from the shackles of their Pack. I couldn't live under the thumb of men who didn't believe I had the brains to think for myself. This wasn't the fifties, and I would never give up my freedom.

I squinted as the wind picked up and sand blew in my face. I checked the dashboard and saw it was almost five in the morning. The sun peaked over the horizon, giving it that mesmerizing, orange-pink glow.

"Hey, check that sign over there. We're here," Roman said as he pointed.

I looked over to my right and saw a sign that read, **Mojave National Preserve**. Okay, so I knew my location, but that still didn't answer the rest of my questions.

"What the hell are we doing here?"

He sighed. "Damn. Lucian told me you were a pup, but I didn't think you were clueless. We've entered the Mojave Desert, home of the Desert Wolves. Their lineage goes back further than the almighty European Summit you wolves love to worship. Grab a paper and pen and start taking notes, Ace."

"My name is Mackenzie, not Ace, and I don't worship

anything but coffee and possibly bacon," I snapped, feeling good about my declaration. No one had a hold on me, much less the Pack. I was a lone wolf.

"Yeah, okay," Roman snickered. "Listen, once the quest is over, I'll make sure to get you back to your Pack safe and sound. You don't have to act tough around me. Vampires and wolves are peaceful here in SoCal."

"Quest, as in a *vision quest*?" I didn't care that he mistakenly thought I was Pack, but I couldn't believe the audacity of Lucian to arrange a vision quest. I didn't know the exact details, but from what Bash said, I needed a lot of training before I could go through a quest or the consequences could be fatal. If things went sideways, the wolf could consume me and I would lose my humanity. If I managed to complete it unharmed, then it would be the most freeing experience of my life. I wouldn't be angry or have this emptiness in my chest anymore. I'd be whole.

Even so, I wasn't ready.

"What other kind of quest is there? Relax, you pups prep for this your whole youth. Although, you're kind of old to be doing it now. Either way, it's like, one in a million who fail. I haven't met a bugger that's failed yet. Don't be the first, Ace."

He winked and I felt like I was going to throw up.

I just might be the first.

To cover my unease, I quipped, "What's up with your eye? Do you have Tourette's or some shit? Stop with the winking."

He laughed. "You're a funny girl, but you need to relax. You'll pass the quest."

I shifted in my seat. "So ... let's say for argument's sake that I *don't* pass. What will happen ... to me?" As I waited for his response, I seriously debated jumping out of the car mid-ride and making a run for it.

How could Lucian set me up like this? Could I find my way back to the city from the desert? Shit, I don't drink enough water as it is, which means I'm going to be dehydrated. Oh my gosh, I was stupid *to trust a damn vampire!*

"You're looking a little pale over there, what's going on?" Roman asked as he pulled onto the shoulder of the road and cut the engine off. He jumped down from the Jeep, adding, "Listen, it's no big deal. You go out there, be one with your wolf, get a vision, and you're done. It's gravy."

Shit, shit, shit. "Uh, where are you going?" I stumbled out of the Jeep and followed Roman to wherever it was he was headed.

"We have to walk from here. The Desert Wolves aren't too far off the main road. Come on; no worries, Ace."

The early morning was windy, and I squinted to avoid getting sand in my eyes. My hands itched from the dry air and I already missed the East Coast humidity.

We stepped over parched plant life and small cactuses, but what worried me was the idea of running into a snake or scorpion. As a city girl, rats and cockroaches were the vermin I was used to. I tip-toed behind Roman in my now dusty, black-and-white Converses. Wearing a black V-neck tee shirt and ripped jeans, I certainly wasn't prepared for a hike.

"We're almost there. See the fire up ahead?"

"Yeah." I peered about a quarter of a mile ahead, seeing what looked like a bonfire. "But I don't see anyone. Where are they?"

As paranoid as I was, the first thing running through my mind was that this blood sucker brought me out to the middle of nowhere to slaughter me into tiny wolfey bites and add me to his salad for dinner. Morbid, I know.

After a few minutes, we made it to our destination and the vampire sat on one of the logs that encircled the fire.

"Where—?"

But before I could ask again, a small figure emerged from around the flames. A woman who looked to be in her eighties shuffled toward us. Her salt and pepper hair was divided into two braids on either side of her head that reached all the way down to her hips. Colorful beaded necklaces and bracelets clanked against each other as she walked. Her skin was the color of rotten oranges and as tough as leather—but it was her sharp yellow eyes that froze me in place.

"Hillary Clinton, I'd like you to meet the Alpha of the Desert Wolves—La Loba," Roman introduced us, and from the little bit of Spanish I knew, her name meant *She-Wolf.*

My jaw dropped as I realized what Roman had said—she was an Alpha. How? I guessed things really were different on the West Coast. I extended my right hand to her to shake, and like most wolves I'd met, she stared at it as if I were offering an Ebola sandwich.

The vampire snickered. "Uh, what are you doing, Ace?"

"Ignore him, Mackenzie Grey, Lone Wolf. I am familiar with your customs and admire you for them," she said, her voice that of a three pack-a-day smoker. I was taken aback that she knew my name ... and status. I thought Lucian planned to keep it a secret.

"Wait—lone wolf?" Roman choked out, but I ignored him.

La Loba shook my hand, her skin warm like a freshly brewed cup of coffee on a winter morning. She felt like home, familiar. I could sense her wolf. I remembered how Sebastian told me I'd always be attracted to my own kind.

"You seek a vision quest. Is this true, Mackenzie Grey?"

My eyes fell to my sweating hands. I wasn't one hundred percent sure this was what I wanted to do. I hadn't prepared for this experience, and that was mainly out of fear; fear of the unknown was worse than anything. What if I didn't make it? When I had my first Change, I was furious about the cards I'd been dealt, but now I never wanted to give it up. Not in a million years.

"I'm sure," I said as I stared unflinchingly into La Loba's eyes. I needed to convey my certainty and unwavering resolution, because I couldn't afford to go into this vision quest fearing a negative outcome. If I wanted to succeed, I had to do what I knew best—survive.

"Then follow me, Mackenzie Grey." She turned back around and headed in the direction from which she came.

"Hold on a second, Mackenzie – what Pack did you belong to before?" the vampire asked as his cold hand latched onto my upper arm.

"I've never belonged to a Pack. Didn't Lucian tell you? He's hiding me."

"Wait, what? Shit, wait—that bastard—hold on, Ace. Don't go through with the quest. You'll fail." His brows were scrunched up in concern. "Forget everything I said before and don't go through with this. This is hella-dangerous. You need proper training."

"I thought you said this was gravy?"

He shook his head. "Not for you. Definitely not for you."

"I'll be okay, *Ace*, relax," I mimicked him.

"You don't know that!"

"Why do you even care?" I arched a brow.

"I don't, but it doesn't mean I can't warn you about the potential dangers. This is ludicrous! You're unprepared and you won't make it out."

I shook my head and chuckled. "I won't fail, Roman. It's not in my nature."

This time, I winked at him, leaving him frozen in my wake as I followed La Loba out into the cold, unforgiving desert.

Its black fur bristled against the wind, silver eyes shining against the crescent moon. It stalked across the desert dunes, his large paws making indentions in the sand. The wolf sat back on its hind legs and howled to the sky before sharing its vision:

> *Rights are wronged. Screams are held.*
> *Etched scars kill hearts that dare rebel.*
> *Victory eats in the presence of the saved.*
> *Oppression rests in idle hands of the brave.*
> *Lest fear ignite a silence too loud to ignore,*
> *Untie the bonds, reclaim what's yours.*
> *Tides rise in the wake of the unchained moon.*
> *Innocent howls split open the sleeping tomb.*
> *Only one will champion and lead the enraged.*
> *No warrior surrenders. No warrior remains caged.*

1

ONE YEAR LATER

I wondered what Amy was doing right now. Probably dancing at some party or at home stuffing her face with ice cream. Oh, and watching *House of Cards*. I wanted to be back home with her. I wondered where she got a job—most likely Google. That genius kid. She was out there concocting a plan for world domination while I was here, wearing skimpy clothes in a dirty, STD-infected nightclub called *Ground Zero*.

Multi-colored strobe lights flashed around in a frenetic, seizure-inducing pulse. Anyone who thought coming here was fun had to either be on drugs or was mentally unstable. Sweaty bodies groped one another on the dance floor as deafening electronic music blasted from the speakers. I had an itch at the corner of my eye that I'd wanted to rub for the past half hour but had to refrain. If I did, the fucking eye liner and mascara gunked on my face would get smudged, because Lord knew I wasn't delicate enough to scratch it like a lady. I'd get raccoon eyes and scare off the guy I was supposed to be meeting.

Damn demons and their stupid, annoying issues. Why couldn't they just abstain from kidnapping and killing each other? They needed better hobbies, like knitting or golf.

The static from the cordless device in my ear startled me, almost making me trip in the hooker heels I had on. "For fuck's sake, you guys. You scared me half to death! I almost dropped a brick."

"TMI, Ace," the voice in the earbud said. "Are you good?"

"No," I deadpanned. "But that didn't stop you assholes from dressing me up like a prostitute though, so why ask?"

Roman chuckled. "If it's any consolation, you look like an expensive escort. Fancy, like the ones politicians get."

"As if that's supposed to make me feel better, jerk."

"Heads up, you got an ogre coming at your six," he said.

I straightened my back, pushed my itty-bitty chest forward, and leaned a little to my right to add some swag. I felt like an idiot, but this was what I was told would be sexy.

"That'a girl," Third-Eye Lou crackled through the earbud. "Pop that hip."

"If you open your mouth one more time—either of you— when I'm done, they'll have to fish you out of the Pacific," I gritted out just as the ogre I'd been waiting on slid his hand down my lower back.

"Hello there, beautiful," he purred into my ear. "I couldn't help but notice you from my table."

I turned around and met the six-foot-plus ogre who looked like he'd OD'd on steroids. His ill-proportioned body made me raise both eyebrows. "Oh, thank you," I simpered. I wanted to barf.

"Would you like to join me? I'm over in the VIP," he boasted, pointing to where he was sitting.

"Oh my gosh, yes! That sounds like fun," I giggled—maybe a little too hard.

"Take it down a notch, Ace," Roman said in my ear. "You sound like a thirteen-year old who just met One Direction."

I cleared my throat in agitation. "Lead the way," I entreated as the Ogre directed me to his section. I turned around and looked up to the second floor of the night club, flipping my middle finger at the one-way mirror overlooking the dance floor where I knew Roman and Third-Eye Lou were watching.

"Maybe later," Roman replied, and I imagined him winking at me.

"Asshole," I muttered.

"Excuse me?" the ogre asked.

"Oh nothing, sorry." I smiled.

He grinned and unhooked the velvet rope separating the VIP section from everyone else. "I've never seen you around here. Is this your first time?" he asked, leading me to a couch where we both took a seat.

"Yes, it's my first time. I found a flyer on one of the bulletin boards on campus and thought I'd give this place a try."

His grin widened. "I see. And you came alone?"

I attempted a blush. Easier said than done. "Well, my girl-friend was supposed to meet me, but she bailed at the last minute."

"Well, I'm glad I can keep you company." He leaned closer and draped his arm across the back of the sofa. "Would you like a drink?" he offered.

I nodded. "Please."

"I'll be right back." With a lecherous wink, he stood to go to the bar.

Once he was out of ear shot, I sagged into the couch. "His breath smells like something died," I complained.

"Don't worry; not much longer and you can go," Third-Eye Lou said.

"I heard ogres eat the intestines first before anything else. Maybe that's what you smell?" Roman suggested, followed by the sound of their laughter in the background.

"You're both having a *little* too much fun with this. I have to deal with this thing's odor and play bait while you two get to gallivant all up in his office and do the cool detective stuff."

"I know, Ace. I promise you unlimited ice cream and a Netflix binge after this," Roman offered. "Alright, he's on his way back. Stay sharp."

The ogre was dressed in navy blue slacks and a striped, white and blue button up. The first few buttons were undone, revealing a peppering of chest hair. His small waist looked weird compared to the oversized proportions of his muscular upper body. He sat down and handed me a pink cocktail with a pineapple on the rim and an umbrella poked jauntily through it.

I accepted and gave a shy smile. "I didn't get your name ... Can I guess? You look like an Arnold to me. Am I right?"

His laugh was strained, and I saw a vein in his neck twitch in aggravation. "Uh, no, more like Danny."

"Oh!" I giggled and turned away, secretly taking a whiff of the drink he handed me. It smelled awfully salty for a beverage that was supposed to be sugary, which meant he added Rohypnol. *Damn it.* The bastard roofied the girls. I couldn't wait to dig my claws into this creep.

"Do you like the drink? I wasn't sure what you liked, but you seem like a sweet girl, so I got you a sweet drink."

At his wide smile, I threw up a little in my mouth. I wet my lips and pretended to swallow. "Mhm, yes, I love it. How'd you know?"

He chuckled. "Call it a gut feeling. Cheers." He brought his glass between us and I clinked mine against his. When I brought the tumbler to my lips, I only took a small sip. My wolf would burn the drug off quicker if consumed in small quantities.

My phone buzzed in my clutch and I set the drink down on the table in front of us. "Excuse me, I'm sorry," I giggled again and pulled out my cell. The name *Tiffany* was on the screen with the message, **Brad broke up with me!** and a crying emoticon. That was my cue from Roman that they had left Danny's office and were waiting for me in the alleyway.

"Oh, no!" I shrieked in mock horror.

"What's wrong, darling?"

"Tiffany needs me. Her boyfriend just broke up with her." I frowned.

"Well, I'm sure she'll be okay; she's a big girl. Why don't you finish your drink first and then leave?" he said, his expression extra friendly.

I shook my head. "No, I better go now. They've been together for years." I stood and straightened my mini skirt. "Thank you for the drink, Arnold."

"It's Danny." His upper lip twitched. "And yeah, anytime," he mumbled half-heartedly.

I waved and stumbled out of the VIP section. My stupid heels were making my ankles wobbly.

"Ace, report?" I heard through my earbud.

Once I was halfway across the dance floor on my way to the side door of the club, I said, "On my way, be there in two."

I pushed through the people huddled in the sticky hallway waiting to use the bathroom and slammed my shoulder into the back door with the 'Exit' sign glowing above. The brisk Los Angeles night draft would make a normal girl stagger back from its bite, but I was different from your average Jane. My wolf wouldn't fail me.

The alley was dark, the brick walls on either side smeared with graffiti. Trash littered the ground; it smelled like a delightful miasma of piss, beer, and cigarettes. As soon as I stepped into the night, my first mistake was not shutting the door behind me. I realized this when I was caught off guard by a meaty hand grabbing my arm and jerking me back.

"What the fuck?" I exclaimed, tripping over myself and falling into a pair of big arms.

"Sweet girls don't talk like that," Danny reprimanded behind me.

"Shit," I muttered.

"Ace? What's going on?" Roman demanded, but I couldn't answer him. Danny had already stuck one of his fat fingers into my ear and plucked out my communication.

"Let me guess—SIU?" the ogre growled. "I should have pegged you from the get-go. Want to know what tipped me off?"

"Not really." He slammed me onto the brick wall of the nightclub and I grunted. "You mess with me and my business, and I'll end you!" he yelled in my face.

I grimaced. "Oh God, please stop talking. Your breath is killing me already!"

That only infuriated him further. "You're the one they call Ace; the one who doesn't know when to shut up."

"I'm glad my reputation precedes me," I deadpanned.

Danny grinned. "That's all that's going to be left when I'm done with you."

"Sure," I said. "Starting with the intestines?"

"What?"

Catching him off guard, I rammed my knee straight to the crown jewels. He squeaked and loosened his grip on me. "I swear, that should be my signature move," I grunted as I brought my elbow to his face. Maneuvering out of his hold while he was incapacitated, I swirled behind him, and with a little help from the wolf, pinned him to the wall. "Hands behind your back, big guy." I interlocked his wrists and pinned them behind his back.

"Are you okay?" Roman called from the sidewalk.

"Yeah, what took you so long?"

"Sorry, was trying to get Third-Eye Lou in the car before he decided to pay for a lap dance, the old geezer." Roman shook his head and handed me a set of handcuffs. I clipped them onto the ogre's wrist and Roman helped me drag him out to the street.

"You're stupid if you think you'll get away with this! He'll find out. He'll find me, and then he'll kill you!" Danny snarled, the vein in his neck working double time.

"Damn, Ace, you weren't kidding about that breath," Roman exhaled.

My claws extended and seized onto the ogre's neck. "*Who* will find us? What's his name?" I snarled.

For the last four months, Roman and I had been searching for a demon who had been kidnapping and exploiting sucubi in the City of Angels. As partners of a new, covert squad of the LAPD called the Supernatural Investigative Unit—not very creative, I know—it was our job to handle the weird and keep it away from humans. But we were nowhere close to finding out why or who this damn demon was. We didn't even have a name.

Danny chuckled. "You think I'm telling you?" He shook his head. "He'll kill me if I snitch. I'd rather rot in a jail cell."

I released him. "Don't worry, Stank Breath, that can be arranged."

L.A. TRAFFIC WAS THE WORST. The slamming of brakes at the last minute, the unending grid lock, and people jaywalking made me grind my teeth. It was two in the morning and I was already losing my patience—although I was glad when Roman tossed me the keys and volunteered to sit in the back seat with the smelly ogre. If I had to deal with him again tonight, I didn't think I could refrain from punching him in the throat.

To avoid any further traffic, I took a detour through a few mostly empty side streets. We rode in a police-issued, unmarked car—a dark gray Dodge Challenger. The power of the engine was a welcome change to Roman's crappy, beat-up Jeep. We could only drive this beauty while on duty, and I took every opportunity to be in the driver's seat. Third-Eye Lou sat beside me, his light snores breaking the silence as he laid against the headrest with his mouth slightly open. His tilted fedora covered most of his face, but I could see him opening and closing his mouth as if he tasted something.

When I turned my head back to the road, I slammed on my brakes, jerking us to a screeching halt. Lou gurgled his last snore and Roman reached for my shoulder to keep me from flying through the windshield. Two black SUVs blocked the path before us. If I hadn't stopped when I did, we would have smashed into them—we were only a few feet away.

"I told you they'd come for me," Danny gloated from the backseat. Roman did what I had been itching to do: he grabbed the back of the ogre's neck and slammed his face into Lou's seat—finally waking the old man from his sleep.

"What—what did I miss?" Lou sat up and adjusted his hat. "What's going on?"

I pointed to the windshield just as the doors of the SUVs opened and four ogres stepped out. "Stay in the car, Lou."

"You don't have to tell me twice," he grumbled and strapped his seat belt tighter.

I rolled my eyes. As if that would make a difference. Before I stepped out of the vehicle, I peered over my shoulder and caught Roman jamming his elbow into Danny's face for good measure, knocking him unconscious.

"I'm coming with you," he said as we both exited the Challenger.

"There's a gun in the glove compartment," I whispered to Lou. "Just in case." He nodded, but I saw his trembling hands as he cupped them together. Third-Eye Lou wasn't used to being out in the field with me and Roman.

"Looks like we got ourselves a party, Ace," Roman quipped as we walked toward the ogres.

"Aw," I pouted. "And I didn't bring my dancing shoes."

One of the ogres smirked. "A vampire and a wolf, how cute." He pointed to our car. "Give us Danny, and we'll forget this ever happened."

I hung my arm over Roman's shoulder and leaned into him. I had long ago swapped my hooker heels for a pair of sneakers. It was a fashion statement I wasn't pulling off well.

"They think we're cute." I pinched Roman's cheek. "And besides that, they think we're here to negotiate."

Roman chuckled. He was just as, if not more, cocky than I was. We were quite a pair.

"Silly ogres," he taunted. "Tricks are for kids."

We both laughed as the four of them ran toward us. Pushing off each other with practiced ease, we rammed into the oncoming boulders. I tackled one to the ground, slashing my claws over his face and chest. Another pulled me off and I caught air until he set me down none too gently. My back slammed onto the ground as I tucked my chin into my chest to avoid cracking my skull against the concrete street. I didn't have enough time to scramble to my feet before he snatched me by my flimsy shirt and hauled me up.

"I beg of you, don't speak," I pleaded. Another encounter with their breath was not something to be desired.

"What Pack do you belong to, little girl?" he demanded. "Lunas aren't supposed to play with the big boys."

Instead of answering, I placed my hands on his shoulders and kneed him in the stomach. Wrapping my arms around his meaty neck, I flung myself around until I straddled him from behind. With my other hand I palmed his forehead and twisted his head, snapping his neck instantly. I added another notch to my mental kill list.

Number four.

The ogre crumpled to the ground and broke my fall. The first one I had tackled managed to get up and jam his elbow into the backseat window where Danny was.

"Hey!" I yelled. Roman was still dealing with the other two ogres and I debated what to do: help Rome or stop them from grabbing Danny. I didn't have much time. One of the ogres had Roman by the neck while the other was breaking off a tree branch to ram through his heart. *No!* I slipped out the pocketknife that was clipped to the inside of my bra and flipped it open, ramming it into the side of the ogre who held Roman. He roared and back handed me, but it was enough to break Roman free. I landed on the asphalt for the second time tonight and shook out the stars that clouded my vision.

The sound of someone tapping the hood of a car stirred me into action. "Come on!" an ogre yelled. I looked over at our Challenger and saw Lou's distressed face and knew Danny was no longer inside. The other ogre tossed Roman to the side and ran to the SUVs. Before we could do anything, their tires squealed and they rocketed down the street, leaving us in the dust.

Roman was lying on his side with his fangs out, hacking up blood.

"Shit." I stood and ran to him. "Are you okay?"

"Yeah," he grimaced. "Their blood is fuckin' nasty."

"Gross." I jerked away from him. "Was their breath not enough of an incentive to keep away?"

He rolled his eyes. "When I'm getting choked to death and about to get a stake to the heart, it's my only option."

"Yuck." I gave him a hand and helped him up. "We lost our first and only lead."

He turned to our car and saw the old man wide-eyed in the passenger seat. "I know he all but pissed himself."

"Let's get him back to the station." I clapped Roman on the back. "What did you guys find at the nightclub, anyway?"

"Not much." He shook his head. "Lou was able to hack into some of his files, but all we got was a list of numbers and letters. It'll take him a while to decode it all."

I sighed. "Do you think we have enough time to do it before they snatch up more girls?"

"Probably not."

2

_____

"You think he'll talk?" Roman asked as he tossed his keys on the kitchen counter.

"Probably not, but he'll be fun to mess with." I wiggled my eyebrows and plopped down on the sofa in the living room. I reached for the TV remote and changed the screen from cable to Netflix. "Now about that binge you promised ..."

Roman laughed. "I'm wiped, Ace. Rain check?"

"You know, there's only so many empty promises I can accept," I pouted.

"The sun will be rising in like, an hour. I'll pass out before we even finish an episode."

"Fine," I sighed. "I'll get some shut-eye too. Maybe wake up before nightfall and hit the streets—talk to my informant. There has to be something that we're missing about this case."

"Of course there is, but how about we forget about it for now and do something else?" Roman crawled over the sofa and slid above me. His hip aligned with mine and I felt his arousal against my thigh. "I can't break *all* my promises tonight." He snuggled into me, his lips gliding over my collarbone.

I tilted my head to the side and let him trail kisses up to my ear. "I flicked you off. That wasn't an invitation." I tried to sound annoyed, but it never worked with him.

"Why wait until a nightmare for you to crawl into my bed?" he whispered. "Let's just skip the appetizer and go straight to the main course, shall we?"

I laughed and he lifted his head. "You did *not* just compare me to a meal."

"I'll compare you to whatever you want me to," he smirked.

I sighed as I pulled off his shirt, my fingers already tracing the fine lines of his body. Every muscle was taut and frozen in time. He would never get old or fat. He was pure perfection—and I was going to hell for enjoying him. *One-way ticket for Mackenzie Grey, please.*

"What are we doing, Rome?" I asked as I gazed up into his hazel eyes.

"The same thing we've been doing for the past few months— having fun. What's wrong?"

I encircled my arms around his neck, his arm hooking behind my back to bring me closer to him. "I don't know, I just want to understand us—whatever *us* is."

"Ace, I thought we discussed this already," he whispered over my lips. "We're fooling ourselves if we think a relationship could ever work." He kissed me and I didn't hesitate. I opened my mouth and let his tongue slip inside. My hands were already in his hair as he worked my shirt off and unclipped my bra. He lifted himself and I grabbed his belt buckle, his lips trailing kisses down my neck.

"I just," I moaned, "I just thought maybe—maybe, I don't know." I tried to form a complete sentence, but Roman's tongue had made its way to my breast and I couldn't think straight. I stretched my arms above my head and gripped the armrest of the sofa, my claws latching onto the fabric and ripping it. Soft suckles and licks made my body purr. The sensation was doubled by my wolf, heightening every touch and spiraling my way toward ecstasy.

"I guess we're due for a new couch." Roman's cold breath hardened my nipple.

"Yes," I groaned.

He chuckled. "Ace, don't worry about the future. All I care about is the present and you. Can that be enough for now?"

I didn't care anymore as I nodded my head vigorously. I started to pull his jeans over his ass, pushing them down his thighs with my bare feet. "Hurry," I moaned as he slid my mini skirt around my waist. With no warning, Roman flipped me over and pulled my ass toward his hips. My back slammed against his chest as he wrapped his arm around my stomach, holding me steady. His stony lips lingered on my skin as he adjusted himself.

"None of it matters, Ace, because I'll never get enough of you," he said as he slammed me down onto him.

I screamed into the empty apartment as my eyes flashed silver in pleasure. I couldn't get enough of him, either.

THE AFTERNOON SUN filtered in through the slits of the curtains. Cold arms wrapped me up against a brick of ice. Roman held onto me as if he feared losing me. I wished these small moments were enough, but they weren't.

When I moved to L.A., staying with Roman was supposed to be temporary until Lucian could find me my own place. But as the nights went by and my dreams were plagued by nightmares of Caleb—the skinwalker I had killed—I had trouble falling asleep. I wasn't completely over Caleb, but the nightmares were few and far between. And once I began working with the LAPD, I started keeping a notebook—my own personal kill list. Currently, there were four tally marks in it, a reminder of the depth of bad I was capable of. Roman was the only thing that helped me sleep. What started off as a friendly bedmate to keep me safe and not alone at night, turned to a cuddle here and there, and then full-on getting naked. If Sebastian and Jonah could see me now, I think I'd give them both a damn embolism.

I was okay with our arrangement at first. We scratched each other's itch, without the complication of labels and formalities. Roman didn't want a relationship because it was rare to find someone who would live forever, so I understood why he didn't want to get his hopes up. At the time I didn't care because I wasn't feeling anything. I'd lost my whole life and needed to do something reckless that would make me feel alive, and it worked—until now. Now I wanted more.

I peeled Roman's arm off me, freezing when he stirred. I didn't want to wake him and try to go for another round—I didn't have the stamina to keep up with him. When I felt it was safe for me to move again, I quickly slipped out of bed. Wrapped in a discarded bedsheet, I tip-toed out of his bedroom. The clock on the microwave said it was just past three in the afternoon. I had less than three hours until Roman woke up, and I didn't want to be there when he did.

After a shower, I dressed and slid into my leather jacket—filling the pockets with some cash, my new driver's license, and my TAP card, which was L.A.'s version of a metro card. I still refused to drive Roman's barely functional Jeep. That piece of junk was going to fall apart one day, and I wouldn't be surprised if I was in it when it did—but that was Rome's baby. He wouldn't give her up. Using public transportation also reminded me of being back home—although the train stations in L.A. were cleaner than the ones in New York City. Alas, I took the 733 bus toward Santa Monica and got off on Main and Grand. A seventeen-mile trip to Venice Beach took me almost an hour and a half to get there—go figure—but that was traffic in the City of Angels.

The boardwalk was packed with tourists and locals as usual, the smell of weed as potent as ever. Bikini-clad women rolled around on roller blades while steroid-induced, Speedo-wearing muscle heads lifted weights. A drum circle on the beach pounded out a rhythmic soundtrack, and reggae music could be heard on the mile-long boardwalk. It always took me a while to find Jorge in this chaos. He was never in the same location, but he usually stayed near the drum circle hippies.

"Ay, Ace!"

Hearing my name, I swerved through the crowd toward the pier and found Jorge, a four-foot-seven imp.

"Que pasa? What you doing 'round these parts, chica? I thought it'd be a while before I saw you again." His shaggy hair and overgrown beard were dead giveaways that he was homeless, and if not, his dirty, shabby clothes drove the thought home. I always offered to help him out, but he refused any sort of assistance.

Jorge was of Hispanic descent, but he wouldn't share his exact roots. The thing was, the imp was my CI—Criminal Informant—and a retired soul collector, which was a really nasty demon who fed off the essence of humans. Jorge was one of my first busts when I started working with the LAPD.

"You know why I'm here," I said as I nodded my head toward Zelda's Corner—an eatery off the boardwalk that was his personal favorite. I started walking toward the little sandwich shop, knowing the imp would trail behind at a distance. I ordered two Professor Ted sandwiches, two bottles of water, and a box of mini donuts to go for Roman. He would kill me if he knew I stopped here and didn't bring him some. I sat on the bench outside the shop with our late lunch as Jorge popped a squat beside me. "Twice in one week? Are you trying to get me killed, Ace?" he giggled. Not the reaction I was expecting.

I handed him his lunch and started to unwrap my sandwich. "Sorry, I know this is risky, but I really need your help."

"So, you thought a Professor Ted would be a good bribe?" He offered a lazy smile as he waved the sandwich in the air—a dead giveaway that my buddy was high as a freakin' kite.

My claws extended and I gripped his tattered shirt. "Are you smoking?" I exclaimed.

He laughed and breadcrumbs fell out of his beard, making me gag. "Of course, *chica*. What are you going to do, lock me up?"

"Don't tempt me, Jorge. Your little ass won't get far, and my wolf always enjoys a good chase." I flashed my silver eyes.

He slouched in defeat. "Bueno," he exhaled, taking a hearty bite. "What do you need?"

"That tip to check out Ground Zero panned out. Thanks, by the way." He nodded. "We found some files in the main office with some kind of code, a list of numbers and letters that we haven't been able to figure out. Lou is working on cracking it now."

"*Y que?*" Jorge shrugged. "What you need me for?"

I rolled my eyes. "Do you seriously need me to spell everything out for you? Do you know anything else that can help us? We're at a dead end here."

"What's in it for me?" He gave me a side glance.

"You have *got* to be kidding me," I muttered. "You get to keep your damn freedom, Jorge. *That's* what's in it for you. We have a deal here – you got out on good behavior, and now you're my eyes and ears on the streets. If you back out now, I can always send you back to your cage in Ironwood."

He snarled, "You won't always be able to threaten me, you know. *Un dia*, your threats will be meaningless."

"Yeah, yeah, but until then, my threats stand. So, what'll it be, little guy?"

He rolled up the sandwich wrapper and threw it into the nearest garbage can. His nose flared in frustration, his tan skin darker and dirtier than the last time I saw him. "Los docks," he mumbled. "Check los docks."

"The—?" I paused. "Oh shit, the docks!" I wrapped an arm around Jorge and pulled him into a hug. "Now was that *really* so hard?"

He tried to shrug me off, but I wouldn't let him go. "Get off me, wolf!" he grumbled.

I squeezed him tighter and tried not to breathe him in. He smelled like he hadn't showered in weeks. "You know you lurve me, Jorge. And that's why you're going to head to Skid Row," I whispered as I slid some change into his utility jacket, "go to the shelter, and tell them I sent you. Get a shower, little man, you reek. And then lay low until this blows over, you understand?"

As soon as I released my grip, he pushed off me. "And if I don't?"

I sighed. "Then that ogre on the boardwalk who's been eyeing us this whole time is going to eat your intestines."

Jorge froze. "I knew you'd get me killed."

I shook my head. "If you follow my instructions, you'll stay alive. Now go while I hold him off."

Jorge paused for a moment and stared at me, his glazed eyes searching for something, and once he found it, the imp was gone in a flash.

I turned in the direction of the Speedo-wearing meathead, not surprised to see he'd already dropped his weights and was marching toward me. Except he was staring at Jorge's retreating figure, trying to catch up. I stood from the bench and intercepted the ogre with a palm to his chest.

"Whoa, in a hurry?" I smiled, my canines sliding out. "Running in Speedos is not a good look for anyone. I highly suggest a change in wardrobe."

The ogre growled.

"Easy there, big guy. You don't want to get into a whose-is-bigger contest with me." I winked. "I can guarantee you, mine is."

My fist connected with his abdomen, making him hunch over. Now that he was level with my height, I gripped his neck with my claws and hauled him toward an empty alleyway, slamming his huge torso into the wall.

"Now, let's do this the easy way. Who sent you?"

The ogre spit in my face, effectively shredding the last bit of patience I had. I roared into the quiet neighborhood, my claws and canines extended at full length. The hair on my arms thickened and my face scrunched up like a prune as it morphed into a half-shift—half human, half wolf. The hand clamped onto his neck squeezed tighter, cutting off his air flow.

"Now, you've pissed me the fuck off," I growled inches away from his face.

His hands scrabbled at his neck, trying to dislodge my claws, but it was no use. He wheezed and choked, but I refused to give in.

"Let's try this again. Who the fuck sent you?" I loosened my grasp just a smidge and he sucked in a hearty pull of air.

"Ron," he choked out. "Ron sent me."

"And who is this Ron fellow? Where can I find him?"

The ogre shook his head as much as he could. "I don't know. No one knows."

I squeezed harder. "You're not helping me," I taunted.

He tapped my hand. "The imp," he choked. "The imp was right. Go to the docks—in Long Beach."

My eyes flashed silver. "Thanks for the confirmation," I growled. Twisting my wrist, I snapped the ogre's neck. His body slid down the brick wall, his eyes wide open as they lost focus and fogged over. His large frame slammed onto the ground, unmoving.

Number five.

Times had changed. I was no longer the clueless werewolf who was scared to get her hands dirty. I was tough, confident, and I kicked ass.

I took two steadying breaths and then morphed back to my

human self—tucking the wolf away for when I needed her again. I pulled my cellphone from my leather jacket and dialed the station.

"Hey-yo!" Lou answered.

I cleared my throat. "I need a clean-up."

3

I hauled ass to the SIU. It was already dark out so Roman would most likely be there—at least I hoped so. We needed to hatch a plan and catch ourselves a bad guy, and luckily, I knew exactly where to go. I took the 733 bus back downtown, got off on Main Street and 7th, and ran the quarter mile to the police station.

The Supernatural Investigative Unit was located in a three-story building in a desolate section of downtown Los Angeles. The first floor housed a small lobby with a receptionist who manned the desk. We never took the time to learn their names because the turnover for that position was unreal. The kinds of "people" we caught that passed through this building would give any human nightmares. To the right of reception was a small coffee stand, and to the left were the elevators. I was headed to the second floor, which housed the squad room.

"Third Eye Lou, where you at?" I burst out of the elevator and stomped into the office.

"Back here!" the old man attempted to yell, his voice cracked from age and too much whisky. "Whatda'ya got for me?" He came out of the break room with a newspaper in hand, sauntered over to one of the four desks that was assigned to him, and plopped down. His desk was the only one with three computer screens and a laptop. He was our tech guru. There was nothing Lou couldn't figure out, which was why he had to accompany me and Roman on our excursion last night in the field to hack into Danny's computer. Other than those rare occasions, Lou stayed at home base and out of danger.

"The codes, Lou, I know what they are!" I grabbed the rolling chair from my desk and slid over to him. "They're cargo containers from the docks. I think that whoever is snatching up sucubi is shipping them somewhere. I don't know where, though. I haven't figured it all out yet."

"Hmm." Lou tapped his chin and pushed his reading glasses up the bridge of his nose. "You might be on to something. The numbers and letters are scrambled, but it could be a way to throw someone off in case it's found. Let me play with them for a sec."

I nodded. "Is Roman here yet?"

He grunted. "You two have been quite a pair lately. Anything you want to discuss?"

I leaned back in my chair. "It's none of your business, Lou."

"Everything's my business, Ace." He tipped his fedora back and pointed to the third eye on his forehead. It blinked a few times before it scanned the office. "And I only ask because I worry for ya. Rome is a good guy, but he's not the steadiest mate. Just be careful. I know how you wolves are."

"I'm not like most wolves, and we have an arrangement. It's all good, Lou," I said as I fiddled with the pens Lou kept scattered on his desk.

"Talking about you not being like most wolves ... where is it you said you're from again?" he asked, his gaze crawling over to me from the computer screens.

I sighed. "How many times do we have to have this discussion? I come from a sma—"

"A small Pack in Wyoming ... I know." He turned his attention back to the numbers on the screens. "You still sticking with that story, Ace?"

"I have no idea what you're talking about. Now put that eye away, it gives me the heebie-jeebies." I shivered as he adjusted his fedora.

He laughed. "What happened to the big bad wolf?"

I shrugged. "Whatever, just get me those cargo shipments and I'll be out of your hair."

"Sure thing, Ace."

I wheeled myself back to my desk and walked toward the elevators to head to the third floor—our in-house gymnasium. It had everything from treadmills to a regulation-sized boxing ring. As I pushed the up button, the elevator doors pinged open to reveal Roman standing there, wearing a dark green shirt that brought out the green flecks in his hazel eyes. His dirty blond hair was messy as usual, and that smirk on his face was enough evidence that proved he knew how good looking he was.

"Well, isn't this my lucky day? Just the beauty I wanted to see." With a wink, he pulled on the front of my t-shirt and dragged me into the lift. As soon as the doors closed, he pushed the red emergency brakes to stop the elevator from moving.

"About last night ... are we good?" he asked, his eyes squinted.

"Why wouldn't we be?" I quirked a brow and artfully avoided the topic. I felt silly for even bringing it up and wanted him to forget I mentioned anything. Did I want more than a friends-with-benefits relationship? Yes. But did I want it with Roman? Not sure.

"Ace," he whispered, pulling me closer to him. "Don't do that. Talk to me. I care about you, and the last thing I want to do is mess with your feelings."

I shook my head and looked down at his chest. "I don't know, Rome." My mind recalled what Lou had just said—*Roman is a good guy, but he's not the steadiest of mates.* I didn't need anyone to remind me of that fact. I'd witnessed Roman's flirtatious nature many times. "Are you sleeping around?" Verbal diarrhea got the best of me. As soon as the words left my mouth, I wanted to palm my forehead in embarrassment.

He stilled. "You think I'd do that?" His hazel eyes drilled into me. "Because I wouldn't, Ace."

"This is stupid." I chuckled awkwardly and attempted to step away. "I'm being stupid, let's just forget I brought it up."

Roman slid his hand in mine. "You're not being stupid—you're a wolf. I understand your kind believes in monogamy, but I don't need anyone but you, Ace." He grinned and kissed the corner of my mouth.

"Not now, Rome." I shook my head and tried to cover up my excitement. I was relieved he wasn't sleeping around. I didn't want to end things, but if he was, I knew I'd have to. "I saw Jorge today and he told me where to find our baddie." I changed the subject.

That caught his attention. "Oh?"

"The numbers are cargo containers! Whatever they're shipping, we have to get to it before it leaves," I said. "I also got a name —Ron—do you recognize it?"

Roman shook his head and pulled the emergency knob, opening the elevator doors on the second floor. We exited and walked into the squad room. "Can't say I do, but who knows? Might be an alias."

"Ace!" Lou yelled. "You were right. They're containers located at the port at Long Beach, and they leave tonight for South Florida."

I snapped my fingers. "I knew it! Let's go!"

"Hold on there, Ace, we can't go by ourselves. After getting our butts kicked last night, we need back-up," Roman suggested. "Do you know who the shipyard belongs to, Lou?"

Third-Eye Lou began typing on his computer. "Hold on a sec ... there! They belong to a Ron Goldstein."

Roman and I said at the same time, "*Definitely* an alias."

"Where is the shipment located?" I asked as Roman walked to his desk and made a call.

"Pier G, off the southeast basin," Lou answered.

I nodded, walking to my desk and opening the bottom drawer that held my duty belt and gun—clipping everything on. I headed to the office closet and pulled out two bulletproof vests, placing Roman's on his desk just as he cooed on the phone, "Aw, come on, babe, it was just one time. No big deal." He paused for a beat. "I also have a box of jewelry with your name on it. Do us this solid and it's yours." Roman paused again and crossed his fingers. "Great! Thank you, doll face."

"Who was that?" I asked as he hung up the phone.

"I just spoke with Alana. The water nymphs are on their way."

———————

THE WEATHER at the docks was chillier than it was inland; the Pacific Ocean gave the wind an extra kick. We drove through the tunnels of the port until we reached Pier G. I tapped my ear bud to make sure it was in place and connected with Third Eye Lou back at home base, confirming the water nymphs were already in position and waiting for our command. Once we reached a dead end, we parked the Jeep and walked through the shipyard, eyeing the cargo containers for the numbers on our list.

"Lou said they're closer to the docks." We walked at a fast pace, adrenaline coursing through my veins. I couldn't resist the grin that spread across my face. The anticipation of danger was my new choice of drug.

"There!" Roman pointed to the second-to-last row of containers. "That one's on our list."

He stuffed the paper that had the list of cargo shipments in his pockets and we jogged to the end of the dock. It was only a few feet away from where the water nymphs were located at the southeast basin.

Roman drew a small black pouch from his pocket and unzipped it. Choosing a tension wrench and a diamond pick, he put the rest of the tools in his pocket and went to work on the locked compartment.

"Hurry up," I whispered as I stood as lookout. Hearing voices nearby, I peered around the shipyard. "I think someone's inside, Rome." I turned back and watched over his shoulder.

"It's all about the tension," Roman smirked as he turned the small wrench clockwise until the lock unclicked. "There."

"Will you stop trying to show off your lock picking skills to uh ..." I looked around us, "no one, and just open it up already?"

He chuckled. "Okay, okay, sorry for wanting to bask in the art of breaking and entering." Roman unhooked the rod that locked the door and swung it wide open. Then we both froze.

"Holy ..." Roman started.

"Shit ..." I gasped.

About a dozen women were huddled in the back of the container—their clothes tattered, their skin blotched with dirt and bruises. Greasy hair framed their terrified expressions as an odor wafted toward us that made me swallow a gag. The rancid smell of feces invaded my sensitivity and I wondered how long these women had been kept imprisoned.

"Rome, Ace, report?" Lou said through our ear buds.

"Lou, call the cavalry. We found them ... all of them," I responded as I slowly inched inside, my hands outstretched in defense. "Hey ... we won't hurt you, we're here to help."

Their glassy, wide eyes of terror would haunt me for years to come. I couldn't imagine what they had been through.

"W-Who are you?" one of them asked. Her hands were spread out as if protecting the others from us.

I gulped. "I'm Ace, and that's my partner Roman." I pointed behind me. "We're part of SIU, and we've been looking for you for months."

Many of the women relaxed as understanding dawned on them.

"Are you the sucubi?" I asked.

Several heads nodded in response. "Yes," said the one I

assumed was their leader. "But we need to hurry. These compartments have silent alarms."

"Shit," I muttered. "You heard that, Rome, Lou?" I yelled back.

"I'm on it, disabling them now," Lou said.

"Alright, let's hurry up then," Roman instructed, motioning the women forward. None of them twitched a muscle.

"It's okay," I reassured them. "You can trust him."

With some hesitation, they started moving forward and Roman herded them toward the road where our car was parked and a bus was on its way.

"My name is Sonya," the leader introduced herself. "There are more of us in other shipping containers. I'll show you which ones."

"Lou, we might need another bus," I reported through my earpiece. "How do you know there are more?"

Sonya shivered. "We sometimes hear their screams in the middle of the night."

I nodded and gave Roman a heads up before I left, asking him to stay with the others. Sonya and I walked around a few more cargo containers until she stopped in front of one with numbers I recognized from our list.

While I picked the lock, I asked, "How long have you guys been here?"

"It varies. Some of us have been here longer than others. I was taken around three weeks ago."

I unlocked the door to that container and was able to open three more containers with Sonya's help, when a commotion by the road drew my attention. The shriek of multiple women rang out in the night and I growled, my wolf making its presence known.

"What's going on, Lou?" I said as I ran back around, following the sound of screams.

"Roman has company, Ace. Ogres—lots of them."

I stopped running and looked around. There were many frightened, tired faces who were in no position to fight, even if it was for their freedom. I scanned the area and realized we were only a few feet from the basin.

"Tell Roman to lead the ogres toward the water. And what's the ETA on back-up?" I started running in the opposite direction of the commotion, toward the nymphs.

"They're five minutes out and Rome is headed your way."

"Good." I growled into the night. My canines and claws emerged, and my face morphed to half wolf, half human.

A few seconds later, I saw Roman sprinting at full speed as a gaggle of murderous ogres chased him. His arms pumped at an inhuman speed, his knees almost hitting his chest. "Now!" he yelled.

My thumb and pointer finger pinched my lower lip and I whistled into the night. A splash in the water was the only hint that the water nymphs heard my call.

I crouched on all fours as Roman skidded to a stop before me and whirled around to meet our oncoming threat. "Ready?" he asked, not a bit out of breath.

"I was born ready," I gloated, causing him to roll his eyes.

The nymphs shot out of the water like a volley of rockets and landed on either side of us. Their wild, undulating hair was coiled in a series of intricate knots with shells braided into their strands, and their eyes glowed a menacing shade of fathomless black. They were a mix of cuteness from *The Little Mermaid* and psychotic-serial-killer Helena from *Orphan Black*. If they hadn't been on our side, I would be terrified of them. They were vicious water creatures who could only be appeased if offered shiny things. Luckily, Roman had promised them an array of silver costume jewelry for their assistance. About twenty nymphs joined the battle, baring their razor-sharp teeth at the enemy.

"Can we eat them?" the nymph beside me asked.

I wrinkled my nose. "Uh ... no, sorry."

"Shame," she sighed.

The ogres came to a stop in front of us. "What a treat," one of them said. "A whole feast, just for us, boys."

"Ugh, gross," I groaned. Roman nudged me to shut up. "Sorry."

"Easy there, gentlemen," a voice from behind the ogres said. "I need a word with our intruders before you gorge on their flesh."

"Flesh?" I muttered to Roman. "You told me they eat intestines!"

He glanced at me in disbelief. "As if that's any better, Ace?"

"Ace?" The voice moved to the forefront of the group and we realized he wasn't an ogre. "Why is that name so familiar?"

I took a few steps forward and shrugged, offering a smart-ass smile. "What can I say? I'm a popular gal."

The man who approached appeared human, perhaps sixty years old. He was tall and slender and walked with a cane, and his receding hairline only had a few strands of thinning black hair, streaked with white. His smile was sinister and oily, which matched the filth in which we'd found the sucubi.

"Popular you are, dear. I've heard your name floated around for quite some time. Always sticking your muzzle where it doesn't belong." He rested his cane in front of him, both hands holding it steady.

"My muzzle?" I touched my nose and felt the ridges of my wolf's snout. "Well now, that's just insulting."

"A comedian, I see," the stranger observed dryly.

"I like to think of myself as a Humorist Extraordinaire, but whatever floats your boat." I grinned. "Now, are we going to continue exchanging such stimulating banter, or are you going to tell us who you are? Wait … can I guess?" I asked, not waiting for a response. "You're Ron Goldstein, aren't you?"

"Do you want a cookie?" he deadpanned.

I thought about it for a moment, tapping my finger on my chin. "Only if it's chocolate chip. I don't want none of that oatmeal shit," I stuck my pointer finger in my mouth and gagged.

"Has anyone told you how goddamn annoying you are?" he snarled, his patience growing weary.

"All. The. Damn. Time," I smirked. I dropped to a crouched position and kicked off running on all fours, my wolf growling and canines snapping.

When an ogre jumped in front of me, I slashed my claws across its chest and kicked it out of my way. My silver eyes zeroed in on Ron. "Come back here, Ronnie," I taunted as I ripped the throats of a few more ogres foolish enough to stand in my way.

Six, seven.

Blood dripped from the tips of my fingers as I prowled toward the skinny bastard who was walking backwards—away from me. I heard fighting break out all around me as Roman and the nymphs joined in the fun, providing me with an opportunity to go after Ron.

"You think you're better than me?" he spat, almost tripping as he continued his backwards walk. "You wolves are far worse!"

"All that yapping is makin' me hungry, Ron," I teased, steadily catching up to his unsteady steps.

"Stop! Just stop!" he yelled, his palm outstretched. "You don't want to kill me."

"And why is that, Ronnie? Give me one good reason why I shouldn't, as you say, gorge on your flesh?"

"Because," he screamed, spittle flying out of his mouth. "I have one of yours!"

In two leaps I was in Ron's face, my clawed hand wrapped tightly around his neck. I slammed his body to the ground. "Where?" I growled. The protectiveness of the wolf erupted out of me. It didn't matter if I was a lone wolf or not. I wouldn't let him hold one of my own hostage—or anyone, for that matter.

"Promise," he squeaked, "you won't kill me."

"Yeah, whatever, now tell me *where!*"

"Ace?" Roman approached me. "What are you doing?"

"Speak, you piece of shit!" I snapped my canines in his face.

"Container," he choked, "... container 44-HJK-1579."

I slammed his head on the concrete, making it bounce like a basketball and knocking him unconscious.

"What the hell, Ace? We need him alive!" Roman shrieked as I stood and started looking around the shipyard. Roman crouched beside Ron's limp body and checked for a pulse. "You're lucky he's still breathing."

"That's not luck," I muttered as I spotted the compartment.

A few uniformed police officers ran toward me and I directed them to Roman for the debriefing. I sprinted toward container 44-HJK-1579 and didn't waste time trying to pick the lock. I ripped the bolt off with a loud roar, unconcerned if the human officers saw me. The doors flew open with a force that made the doors bounce off the sides of the container and my eyes switched to night vision. Inside were a few sucubi huddled over a girl who couldn't be older than ten years old. Her face was caked with dirt, her light brown eyes wide and fearful, with strawberry blonde hair that needed a good wash. But most of all—she smelled like a Luna.

4

Forty-eight sucubi from up and down the West Coast were rescued at the raid at the port of Long Beach. Ron was an incubus—a male succubus—who had been kidnapping his own kind to sell overseas as sex slaves. He had been using the ogres as bodyguards, but that plan was eliminated when most of them were slaughtered tonight. A few got away, but most were either dead or incarcerated along with their boss, waiting to be processed and shipped to Ironwood. Good riddance.

I sat behind my desk and stared at the little girl seated in front of me who returned my stare unflinchingly. She was in that awkward stage as a kid when you were so tall and thin, your pants hitched up to your ankles. Which was more noticeable because she kept bouncing her right leg. We were alone, as most of the sucubi were at the bus station headed back home. Only a few others were still milling around the station.

"Do you have a name?" Her eyes barely blinked as she watched me, not saying a word. "Alright, kid, you need to tell me something. Where are your parents, at least? Can I call someone to get you?" Silence. "Do you need to use the bathroom?" Nothing.

I slumped into my chair and rubbed my eyes. I was exhausted and hungry. Fatigue was rearing its ugly head and I was losing patience. The only thing I had left to do before I could go home was take care of this little Luna girl, and I had no idea how.

"She has no one." A voice by the elevator startled me. I turned to see who had spoken and saw Sonya standing at the entrance of the squad room.

"Excuse me?" I said. "Do you know her?"

She nodded. "Her name is Emma. Her mother was a succubus."

My eyes widened. "How?"

"Her father was a wolf. The wolf gene is dominant over every other species."

I nodded. "Okay, well, do you know where I can find them?"

Sonya's smile fell. "They're both dead. Her father was a lone wolf who was killed by the Pack, and her mother was captured by the incubus. She died last week of dehydration."

My gaze went back to the girl. Though her eyes had glossed over, she didn't dare shed a tear. Her resolve was strong. I saw it in the rigidness of her body.

"Are you going to take responsibility for Emma?"

Sonya gasped. "What? I can't!" She inched back to the elevators. "She needs to be given to the Summit. They'll be able to care for her."

"The Summit?" I jerked my head back. "Are you nuts?"

"Are you?" she questioned. "You should know better!"

I froze. *Shit.* Those were the rules all Pack wolves lived by. I couldn't let it be known I was a lone wolf. The only ones on the West Coast who knew my secret were Roman and La Loba of the Desert Wolves, and I needed to keep it that way.

"What I mean is, shouldn't she be with someone familiar?"

Sonya thought about it for a moment. "I can't. I just met her, and I'm not prepared to care for a wolf. The Summit is her best chance of survival. I'm sorry," she apologized to the girl before turning to leave. "And wolf?"

I glared at the succubus. "What?"

"Thank you … for saving our lives. If you ever need anything … you have our loyalty." With that, Sonya turned and exited the room.

"Well, damn. Ain't that a bitch?" I mumbled.

"You got that right," the kid said.

I whipped my head around. "What?"

"I said, you got that right. This shit sucks."

I thought my jaw would drop to the floor. "Uh … you shouldn't talk like that," I said, baffled by her sudden chattiness.

"You shouldn't either," she countered. "And you're not sending me to the Summit. I don't want to be a Luna."

I wanted to burst out in laughter but had to swallow the urge. *Ditto, kid.*

"Well, unless you have some family I can send you to, the Summit is your only option. How old are you, anyway?"

"Eleven and a half, and the Summit isn't my only choice. You *could* just let me go," she proposed. "I'm big enough to take care of myself."

I chuckled. "No, you're not. You haven't even hit puberty yet, so you haven't shifted. There's no way you can survive on your own."

"Yes I can."

"No you can't."

"Yes I can."

"No."

"Yes." She inched to the edge of her seat. "Yes, times infinity!"

"No, times infinity, times infinity!"

She gasped, horrified. "You can't *do* that!"

I smirked. "I'm a grown up, I can do whatever I want."

She slouched into the seat and huffed, "That's bullshit."

"Hey!" I reprimanded. "Language."

"Whatever," she muttered and turned her head away.

With that small victory, I stood and headed toward the breakroom to get her something to eat. She had already gulped two bottles of water.

Roman leaned against the doorway with a grin on his face. "How's it going with the little one?"

"She's impossible," I complained. "And the mouth on her is despicable."

He laughed. "Oh yeah? Seems familiar, don't you think?"

I glanced over my shoulder to find her flipping me off. "That little monster!" I gave her the finger in return. "And here I was about to get her a snack."

Roman covered his mouth with the palm of his hand and suddenly looked like he was about to sneeze. "Holy shit, Ace, don't you see it?"

"See what?" I asked, frustrated. "That she's an annoying little girl with no manners? Yeah, I caught on."

"No, Ace, she's a mini you."

I was taken aback. "Excuse me?" I placed a hand over my chest in mock horror. "That kid is nothing like me!"

Roman shook his head. "She is *exactly* like you." He leaned forward and whispered, "Right down to the rebellious part that prefers to be a lone wolf rather than conform." He pushed off the door frame and walked over to Emma. She smiled brightly at him as he extended his hand in introduction.

That conniving little person ... she was going to be trouble.

"Do you need to use the bathroom?" I yelled to her. That bouncing leg was driving me nuts.

"I don't use public bathrooms!" she screamed.

What the fuck?

"Well, aren't you a bundle of rainbows and sunshine?" I mumbled.

I headed to the break room and grabbed a roll of Ritz crackers that I had started eating last night, and another bottle of water for Emma. When I came back, she was giggling at Roman and I had to swallow the urge to growl. How come she was sweet with him and not with me? I was pretty darn lovable.

"Alright, kid. Eat up, because we have to go." I dropped her snacks on her lap.

"Go where?" she asked.

"Mojave Desert."

Roman's eyes snapped to me. "You're taking her to the Desert Wolves?"

I nodded.

"So soon?"

"Yes, Roman," I huffed. "I can't take care of her, and she's better off with the Pack, anyway."

His hazel eyes narrowed as he grabbed me and pulled me to the side, out of Emma's earshot. "Isn't that a bit hypocritical of you? You know she's not better off with them."

"What do you expect me to do?" I whispered. "You want her to shack up with us, and we become all domesticated and shit?"

He blanched, as I expected. "Of course not."

"Then what other options do we have?"

"All I'm saying—"

"I know what you're saying, Rome, but we don't have any other choice. I'm sorry." I pushed past him. Emma was munching loudly on the crackers, crumbs decorating her face and shirt. "Ready, kid?"

She pouted. "Can I stay with you? Pretty please?" she pleaded. Her glassy eyes were almost my undoing. The last thing I wanted was for her to lose all that attitude and independence by joining the Pack. But if she was alone on the streets when puberty hit, she could hurt someone. She needed to be taught the *right* way, unlike me.

"Sorry, but you can't stay with me. I'm not an adult," I admitted. I still had a lot of growing up to do before I could take on the responsibility of caring for a child. I squatted in front of her. "But I promise that the wolves will take you in and love you. Just don't ever lose that spunk." I winked at her, hoping to soften the blow.

"My mom told me I was different from the Lunas."

I smiled. "You're definitely something, kid, but that's what makes you special. You're going to kick ass as a Luna, you hear?"

She cracked a smile and nodded.

"Good. Now get your stuff and let's go. It'll be a long drive."

THE DRIVE to the Mojave Desert was always a pain for me. I hated sitting still that long, and I dreaded meeting with the Desert

Wolves. Even though I shifted with them on full moons, I wasn't part of their Pack so I was still considered an outsider. But even with all that drama, I appreciated La Loba and everything she had done for me. She was the reason I survived my vision quest. That day was forever ingrained into the forefront of my mind and I got chills every time I thought about it.

I spent the day in a sweat lodge with La Loba guiding me through the ritual. When it was finally over I spent the rest of the day puking, about to pass out from heat stroke, and kept mumbling a riddle I had been gifted with—my vision. To this day, I still had no idea what it meant and didn't care to figure it out.

Roman pulled over on the side of the road nearest the encampment. I slid out of the Jeep and pushed the seat forward to allow Emma to get out. She didn't move.

"Come on, Emma. This isn't the time to mess around. It's almost morning and Roman needs to get home."

"Why?"

"Because he's a vampire."

"So he can't be in the sun?"

"He can, but it just makes him tired."

"So why didn't he stay home?"

I sighed. "Emma, stop with the million questions. Please just get out of the Jeep."

Her small eyes widened. "Please, Ace, *please* don't take me to them! I'll be nicer to you, I promise," she gulped. Her little eleven-year-old hands gripped the back seat of Roman's beat-up Jeep. Her knuckles whitened with fear of the unknown. I could relate.

"Hey, Rome?" I called out. "Why don't you go on ahead? We'll be there in a minute." He nodded and walked toward the fire of the Desert Wolves. I climbed into the Jeep again and slid next to Emma.

"I'M NOT SCARED," she said. Her voice sounded impossibly small.

"I know you're not. You're too tough to be scared. I mean, what eleven-year-old has the balls to stand up to *me*?"

"Eleven and a half," she corrected.

"My bad, I meant eleven and a half. You see? Balls of steel you got there."

There was a pause as she looked away from me. "What are they going to do with me?"

"They're going to give you a home, Emma. A home with your own kind."

She gulped. "My mother said Lunas are slaves. I don't want to be that."

It was my turn to freeze in uncertainty. Lunas weren't slaves, but they weren't free to be who they wanted to be. The wolves had a defined, hierarchical structure that Lunas were forced to follow. It was the main reason why I was on the run and not part of the Brooklyn Pack. I couldn't live like that. I'd rather be dead.

"You won't be a slave, Emma," I lied without looking at her. "Whatever Pack you belong to, don't let them change you—and you give them hell if they try."

Through my peripheral vision, I saw her scoot closer and wrap her arms around me. She exhaled a tiny sigh of relief as she rested her blonde head on my arm. "Thank you," she muttered, still embracing me.

I wrapped my free arm over her as a single tear escaped my

eye. I didn't deserve a thank you. I was putting the last nail in her coffin.

EMMA WOULDN'T LET GO of my hand as we walked across the open land to the entrance of the camp. The Desert Wolves lived freely, most of the time in their wolf form. You would have thought being a wolf full-time would make them less human, but it didn't. They were incredibly in tune with the earth. If anything, they were more human than wolf. I envied that sometimes.

La Loba and her son Emmanuel stood by the bonfire with Roman. While she was old and weathered, Emmanuel was tall, strong, and a warrior. He was shirtless, wearing only a pair of basketball shorts. His long black hair was braided behind him, falling to mid-back. And like his mother, his eyes glowed yellow —the only inkling that his wolf was present.

Everyone knew La Loba was the Alpha of the Desert Wolves, but Emmanuel assumed the role when they met with the Summit, since women couldn't officially hold that position. Their tribe believed the oldest in their community were the wisest, and as such were the only ones qualified to be Alpha. I liked their way of thinking, even if they had to practice their ways in secret.

"We missed you last month," Emmanuel said as he smiled, his canines peeking over his bottom lip.

I shrugged. "Was busy with a case, but I'll be around next time."

He nodded. "Good. So what brings you around on a non-full moon?" His pale eyes glided over to Emma and then back to me.

I cleared my dry throat. "Emmanuel, La Loba, I'd like to introduce you to Emma ... a Luna."

Emma's hand tightened as it held mine and she stepped closer to me, hiding part of her face behind my arm.

"Hey ..." she mumbled.

"Hello, little one." La Loba smiled at her, lines of age and wisdom indented around her mouth. "Welcome to the Mojave."

Emma peeked between the gap in my side and arm. "Yeah ... thanks."

I had to stop myself from laughing. This little girl would be a tough nut to crack.

"Her father was a lone wolf and her mother was a succubus," Roman explained.

"Was?" Emmanuel asked.

"Yes. They were both killed," I said. My gaze roamed around the desert. "I-I came to you since I am unable to contact the Summit myself, but I was hoping you would be willing to, uh ..."

"Mackenzie," La Loba stopped me. It was the first time I'd heard someone speak my given name in over a year.

"Yes?"

"I know what you want," she said, "but unfortunately it cannot be done."

My chest caved in on itself. I had hoped to ask her if she would take Emma into her Pack instead of reporting her to the Summit. With the Desert Wolves, Emma would have a freedom unlike the Lunas in other Packs. Their way of living in private was different, more compassionate to Lunas.

"Why?" my voice cracked.

La Loba's yellow eyes were sad as she walked toward me,

clasping my free hand in hers. "My beautiful girl." She smiled. "That is not my journey to take, dear."

"What?" I hadn't realized I was crying. I licked my salty lips as a hiccup escaped me. "But that doesn't make any sense."

Her hand reached to wipe away my silent tears. "You, Mackenzie Grey, must take that journey. Only *you* can save her."

I shook my head, pushing away from her and dragging Emma along with me. "I can't do anything!" I yelled, slamming my palm on my chest. "I'm stuck, powerless to help anyone."

"That's not true and you know it." She paused. "You were given a year to prepare, and I've kept quiet to allow you time for it, but now it is time."

I froze. I hadn't shared my vision quest with anyone but La Loba, and I only spilled the beans because she was there and I didn't understand what it meant. At this moment, I regretted having confided in her.

"What are you guys talking about?" Roman interrupted.

I stared at La Loba, but all she did was quirk an eyebrow and wait for me to respond. I had no choice but to tell him.

"My vision," I started. "It said some stuff that I have no clue about."

"Can you tell me about it?" he asked.

I shifted on my feet and sighed. "Look, it's no big deal. It's a bunch of jumbled words that have no significance. Can we get back to the issue at hand?"

"Fine," Emmanuel said. "We'll take the girl to the Summit."

I shut my eyes and squeezed Emma's hand.

"Ace," she mumbled. "It's okay. I'll be fine." She peeled her sweaty hand out of mine.

"I know you will be." I squatted before her. "Don't forget what I told you. Give them hell."

Her smile never reached her eyes. "I will. Balls of steel, remember?"

I chuckled. "Right on." I straightened and glared at the two Desert Wolves. "What's going to happen now?"

"We'll take her to the Summit, and they will place her with a Pack that suits her better. We have no say in where that is," Emmanuel explained. "I'll escort her personally. You don't have to worry."

"Okay." I nodded. Emma wrapped her fragile arms around my waist and squeezed me tight, reminding me of Amy and her bear hugs.

"I still don't like you," Emma joked, "but thank you."

"I don't like you either, kid, but you're welcome."

5

Since wrapping up the case with the sucubi and transferring the rest to Homeland and the FBI to investigate the human trafficking, I was left with not much else to do. Nothing more exciting than petty thefts and complaints trolled the supernatural streets of L.A. Whenever we had slumps between cases, Roman and I usually went up to Big Bear Mountain or Malibu, depending on the weather. This time around I was in a foul mood, making any vacation impossible.

I relieved some stress at the punching bag. I couldn't sleep, so I ran to the station and headed straight to our third-floor gym. With my hands wrapped in gauze and white tape, I hit the bag for hours until my knuckles were numb and I could barely stand. I had never been the type to go to the gym—my workout typically consisted of sitting in front of the TV being lazy, but out here in L.A., I found myself in there more times than I could count. The first thing Roman did when I arrived from New York was train me to fight in this very gymnasium. As a lone wolf, self-defense was important.

"Need a partner?" Roman called from the doorway.

I shook my head. "Nah, I'm good."

I heard the thud of his heavy combat boots as they made their way towards me and stopped right behind the punching bag—holding it in place.

"You're gonna have to talk to me, Ace. I worry for ya."

"I'm fine," I grunted as I kept hitting the bag.

"Sure you are. That's why you're in here almost every day, not sleeping or eating. You look like shit."

"Don't sugar coat it," I grumbled.

"This isn't a joke, Ace. You're not taking care of yourself. Of course I'm going to be concerned."

"Why?" I exclaimed, raising my hands in the air. "You're not my boyfriend. Why the fuck do you even care?"

He scoffed as if I'd kicked his puppy. "Stop misplacing your anger and just tell me why you're *really* pissed. It's Emma, isn't it?"

I cracked my knuckles impatiently.

"I might not be your best friend Amy, but I'm the next best thing, Ace. Stop bottling stuff up and just tell me!" he pleaded.

I'd never seen Roman like this before. He raked his hands through his dirty blond locks, obviously frustrated. His hazel eyes gleamed with concern.

"It's what La Loba said," I relented. "About my vision quest."

"What about it?"

Contemplating whether I should tell him or not, I huffed and turned toward the boxing ring in the middle of the room. I dug through my messenger bag for my wallet, searching for the folded sheet of paper I'd crammed in one of the credit card slots. I pulled it out and handed it to Roman.

"What is it?"

"My vision."

His eyes widened slightly but he composed himself, unfolding the paper and flattening out the wrinkles. He cleared his throat before reading aloud:

"Rights are wronged. Screams are held.

Etched scars kill hearts that dare rebel.

Victory eats in the presence of the saved.

Oppression rests in idle hands of the brave.

Lest fear ignite a silence too loud to ignore,

Untie the bonds, reclaim what's yours.

Tides rise in the wake of the unchained moon.

Innocent howls split open the sleeping tomb.

Only one will champion and lead the enraged.

No warrior surrenders. No warrior remains caged."

"That's what the wolf told me during my quest. I sweated enough to hydrate a third-world country, and that was the shit it told me. It doesn't even make sense!" I whined. "And then La Loba, after more than a year later, tells me saving Emma is the journey the vision was talking about? What the actual fuck?"

Roman chuckled. "Calm down, Ace. Your blood pressure."

"Fuck my blood pressure, I'm a goddamn wolf. That shit doesn't faze me."

"Well, chill. There's no need to get riled up. We can figure this out together," he suggested.

I shook my head. "It's too late, Rome. It's been two weeks since Emma left. There's nothing I can do now." Just then, my cell phone rang and I dug it out of my bag. The last person I expected to see on the caller ID was highlighted on the screen.

"HOLY SHIT," I muttered as I looked up at Roman, who approached me warily.

"Who is it?"

The phone stopped ringing, but within two seconds it started again.

"It's Lucian." I swiped the button to answer the call. "Hello?" I pressed the speaker button so Roman could hear.

"My dear Pet, it's been so long! Why didn't you answer the phone right away? I would have thought you'd be absolutely *thrilled* to hear from me." Lucian's cheery and accented voice echoed around the gym.

"I don't know about thrilled, Lucian. Last we spoke, you said if you ever called it was because shit had hit the fan. I'm sure you can understand my hesitation."

The only other time I had spoken to Lucian since arriving in L.A. was the day after my vision quest to let him know I survived. He informed me of my living arrangements and about getting me a new fake ID, since the one he made for me said my new name was Hillary Clinton. I rolled my eyes just thinking of his absurdity.

"Shit *has* hit the fan, as you say. But first, the pleasantries," he chimed.

I stilled. "What the ...? What happened, Lucian?"

He gave an exaggerated sigh. "Oh, hush, Pet. The Summit won't arrive for another two days, you have plenty of time. Let's chat. What have you been up to?"

"The Summit?" Roman and I both exclaimed.

"Roman? Is that you, boy?"

"Yes, Luce, it's me."

Lucian chuckled. "Well, isn't this a bloody treat! My two favorites together at once. I've heard rumors of your lavish love story. I want *all* the juicy details."

"Uh, no, there's not a love story," I muttered as I peered over at Rome, who was holding back a grin. "Can we please get back to the Summit?"

Lucian huffed, "Fine, don't share. But you screwed up, Pet."

"Excuse me? My cover hasn't been blown."

"Oh, yes it has." He paused. "A child was brought to the Cadwell Estate in Little Falls a couple weeks ago. Your scent was all over her, and one of the wolves recognized it."

I slapped my palm to my forehead. "Damn it – Emma!"

"She couldn't have known," Roman said.

I nodded. "I know, but *fuck*, what am I supposed to do, Lucian?" There was a pause. "Hello?"

"What do you *think* you have to do, Pet? You have to run."

"What?" I shouted. "I can't!"

"You can, and you will. In two days' time, Los Angeles will be crawling with wolves from the Summit, all intent on hunting you down. I've already started preparations for your new location. How does South America sound? Colombia is beautiful this time of year."

"Lucian, please, I can't leave." My eyes pleaded as if he could see me, though I stared at Roman instead. *I don't want to start over again. It's not fair!* Roman reached for my hand and gave it a squeeze.

"It's either South America or get captured by the Summit.

Your choice, Pet. Call me when you've figured it out." With that, Lucian disconnected the call.

I stood motionless, letting my cell phone slip from my hands and clatter to the ground. I always knew Los Angeles wouldn't be the place I called home, and that I'd probably have to run someday, but I foolishly thought it would never actually happen.

"Talk to me. You're freakin' me out." Roman waved his hand in front of my face. "At least blink."

I blinked and had to swallow a few times to avoid letting the tears fall. Lately I'd been way too hormonal. I needed to stop the waterworks.

"Come on, Ace, you need to pack." I still couldn't believe it. He turned to leave, but my feet were glued to the ground. "Ace?"

"I can't go, Rome," I choked out. "It's only been a year and I already have to move? I can't run forever. This is madness."

"Hey," he whispered as he cupped my face in his hands. "I know this is messed up and unfair. The last thing I want to do is lose my partner-in-crime," he said. "But your safety is the top priority right now. I won't let you get taken by the Summit. Not if I can help it."

Everything Roman said went in one ear and out the other. I understood where he was coming from. He just wanted to keep me safe. Yet all I could think about was how many times I would have to do this in my lifetime. The Pack recognized my scent on a little girl who shared a short encounter with me, and I was discovered. How fucked up was that? I wasn't safe anywhere.

"La Loba," I stammered, nearly tripping over myself. "She-she might be right."

"What are you talking about?"

My chest rose up and down in quick succession and I gasped

for air. My mind ran at warp speed as I processed the riddle of my vision quest and what happened with Emma. I felt like I was trippin' on speed as my mind raced and tried to connect the dots.

"She said this was my journey to take. What if she means I need to go back to the Pack? Look!" I reached for the paper where I had written my vision and pointed to a line in the riddle. "*Oppression rests in idle hands of the brave.* Not to toot my own horn, but I'd like to think I'm brave," I joked.

"What are you saying, Ace?"

"The oppression of Lunas! What they're doing is wrong, and I haven't done a thing about it. What if it's my job to change things ... for Emma?" I could only imagine what I looked like to Roman. All wild eyes, sweaty from a workout, and possibly diagnosable. I was probably losing my mind.

His laugh was strained. "Ace, come on, even *you* have limits. The wolves haven't changed their ways in a thousand years, and I don't think they will anytime soon."

I shook my head. "Look at this part: *Only one will champion and lead the enraged.* I know I'm not the only Luna who is sick of their misogynistic ways. I can do this, Rome, I know I can. I have to—for my own freedom."

His hazel eyes were filled with unspoken concern. We weren't the overly emotional type, and although we weren't technically a couple, I knew deep down, I claimed a special place in Roman's heart—as did he in mine. We weren't forever, but we were something. And making sure I stayed alive was something I knew he would do.

"Are you sure you want to do this?" he questioned. The good thing about Roman was that he never told me what I had to do. He acknowledged I had a brain of my own and trusted my instincts, even when he wasn't sure. It was a trait I wished Sebastian and Jonah could have one day.

"Yes." I nodded. "I don't want to be on the run forever, and I can't throw Emma to the wolves."

His eyes narrowed as he gazed at me. I knew just by the rigidness of his indestructible body that he wanted to disagree, but that wasn't Roman. "Fine," he conceded. "What are you going to do?"

My gray eyes glistened with excitement. "I'm going to start a riot."

6

As we drove back to the apartment, I called Lucian and told him about my plan. Needless to say, I was his least favorite person at the moment. I hadn't even placed the call on speaker and Roman could hear every scream coming from the Head Vampire of New York City.

"Pet, I cannot protect you in the city! I won't be able to get involved," he explained.

"It's okay, Lucian, I'll be fine."

"No—no, you won't. You don't know the whole truth yet, and it's better if you disappeared to Colombia. Believe me when I tell you, Pet, it's for your own good."

I groaned. "I don't care. Call me stubborn, but I can't move every time someone catches a whiff of me." I tried to divert the topic, though I knew what truth he was referring to. I was pretty sure it had something to do with my parents. Charles—Jonah's father and the Alpha of the Northeast region—told me I was adopted before I left New York. I wasn't stupid; I realized there had to be some truth to it, but it didn't matter. I didn't want to know. My parents were the ones who raised me. Anyone else was just a damn stranger I didn't care to meet.

"Mackenzie!" Lucian blurted in a very uncharacteristic way. He'd never used my government name.

"Lucian!" I mimicked.

"There are a lot of people out there who know of your ... identity. Once you step foot in the city, the Brooklyn Pack won't be the only thing you have to worry about. You'll be in serious danger," he warned. "This isn't a game, Pet."

There was a pause in the conversation. *Who the hell was I that would cause bigger problems than being a lone wolf?* I wondered to myself.

Roman found street parking two blocks down from our apartment building. We sat in the Jeep in silence with my cell phone still glued to my ear.

"I understand, Lucian," I whispered, "but there's something telling me I have to do this. As if ... as if this is what I'm meant to do. Does that make sense?"

He didn't answer. "I'll do what I can, but I make no promises." The line went dead. I looked at my phone as it went back to the home screen—my reflection staring back at me.

"I understand why you have to do this," Roman said. "You have to stop running and stand up for yourself. So what's the game plan?"

I turned to him and reached for his dirty blond hair. My fingers slid through his tousled locks as he leaned his cold cheek to my forearm. His hazel eyes bored into me with desire, sending prickles of goosebumps across my skin.

"I spend one more night with you," I said as I leaned over the console and brushed my lips over his. "And then I stop running."

I BOOKED a red eye flight to the East Coast for the following night. I couldn't leave until I spent time with Roman. I wasn't *in* love with him, it wasn't like that with us, but I did love him. And if he ever needed me, I'd be there in a split second—or more like five hours, since that was how long a damn flight back west was. He made me promise to call him often so he knew I was safe, and then he offered to come with me. That was definitely a no-go. Bash and Jonah would have a fit. They barely tolerated Lucian. If I brought yet another vampire into the mix, I would never hear the end of it.

The warehouse hadn't aged a bit. It felt as if just yesterday I was prancing around the first floor, overflowing with the confidence every young adult in their early twenties thought they had, oblivious to the repercussions of my actions. Not just turning my back on the Pack, but taking the life of someone else—no matter how much the skin walker deserved it. I fled to the West Coast so I'd never have to think about this dump in Brooklyn again—but here I was, pushing through the double doors.

Blasted by the freezing air of the A/C and the smell of brimming testosterone, I entered the main floor as wolves from the Brooklyn Pack milled through the cafeteria-style room. For the first few seconds, no one noticed me standing under the threshold, but after my scent filled the air, one by one, heads turned in my direction. None of them mattered to me. There were only two people I had been scanning the area for, and I shouldn't have been surprised when I found them in the middle of the main floor, drilling holes of pure hatred in my direction.

"Honey, I'm home."

Chaos ensued.

A BLUR of faces whizzed past as Sebastian strode toward me, clutching my arm and dragging me to the basement, while Jonah marched on my other side. Being between the two best friends—the Alpha and the Beta—I felt at home.

"You *do* know I'm able to walk on my own, don't you?"

"Shut. Up," Bash growled. I felt the heat—and not the sexual kind—seep out of his pores. I guessed things hadn't changed around these parts. I would be forever cursed with the ability to piss Sebastian Steel off simply by entering a room.

"Well, this wasn't exactly the welcome wagon I expected. I was hoping to at least get a hug, possibly a cake. I'll take either or, really." I grinned, but I was the only one.

"If you know what's good for you, you'll shut the hell up, Mackenzie," Bash gritted through his teeth. "You're a real idiot."

"Hey! I resent that!" I scoffed.

"I can't believe this ..." Jonah mused.

They pushed me into Sebastian's small office, just as messy and cluttered as I remembered, and slammed the door shut behind us. I turned around to catch them both pacing the room. I wanted to sit down, but then I recalled what kind of extracurriculars Bash was into with the resident mean girl, Vivian. I wondered if they had mated during my absence, and if she was the Alpha for the Lunas. I prayed she wasn't, because if so, we were going to war.

"What the hell were you thinking? Are you mentally unstable? Have you lost your bloody mind?" Sebastian roared and I had to take a step back. His fury hit me in waves, and I was forcefully reminded who was the true Alpha here.

"Easy there, champ. I haven't lost my marbles—at least not yet."

"Then what would make you resurface after all this time? We lost your trail months ago! You were free," Jonah blurted, ever the pacifist, but I could tell he was just as upset.

I savored that tidbit for a moment. I was free. I had successfully fled the Pack and all their misogynistic ideologies, but because I was a glutton for torture, I returned to where it all began.

"I was never free," I declared as I straightened my posture. I wouldn't let them intimidate me—not now and not ever. "No matter where I went, I would always be looking over my shoulder. The minute I seemed or smelled familiar to anyone, I'd have to pack up and run. That's not freedom."

"You know what we mean, Mackenzie," Jonah sighed. "You aren't giving us any choice in what happens next."

"I know." I nodded. "Whatever you have to do, I understand."

Sebastian's nostrils flared. "What do you have up your sleeve? It can't possibly be this simple."

"So glass-half-empty. Why can't a gal come by and visit her pals?" I smirked, which only angered them further. "If it's such a big deal, I can always go." I moved to leave, but the two wolves blocked the door.

"You know we can't let you leave now," Jonah said.

"Well then, pop the champagne, because I'm back, bitches!"

I plopped myself down on one of the office chairs, hoping it had been cleaned, and interlocked my hands behind my head. Stretching out my legs and crossing them at the ankles like I didn't have a care in the world, I waited for the boys to do or say something. I had to tread carefully. Sebastian was already questioning my motives. Because, let's be honest, no one in their right mind would come back to this—but I had—for Emma and everyone else like her, like me.

"Did you at least miss me?" I asked with a sweet smile. I shouldn't goad them, but I was curious. Did I leave an impression on them like they had on me?

Sebastian wouldn't look at me, but Jonah's milk chocolate eyes softened, and that one dimple peeked out. "Of course, Kenzie."

"Good," I smirked. "So what's the plan?"

"We take you to the estate. Charles needs to talk to you before anyone else knows you're here," Sebastian said. "We leave at first light tomorrow."

I clapped my hands together. "Perfect!" I stood to leave. "Now, if you boys will excuse me, I have someone else to see." I inched toward the door but they both blocked my exit. "Relax guys, I'll be back."

"Who are you going to see?" Sebastian clipped out.

I crossed my arms over my chest. "Amy, duh?"

Jonah diverted his gaze and Sebastian stiffened. Something was wrong.

"What? What aren't you telling me?" My hands clenched into fists. The energy in the room shifted, giving me a touch of claustrophobia.

"About Amy ..." Jonah started, and my heart began to race. *No, God, please not Amy ...*

"Calm down, Mackenzie," Sebastian warned.

"Do *not* tell me to calm the fuck down! What happened to Amy?" I barked.

"Nothing's happened to her," Jonah quickly retracted. "But ..."

"But what? Spit it out already, damnit!"

"She's here," Sebastian finally said.

I froze. "What do you mean, she's here?"

A million scenarios raced through my mind at lightning speed. Were they holding her prisoner? Did she become a werewolf? Was she ... dead?

"She's in the warehouse," Bash said, "with Jackson."

"Why? Is she here against her will?"

"What? Of course not!" Jonah exclaimed. "She's here of her own volition. She's *with* Jackson," he added, wiggling his eyebrows suggestively.

I didn't care who the hell she was boinking, but I told Jackson to *look out for her*, not *get in her pants!* She was supposed to stay far away from all things supernatural! It was the whole purpose of me leaving her behind.

"Where is she?" My body vibrated with rage, though I tried to keep my anger in check.

"She's upstairs, in Jackson's room," Sebastian answered, his gaze following my every twitch.

I didn't waste any time excusing myself or apologizing. I pushed past them and sprinted out of the basement to the main floor. Wolves were huddled around, waiting on their Alpha to give them instructions on whether to keep me a secret or not.

Like it mattered. I planned to make myself known whether they liked it or not. But first, I needed to find Amy.

I took the stairs to the second floor two at a time and pounded my fist on every single bedroom door until everyone inside came out to see what all the ruckus was about. It wasn't my proudest moment, but goddamnit, she wasn't supposed to be involved.

"Jackson, you son-of-a-bitch, you better come out and face me!" I yelled to draw him out. It didn't take long for a door at the other side of the warehouse to pop open and a burly, shirtless man with a stupid hipster beard emerged. Those familiar chocolate eyes flashed gold as recognition hit him. There were too many wolves in the warehouse for me to zero in on just his heartbeat, but it didn't matter. He knew I was pissed.

"You!" I pointed at him from across the way. "You're dead!"

He held the door slightly closed, keeping something or someone, from my vision. It didn't take a genius to figure out who that was. This certainly wasn't the reunion I had in mind.

"Mackenzie," he said loudly. "Just hear me out," he tried to plead.

But all I saw was red.

Jackson couldn't keep Amy back any longer; she pushed out of the room and ducked underneath his arm. Her petite, tattooed frame looked the same as the last time I saw her. Flaming red hair was pulled up in a messy bun, and luckily, she was completely dressed. Her wide eyes and slack jaw were frozen as she saw me.

"Mackenzie," I saw her lips form my name.

"Amy," I sighed. "What are you doing here?" The anger in me washed out and I could no longer stay mad at her. This was my best friend and I'd missed her terribly. The last thing I wanted was for her to see me for the first time in over a year and see a monster.

Without another word, Amy strode over to the stairwell closest to her and made her way to the main floor—Jackson trailing behind her.

I took the stairs to the first floor where Sebastian and Jonah stood in Amy's way.

"Get out of my way," I gritted, not understanding why everyone was acting like this.

"We'll let you near her as soon as you calm down, Mackenzie," Sebastian chastised, and I wanted to throttle him.

"I *am* calm!" I yelled. "What the hell is going on? Amy?"

She stood between the Alpha and Beta and put her hand on Bash's shoulder. "Don't worry, she won't hurt me."

"Obviously." I rolled my eyes. "Is that what you morons think? That I'll hurt her?"

Sebastian straightened. "We don't know where you've been, Mackenzie. You could be feral, for all we know."

"Feral? Like a fuckin' cat?" I cocked my head to the side and scrutinized their faces. They couldn't be serious.

"You could be dangerous. You have to understand our concern. We don't know you anymore," Jonah said.

My body heat ratcheted up a notch, my neck and cheeks a blazing red. I left for a year, and now I was a stranger all over again. I shouldn't have been surprised, but I was. Especially to receive this treatment from Amy.

"What do I need to do to prove I'm not the next Unabomber?" I crossed my arms over my chest and waited for them to respond.

Sebastian nodded his head back to the basement. "Follow me."

Before following Bash to his office, I paused and looked at my best friend, seeing disappointment and anger directed at me. I wasn't stupid. I figured she'd be pissed that I left her behind. My gaze bypassed her angry face and flitted over to Jackson's guilty one, and my eyes flashed silver.

"You're dead meat, Cadwell," I said before I left.

IT WAS JUST me and Sebastian in his office, and thankfully, he had calmed down a bit from earlier. I expected him to be frustrated with me like always. My immaturity was a recurring pet peeve of his. On the way to his office I took the time to check him out—all of him. The body of a fighter and the face of a fallen angel. All square jawed and Roman nose, his hair the color of ink with icy, pale blue eyes that would strike the fear of God in anyone.

"So, what's the game plan, Bash? Torture me until you deem me trustworthy?"

He shook his head and sat behind his desk. "I wanted some time alone with you. How have you been?" His crystal blue eyes warmed a centimeter. His large frame relaxed a fraction when I sat across from him.

"I've been better," I answered honestly. "What's the deal with keeping me from Amy? She's not pregnant, is she?" I could barely keep the look of horror from my face.

"No, but you're a wild card right now. Your temper is erratic, and you need to cool down."

"I would *never* hurt her," I said earnestly. If I could tell a single truth, that was it. I would do anything to keep Amy safe—like move across the country without her, just to keep the bad guys away.

"You shouldn't have come back. It's not safe for you."

I quirked a brow. "Why? Because I'm a lone wolf?"

Sebastian huffed impatiently. "Do you think that even matters anymore? You've been a free lone wolf since we met you, Mackenzie. You've had special privileges that others have not been afforded. Aren't you curious as to why?"

I rolled my eyes. "Does it matter? You're gonna tell me anyway."

"I'll only tell you if you honestly want to know."

"I only want to know what kind of danger I'm in. Everything else is irrelevant."

"You're a hot commodity, Mackenzie. Alphas all over the country are going to want you to join their Packs—and they may not be as reasonable or considerate as I have been. They might just take you by force."

I scoffed, "Let me guess, you want me to join the Brooklyn Pack for my own safety?"

Sebastian shook his head. "No, Mackenzie. I've already asked you, and you *literally* ran away. I've learned my lesson, you can't be tamed," he smirked. "I'm just giving you a heads up—as a friend."

I couldn't resist the grin that spread across my face. "Right ... friends."

"Exactly." He paused. "Now, do you want to tell me where you've been?"

I shook my head no.

"I figured. Well, as we told you earlier, I have no choice but to hand you over to Charles. Do you understand?"

"I'm not an idiot, Bash, I know."

"That's what I don't understand," he muttered. "Why?"

I smiled. "I have my reasons."

"You know you can trust me, right?" His eyes narrowed suspiciously.

"Like you trust me?"

He laughed. "Touché."

"So, what happens now?"

Sebastian stood from his chair and walked around to lean against his desk. "Now, I let you catch up with your best friend, but I expect you back here tomorrow before sunrise. Got it?"

I stood from my seat and stepped between his legs, planting my hands on his shoulders. "Thank you, Sebastian," I whispered, taking him by surprise.

His blue eyes crinkled at the corners and I was graced by an unexpected smile. "You've changed."

"For the better?" I asked.

"I think so."

I smiled wider. "Good." I kissed him on the cheek and left his office.

I EXITED the basement and touched my lips, the feel of Sebastian's scruffy five o'clock shadow sending tingles of electricity through my sensitive skin. I shook the feeling away. As I emerged onto the main floor, the only ones left were Jonah and Amy. Everyone else had scattered to God knows where. Jackson had ghosted, and I was glad. I was tired from my flight back to the

East Coast and didn't have the energy to kick his ass for breaking his promise to me.

Amy and I took a cab back into the city, and the silence between us awakened my ADD. I couldn't sit still, much less keep quiet.

"Are you going to ignore me the whole ride home?" I asked as the taxi driver made a sharp turn.

"It's not your home anymore, Mackenzie," she said as she looked out the window.

"Ouch." I cringed. "Right in the feels."

"I don't care," she mumbled as she nibbled on her lip ring.

I shifted my body, placing my back against the car door so I could face her. "Listen, Amy, I know I messed up, but I thought what I was doing was for your own good. I didn't want you to be involved and put in harm's way. I realize now that it was pointless, because you're all up in the Pack, but whatever. The point is, I messed up and I'm sorry. I didn't mean to disappear." I gasped for air. Verbal diarrhea was a hazard of mine. "Amy?"

She whirled around, her eyes blazing with fury. "You can't just dictate everything, Mackenzie! And you also can't come back and expect everything to be normal again!"

"I didn't say that I expected anything!"

"Well, good, because saying *sorry* isn't going to cut it. Not this time." She huffed and crossed her arms.

I scooted a little closer to her. "I missed ya, Amy." I grinned. I was itching to pull her into a huge bear hug, but I knew she needed her space.

Her gaze turned to me and I saw her inner struggle. She was trying hard to stay mad at me, but I was sure I could break her resolve.

"I didn't watch the latest season of *House of Cards* because I couldn't watch it without you," I pouted.

Her eyes softened. "Damn it, Mackenzie Grey! I missed your ass too!" She pulled me into her little tattooed arms and I hugged her back just as fiercely.

"Yes! I knew it!"

"You're such an asshole. You couldn't even give me a day to be pissed. I deserve at least a day!"

"I know, Aims, but I don't have a day. Sebastian has to take me to the estate tomorrow morning. I don't know what Charles is going to do, but I wanted us to be on good terms before I headed out."

The taxi pulled to a stop in front of our apartment building. While Amy paid the cab driver, I got out and scanned the neighborhood. Everything looked the same. Even the bodega down the street that was owned by Mr. and Mrs. Mejia was the same. As I stepped into our apartment, I was struck by a wave of nostalgia. Our quiet, sparse apartment had been perfect for us when I was still moon-bound. I remembered many nights of having to rush home and lock myself in my cage because the wolf had a hold on me during every full moon. Those were some tough times, but I'd learned to shift at will and was no longer bound to the Change or to the moon.

"Welcome home, Kenz."

OUR APARTMENT LOOKED THE SAME, except now there was an occasional article of men's clothing lying around. *Is the bastard sleeping here?* My eyebrows scrunched inward, but I kept the inquisition to myself. I had no desire to start another argument with Amy this soon after our reconciliation.

"What have you been up to?" I asked. "You know, post-gradua-tion and all." I walked around the living room, running my hands over the familiar red brick walls. This was home.

"Not much. I mainly do remote IT work, so I can work from home." She shrugged. "It pays the bills." Amy peeled her coat off and hung it by the door. "Are you going to tell me why you're back?" she asked as she headed into the kitchen to start a pot of coffee.

She knew me so well.

"Of course I am!" I said. "I have to fill my bestie in on my master plan for world domination!" I did my evil laugh with my fists planted at my hips.

"Alrighty then, I'm all ears, Wolfey."

I hopped onto the kitchen counter and got comfortable. "I can't run forever, Amy," I started. "A few weeks ago, I found this little eleven-year-old Luna. Her mother was a succubus and the father was dead—killed because he was a lone wolf."

Amy sucked in a breath.

"Yeah ... apparently the werewolf gene is stronger than any other species out there. It seeks dominance, so the girl never stood a chance at being anything but a wolf. When I rescued her from a guy who was exploiting sucubi in L.A., I was left with the girl; her mother had died while they were being held hostage." I paused and swallowed the lump that had formed in my throat.

"Kenzie?"

I brushed off her concern, plunging back into my confession. "I didn't know what to do, so I took her to the Desert Wolves, which was a Pack that had been helping me out since I arrived in

Los Angeles. They had no choice but to report her to the Summit, and those bastards caught my scent on the little girl."

"You got caught?" Amy breathed.

"No, Lucian called to warn me and give me a head start before they arrived. I was about to run when a friend of mine told me I'd eventually have to stop running, that I'd have to stand up for myself."

Amy nodded. "So you decided it would be today?"

"Yeah." I sighed. "I'm tired, Amy. You know, Jonah asked me earlier why I chose now to return. He said I was free, and that they'd lost my trail a few months ago. But was that real freedom? If something doesn't change, I'm condemned to play a game of hide-and-seek for the rest of my life."

"Oh, Kenz." Amy hopped onto the counter with me and wrapped me in one of her hugs. "I'm sorry."

I snorted. "Don't be. It's not your fault."

"If you're not hiding anymore, then what are you going to do?"

She pulled away from me and I smirked. "I've decided I'm going to change the system—not just for me, but for every Luna out there."

"Alright then, Che Guevara, when does the revolution start?"

I rolled my eyes. "Before I do anything, I have to find out what Charles plans to do with me. I'm not out of the woods just yet." My future was uncertain, which meant I couldn't plan anything until I knew what would happen to me. I wasn't Charles' favorite person in the world, and I knew that was mostly my fault. Let's just say my mini freak-out about whom he thought my parents were didn't bode well with the Alpha.

"Well, enough with the heavy." Amy marched to the fridge

and pulled out a tub of ice cream. "Time to spill." She grinned.

"No deets to spill, homie." I chugged the rest of my coffee.

"As if I'd believe that load of horse shit." She waved a spoon at me. "You've been gone for a whole year. Don't tell me there aren't any residual wolfey feelings somewhere inside."

"For who? Bash or Jonah? I'm so over them," I scoffed, grabbing the Chunky Monkey to throw her off the trail. Sure, it was a total lie, but she didn't need to know that. Seeing them today was like a punch to the gut. Every wistful feeling and heated memory came rushing back like a tidal wave. But none of that mattered. I had a goal in mind, and I couldn't afford to be distracted by boy issues.

Amy smirked. "If you're so over them, then who in L.A. was making my girl ARH-WOOOO!" she fake-howled to the ceiling.

I threw my head back in laughter. "You did *not* just do that."

"Oh, yes I did." She snatched the ice cream container from me. "Now spill."

"I don't know, Amy. Things are confusing right now. Why couldn't they have gotten fat and ugly while I was gone? Life is so unfair!" I covered my face in my hands.

She patted me on the back. "There, there, babe. I'm sure they'll get a receding hairline any day now."

"Yeah, right." I rolled my eyes. "I can see them now – old as hell and looking like a bunch of silver foxes," I grumbled into a mouthful of Chunky Monkey.

"And you'll probably look like Sofia Vergara, so stop your whining." She stole my spoon as the apartment door unlocked and swung open.

I jumped off the counter, already baring my canines as I lunged into a crouch, a growl ripping through me that made Amy flinch. Jackson and Jonah walked in, their hands raised in defense.

"Easy there, Kenz, calm down and breathe." Jonah stretched his hand out to me as if I were a wild animal that had escaped its cage. He was always the one who helped me when I lost control —except I didn't need his assistance anymore.

I retracted the wolf and stared at him. "Seriously?" I deadpanned. After all this time, did they think I was *that* out of control? "Well, if it isn't Dumb & Dumber." I sauntered back into the kitchen as if nothing had happened. Amy was frozen in a corner while I reached for my mug to refill it. "What do you guys want?"

"You ... you can shift at will?" Jonah asked, standing in shock.

"What can I say? I'm skilled like that." I winked at him and took a sip of coffee.

"Well ..." Amy floundered with what to say. "That is, uh ... good to know. Definitely a detail you forgot to tell us before."

I chuckled. "I'm not some rabid animal who's been living on the streets and eating out of trash cans. I was very comfortable in my downtown apartment and cushy job, so take a breather."

Jackson was the only one who didn't seem surprised. That made me raise a brow until my phone started to vibrate in my back pocket. I looked at the screen and Roman's name appeared. I hit the silent button and ignored his call.

"Are you serious?" Jonah asked. He wore fitted jeans and a flannel button-up. Same ol' Jonah. For a moment, I was sucked back into old times and had to recall what we were talking about. Oh, yeah, me living it up in L.A.

"As a heart attack," I smirked. "So, to what do we owe this impromptu visit?"

Amy cleared her throat. "Sorry, Kenz, that might be my fault. I made plans with Jackson."

"Speaking of which," I glared at the traitorous wolf, "you and I need to have a chat."

Jackson scratched the back of his head, his brown eyes looking anywhere but at me. "Mackenzie, don't be so dramatic."

"Dramatic? You ain't seen *nothing* yet, Cadwell."

"It's not like I planned to bone your best friend, it just happened!" he yelled. "Sue me for thinking with the wrong head!"

I scoffed, "Of course! Blame it on your dick! Real smooth there, Casanova."

Amy giggled. "Kenz, relax. We can talk about this later."

"No way, Aims. He told me he'd look out for you. I left you behind for this specific reason, making my grand gesture moot."

"Maybe you shouldn't have left me, then," she retorted, still hurt.

"I see that now," I mumbled. "Does he at least treat you right?" I turned to her, softening my voice.

"Yes. He's a real ... gentleman," she laughed as they eye-fucked each other.

"Oh, gross." I rolled my eyes. "Get a room."

Everyone laughed except Jonah—he was watching my every move. I felt it.

"You've changed," he cut into the conversation. "You're not the same as when you left."

"Well, that's the definition of change, Jonah. It's been over a year; of course I'm not going to be the same, but I'd like to think I'm still just as charming." I grinned. "Now, I don't know about you guys, but I could seriously go for some New York pizza."

7

E mpty pizza boxes littered the living room floor as I
lounged on the couch rubbing my very full belly. Amy and
Jackson had already retreated to her room for the night, and
Jonah and I had just finished watching a rerun of *Lost*. He turned
the TV off as I glanced over at the clock on the stove. It was two in
the morning and I wasn't even tired. Sleep would be a real pain in
the ass to fix. I was regretting those vampire hours now.

"Aren't you tired?" Jonah asked as he started cleaning up.

I sighed. "Nope. Sleep is gonna be a bitch. I used to work
nights."

"Ah, I see," he said, quickly looking away. "Well, I don't mind
keeping you company."

"Aren't you tired?" I inquired. "Or are you hoping I'll spill my
guts to you?"

He shook his head. "No, of course not, Kenz, but I did miss
you."

That dimple peeked out and I couldn't help the broad smile that stretched over my face. Jonah Cadwell was every girl's Prince Charming—with a dash of over-protectiveness. And I'd be a liar if I said I didn't think about him while I was gone. On the contrary, not a day went by without the thought of either wolf that tugged at my heart strings. Unlike Bash, Jonah wasn't afraid to tell me how he felt, even if it was too intense for me.

"So, what's been new? Any special girl in your life?" I asked, my smile feeling tight on my face. Did I really want to know? Probably not, but I couldn't help but ask.

He whispered, "You know there will never be anyone else for me."

Part of me was disappointed that he hadn't moved on, while another part felt relieved. I knew it was wrong and I hated feeling this conflicted; it wasn't fair to him. "Are you planning on spending the night?" I changed the subject.

"If it's alright with you."

I tilted my head. "Of course you can, Jonah."

He smiled. "Thanks. I'll grab a blanket and pillow from the closet."

I was on my way to my bedroom when I stilled. "This isn't your first time sleeping over, is it?"

I saw a small blush creep up his neck as he looked away. "Uh ... no."

"And where did you sleep?" I asked, trying very hard not to laugh at his bashfulness.

He cleared his throat, still avoiding eye contact. "Your room."

"Figured." I nodded. "Well, come on then. It's not like we've never shared a bed."

I knew I was sending him through an emotional roller coaster. It was just a year ago that I could barely look at him—or Bash, for that matter—without my ovaries kicking into overdrive. I'd been trying to get over my ex, James, and wasn't ready to get physical with anyone. I quickly learned these wolves were the definition of physical. There were nights I still dreamed about me and Bash at the library, or that heart-stopping kiss Jonah gave me in the middle of the street. Both men had vied for my attention and I couldn't choose either one. But now things were different. I'd like to think I've grown up a bit.

Everything in my room was as if I'd never left. My laptop sat on my desk, waiting for me to log on and Skype my brother, Ollie —but that would have to wait.

I was pulling off my t-shirt when Jonah walked in. Although my back was to him as I rummaged through my closet, I felt his heat enter the room. I unbuckled my jeans right as he knocked on the door frame.

"Just come in," I said over my shoulder. "I'm looking for some jammies." As soon as I found a pair of sweatpants and my Nirvana t-shirt, I changed without a care that Jonah might be watching. That modesty ship had sailed.

He closed the bedroom door and peeled off his flannel shirt. I could feel the familiar blush that used to creep up whenever I was around him. It brought back memories of when I first met the Pack—or more like when they first kidnapped me.

"Haven't you ever heard of an undershirt?" I joked, repeating my words from the first time I saw him shirtless.

"You're a real smartass, Mackenzie Grey." He balled up his shirt and flung it at me.

I caught it before it hit my face, taking a whiff of his scent. That woodsy smell was something I missed. I slid his flannel shirt on over my Nirvana tee and climbed into bed. "What do you think? Real nineties grunge?"

He chuckled. "I'm glad you haven't lost your sense of humor." He laid on his side, facing me.

"How could you believe I would be anything *but* sarcastic? It's so ingrained in me, I'll be ninety years old and still annoying the shit out of Bash," I laughed.

Jonah barely smiled as his brown eyes drilled into me. "Mackenzie?"

"Yeah?"

"Why are you here?"

"Ya know," I started, "I'm beginning to get the feeling you guys don't want me around."

He shook his head. "That's not what I mean. I'm ecstatic you're here, Kenz, but I also know you weren't struggling wherever you were. Which begs the question, *why the hell would you come back?*"

I paused for a moment before answering. I had to be careful with what I said. The last thing I wanted was to implicate Bash or Jonah in anything I did.

"Let's just say I have some business to take care of," I answered cagily. "And I won't expand beyond that."

He looked as if he wanted to argue, but I narrowed my eyes, effectively shutting the conversation down.

"Just answer one question," he said. "Are you planning to start trouble?"

I couldn't resist the belly laugh that erupted from me. My eyes teared as I gasped for air, and I was almost positive my cackles could be heard blocks away. When I found my voice I said, "Jonah, what kind of question is that? Of course I'm gonna start trouble."

WITH JONAH just a few inches away, his body heat crawled over to me, making it impossible to fall asleep right away. The itch to scoot over and huddle against him was unbearable, but after a while I finally drifted into blissful sleep ... until he started nudging me awake. With my head under the covers, I tightened my fists on the comforter to keep the covers from getting ripped off. This was something I was used to doing with Roman.

"Kenz, you have to wake up. I need to bring you to the warehouse before sunrise," Jonah mumbled as he tried to pry the sheets away from me.

"Is that why you're here? Bash sent a babysitter?" I grumbled, my eyes glued shut.

"Well, I wouldn't put it that way, but yeah, I'm here to make sure you get back as planned."

"But I *just* fell asleep," I whined. "Five more minutes."

I felt the bed dip and then realign, and I smirked to myself and started to settle back into sleep. Suddenly I was thrown into the air, landing face-first on the floor. Jonah had tipped the mattress over, which was a rather effective method of getting me up. I wiped the drool off my cheek and stood, glaring at the asshole before me.

"Seriously?"

"Kenz, you told me to give you five more minutes an hour ago!

Get in the shower and let's *move*. We're already late. You can sleep on the way to Little Falls."

SEBASTIAN, of course, was as cranky as I was—though his reason was different from mine. Jonah and I were late, but in my defense, I was severely lacking in the sleep department.

They left Jackson in charge of the Pack while we were gone, as the Alpha and Beta escorted me to see Charles. The last time I'd been in Little Falls was the first time I shifted with other wolves. The experience was like none other—like a cleansing, of sorts. Those were good memories, but the not-so-good memories? Those were my interactions with the Alpha of the Northeast region—Mr. Charles Cadwell.

The tall, wrought iron gate with concrete pillars on either side provided a formal welcome to Cadwell Estate. The familiar three-mile drive through the estate was just as beautiful as I remembered, and I watched as wolves ran beside our car as bodyguards. Their glowing eyes flashed through the car window as they watched me, so I flashed mine back to establish dominance. Once they couldn't handle my glare, the wolves turned away and ran faster. I faced forward again and met a pair of icy blue orbs through the rearview mirror. Creases at the corners of his eyes told me he was laughing, but the quirk of his brow hinted that I had surprised Sebastian Steel. Another point for Team Kenzie.

Unlike last time, Charles was already waiting for us by the front door as we drove up the massive, circle-shaped driveway. The signature Cadwell eyes followed us as we exited the vehicle. He stood in jeans and a tucked-in button up, with his brown hair slicked back in waves. The only difference between him and his sons was the dash of grey hair that peppered the sides.

Since it wasn't a full moon, the surrounding silence and emptiness of the estate made it appear much larger than it was. The Alpha walked down the front steps and whistled at the wolves who had escorted us inside the property. Some ran inside the house, and others dispersed into the woods. But none remained besides Charles, Jonah, Sebastian, and me.

"I think this is a first. I've never seen a lone wolf come out of hiding to get captured," Charles quipped. "You are quite peculiar, Mackenzie Grey."

"Right back atcha." I pointed my finger at him and winked.

"*Mackenzie*," Sebastian growled as he elbowed me in the ribs.

"Ouch," I scoffed. "Easy there, it was a compliment."

"Behave," he whispered and turned to Charles. "My apologies for our tardiness. I was dealing with some things that took up more time than anticipated." Bash took the blame.

"No worries, I expected it." Charles glowered at me and then shifted his steely eyes back to his son. "You look well, Jonah. I presume Miss Grey's arrival has brightened up your mood?"

What the hell is the old man talking about?

"I'm well, Father," Jonah said stiffly, looking embarrassed. "The office?"

"Yes, you know the way," his father answered, and we followed him inside.

I kept my head down as we walked in, only glancing at the foyer with the double curved staircase. This place was so damn fancy I was scared to breathe, afraid I might knock over a priceless vase with the force of my lungs. Charles already looked ticked as it was. I certainly didn't need to piss him off further.

We entered his office and it smelled just as I remembered—wood, rain, and cigars. It seemed like things never changed with these wolves—which was downright depressing. They were going to get a rude awakening with me. We sat in the formal sitting area near the liquor cart and Charles poured himself a drink. He offered drinks all around, but we refused.

"Mackenzie," he started, "what brings you back to New York? I'm sure it wasn't the weather. You look tanned."

I smirked. "What did me in was the pizza. The thought that anyone could ever survive without New York pizza is blasphemous, don't you think?"

Those brown eyes hardened. "Of course. Such a tragedy."

I waved him off. "But let's skip all the passive aggressiveness, shall we? Let's get down to what you *really* want to know."

"Direct, just like your—never mind." He smiled. "Please tell us where you've been this past year."

I sat between Sebastian and Jonah and felt the stiffness of their bodies. They weren't fond of the banter between me and Charles, but I didn't care. Something had been nagging me since I returned, and this was the perfect time to test my theory. I knew lone wolves were killed on the spot, no questions asked. Prime example: Emma's father. But I'd been prancing around for the last thirty-six hours and sashayed right into a wolves' den, yet the worst affliction I had was clogged ears from the flight back east. Why was I getting special treatment from someone who had the power to order my death in a split second?

"That's where we might hit a snag," I said. "I can't tell you *where* I've been, but I can tell you what I've done." I grinned. There was no way I was going to spill the beans on Lucian. I wouldn't put it past them if they killed him just for aiding and abetting. And that would lead to Roman, and I didn't want him involved. Hence all the unanswered voicemails and text messages I'd been avoiding.

"Pray tell, what have you done?" He chuckled as if my antics amused him, when I knew they did the opposite.

I stood from my seat and paced in front of them, ticking off everything I'd done on my fingers. "First, I went on a vision quest," that got a gasp out of them, "and boy, was *that* one hell of a trip. Like being on acid or some shit, not that I would know." I laughed. "Then I got to chill and enjoy my quasi-freedom. You know, typical shit like sippin' mojitos pool side, sleeping in, and binging on episodes of *The Gilmore Girls*. Have you seen it? Seriously, give it a shot."

"Mackenzie," Sebastian warned, but I didn't look at him, afraid I would lose my nerve.

"But I digress. I had an interesting chat with my wolf, and man, she's awesome. We're so in tune with one another, I'm no longer moon-bound. Oh, and I also got to meet some cool supernatural peeps. Like nymphs, warlocks, imps, ogres, and even a ton of sucubi—which brings me to my last thing. Emma."

"That *was* your scent we caught on her?" Charles asked, slightly surprised.

"Her scent?" Jonah interrupted, but his father ignored him.

That told me the boys didn't know that Charles had gotten a lead on me. *Interesting.*

"Bingo, daddy-o," I joked. "And now I want to know where she is."

My stare met Charles head-on as he tapped a hand on his chin, contemplating everything I'd divulged. "That's why you're here? For a child?"

"Wow, you sure are on a roll there, Mr. Cadwell. You should play the lottery."

"She was reported by the Desert Wolves—any relation to you?" His eyes narrowed to slits.

I scrunched my brows inward. "The what?" I lied. I refused to implicate La Loba. She had been too good to me.

"Guess not." He paused. "If you must know, the child is here, under my order."

All the confidence and cockiness that pumped through my veins chilled into ice and I felt the blood drain from my face. Why would they keep her at the estate all this time? I was told she'd be given to a Pack. I inhaled deeply, trying to catch a whiff of her scent, but the smell of cigars overpowered all my senses.

"Oh, don't fret, Miss Grey. I assure you she is in excellent hands. Quite a spitfire, not unlike yourself," Charles said. "I'll let you see her before you leave—but only if you do as I say."

Deals. *Of course he wants a bargain.* My loyalty for a quick visit. I hated to say it, but I wouldn't do that—not even for Emma. That thought made me sick to my stomach.

"Dad, this isn't necessary," Jonah said. "We aren't here to play games." Sebastian only watched me, always the observer.

"No games, son. There is only one thing I want from Miss Grey, and then she is free to go."

That piqued my interest. "Free?" I inquired. "Like, lone wolf free?"

He nodded. "Yes. Free."

I half coughed, half gasped when Charles said the one thing I never thought in a million years I'd ever hear him say.

"What do you want?" I asked.

He leaned back in his chair and took a sip of bourbon from

his tumbler. "I only ask that you take a seat and listen to a story. When I'm done, you can decide what you deem to be best for yourself. And if being a lone wolf is what you think is right, we will not hunt you. Do we have a deal?"

Without hesitation, I extended my hand to Jonah's father. "Deal."

8

"The American Summit consists of the five region Alphas of the United States, two Alphas from Canada, and one from Central America," Charles stated. "Many lone wolves believe South America is a haven because no designated Packs live there, but that's a mistake. We have a team of trackers positioned there, keeping that continent free of lone wolves."

I sat by myself as I listened to Charles, but carefully watched Sebastian and Jonah on the sofa in front of me. It couldn't be this easy. There was no way Charles would let me go after listening to a story and receive my freedom. It had to be a trick.

"Why are you telling me this?" I interrupted, impatient.

"Just listen, Miss Grey," Charles admonished. "Europe, on the other hand, is different from the New World. They still live by very old laws—and still rule under a monarchy."

"Charles, no," Sebastian interrupted as he stood. "She's not ready." His blue gaze flickered between me and the Alpha in concern.

"Sebastian, you don't give Miss Grey enough credit. If she wants to keep her freedom, then I'm sure this small story won't do much damage, yes?" He motioned to me.

I looked between Bash and Jonah, noticing they both looked like they would throw up at any minute. How bad could this story be?

I nodded for him to continue, though my gut told me to call off this deal. However, I wanted to be free more than anything. I'd pay the consequences later.

"Very well," Charles continued with a grin. "As I was saying, the European Summit does not consist of a committee like here in the New World, but rather a monarchy. One that has been ruled by the same family for many centuries. Although we have a Summit, the European one can overrule us whenever they like because they are *the law*."

He paused to take a drink and I couldn't stop bouncing my right leg the same way Emma did. He was building up for something major, and it only pissed me off further that he was being so dramatic about it.

"Any day now, Charles. I'm getting old here." I faked a yawn.

Unperturbed, he continued, "There was a rumor, less than twenty-five years ago, that our King was having an affair. An affair with someone who wasn't a Lycanthrope, which is a huge no-no for the royal family, and an even bigger no-no to betray your mate."

"Wow, real scandalous," I laughed. "Would be an amazing reality TV show."

Charles smirked. "Right. Well, the Queen heard of the King's betrayal and had the mistress executed at once. Some said his lover was with child at the time, but there was never any proof."

My smile fell, as did my heart, lodging somewhere in the pit of my stomach. My gray eyes widened and I whipped my head around to Bash and Jonah, but neither of them would look me in the eyes. I didn't want to hear what came next.

"There was never any proof of a love child until a year and a half ago, when a lone wolf strolled into the Brooklyn Pack," Charles said.

"No," I whispered. "You're full of shit." My feet stumbled over each other as I stood. My body shook so much, I could no longer stay seated.

"Mackenzie Grey," his voice boomed, "you are the illegitimate daughter of Alexander MacCoinnich, King of the Lycans."

"No," I mumbled as I shook my head. "You're lying. My father is Thomas Grey ..."

"He is not your biological father," Sebastian murmured beside me. I hadn't even seen him move. "Take deep breaths."

I was hyperventilating. The oxygen in the room felt like it was getting sucked out by a vacuum and it burned my chest. My eyes watered, blurring my vision. Though I gasped for air, I still couldn't breathe.

"You are in great peril, Miss Grey," Charles stated. "What others would do to have you join their Packs—"

"Shut the fuck up!" I growled, clutching my chest. "Just shut the fuck up!"

"Kenz," Jonah tried to comfort me, but I brushed him off.

They couldn't just drop a bomb like that and not expect me to freak out! I had been left in the dark my whole life, which made it easy to pretend I wasn't adopted. But now? Things were becoming real. The bastard knew it would get a rise out of me.

"Don't *Kenz* me! This is some serious shit! And you all knew!"

"You said you didn't want to know," Bash rebutted. "When you left, keeping you in the dark was okay because no one knew where you were, but now that you're back," he paused, "it changes everything."

"Why? We can keep this a secret between us. No one else has to ever know," I said. "I'll go far, far away. You'll never have to worry about me!" I attempted to bargain, but the looks on their faces told me everything I needed to know.

"Do you remember the Summit meeting I had to attend while you were home during winter break with Jonah?" Sebastian said.

I nodded.

"That was when I presented your lineage to the Summit. Everyone already knows. Your arrival in New York makes you fair game to any Pack that wants you."

I froze. "Excuse me? What the hell is *that* supposed to mean?"

"It means," Sebastian started, "that you're unclaimed and in American territory. Any Pack can easily force you into fealty."

"Force me?" I repeated.

"Yes, Miss Grey. Sebastian has been very kind with you, but if he really wanted, he could force you into the Pack," Charles said. "Because of my son's ... fondness of you, I have put all North-eastern Packs on alert that you are hands-off, but I cannot speak for other regions."

I could only imagine how I looked—like a red hot chili pepper. Terrifying scenarios ran through my mind and before I knew it, I was running out of his office. My earlier fears came to life as I stumbled and knocked over a vase of flowers. The sound of shattered glass was a distant noise as I rushed out of the house to the driveway. Hands on my knees, hair in my face, I bent over and tried to even out my breathing. I knew I was probably overreacting, but Charles played his cards. He expected me to join the Brooklyn Pack for my own safety, and I would be stupid if I didn't contemplate it.

"Mackenzie, are you okay?" Sebastian came up behind me as I dry-heaved. His presence provided a wall of concern.

"I just ... I couldn't stay in there," I panted.

"That's understandable. Sit down before you pass out." He motioned me over to the front steps of the mansion and sat beside me as we both stared off into the winding driveway. He kept a respectable distance, his posture rigid.

I shook my head as if that would make everything go away. "Bash," I whispered. "Is it true? Am I adopted?"

Those cold blue eyes softened as he stared into mine. He only nodded.

"I need to go home and speak with my parents," I said as I tried to stand.

"You can't just barge into your parents' home and demand answers." He gently pushed my shoulder to sit down again.

"And why the hell not?"

"Because they think you've been missing for the past year."

"What?"

"Mackenzie, I know you want to figure all this out. I see now why you didn't want to know, but aren't you concerned about the other thing Charles mentioned? Not all Packs are like mine. Some are aggressive and dangerous."

I was scared. I would be stupid if I wasn't, but that didn't mean I had to make a rash decision, either. I'd been free no more than ten minutes and my liberty was already being threatened. It almost seemed comical.

Jonah walked out but didn't hover. He stood at a distance,

leaning against one of the statues by the front stairs. "My father needs an answer, Kenz. Do you plan to stay a lone wolf?"

I felt my jaw slacken. "Are you serious right now?"

"Jonah, I don't think now is a good time," Bash said.

Jonah rolled his eyes. "I know, Bash, but she can't leave the estate without telling Charles her decision."

"Tell him to wait!" he barked.

"I'm not the bad guy here! Don't shoot the messenger."

Sebastian stood and glared at his Beta. "That's right. You're not a messenger, you're her *friend*."

"Okay, everyone chill," I cut between them. The last thing I needed was for them to get in a fight. I needed them both on my side. "Tell your father that nothing's changed. I won't be joining the Pack."

"Kenzie!" Jonah exclaimed. "Think about this. You won't be safe on your own."

"I'm not going to let someone own me!" I shrieked. "My freedom, my life, my goddamn decision. If you don't like it, you can kick rocks barefoot. I refuse to let anyone intimidate me, you hear?"

Sebastian wore a shit-eating grin and for a moment, I felt like I'd been thrown into an alternate universe. I thought for sure Bash would have been begging me to join the Pack.

"You're just going to let her do this?" Jonah asked his Alpha.

"You heard her, Jonah. It's her life, her decision. We will respect it and do what we can. You understand?" he ordered. Jonah could only nod and go back inside to tell his father.

"What was *that* about?" I asked.

"Nothing," he grumbled. "You still want to see your parents?"

I turned back to the house where Jonah stood at the doorway, a grim look on his face. Then I slid my gaze to Sebastian, who was already opening the car door. Once again, I was stuck in the middle, but this time I made a choice.

"Yeah, I still want to see them," I said and followed Bash.

———

A TWO-HOUR DRIVE of pure silence in which Sebastian gave me the space I needed and provided me an opportunity to calm down from my outburst in Little Falls. I was no longer having a total meltdown. I swear I could have been nominated for an Oscar with that scene I pulled at the estate. It was one thing to find out you were adopted, but to find out you were the bastard of a King, and that others were gonna come and try to kidnap you? Yeah, it was just too much for dear ole' Mackenzie Grey.

"What's going on between you and Jonah?" I said as we entered Cold Springs, my hometown.

"Nothing."

"No, there's something, and I feel like I'm entitled to know. So spill, because I won't shut up until you do."

He sighed. "We haven't been seeing eye-to-eye lately, that's all."

"Why? You guys are best friends."

"Sometimes that's not enough, Mackenzie. People change."

"Do I have anything to do with it?" I fiddled with the radio station to occupy myself.

"Yes," he whispered.

"Bash, don't mess up your friendship with Jonah because of me. Trust me when I tell you, I'm not worth it," I said, my heart shattered by this news.

He pulled the car into a random parking spot on the street and put the car in park. Sebastian turned and his gaze pierced me in place. His mouth was a firm line that hinted he was pissed.

"Mackenzie, you *are* worth it. And it's not because of who your father is, but because *you* are a very special woman. Jonah and I haven't been seeing eye-to-eye because he's letting his father fill him with all these thoughts that aren't in your best interest." He paused as if wondering whether to tell me or not. "I stopped looking for you within a month of your disappearance," he admitted.

My eyes widened. "Why?"

"Because whether I agreed with your decision to leave or not, it didn't matter. You didn't want to be a Luna, and honestly, I didn't think you'd be a very good one anyway," he chuckled. "Letting you go was the best thing I could do for you. But Jonah...he never stopped searching for you."

I didn't know whether to be insulted or not. Bash gave me what I wanted, but Jonah kept hope that I would still come back.

"Charles fed him a story about how he should get you back so he could mate with you to keep you safe. Don't get me wrong, Mackenzie, the idea has merit and Jonah is doing it with all the good intentions we both know he has. But his father's intentions aren't pure—not in the least."

"What does Charles want?"

"I don't know, but I can only guess he wants what all the other Packs want from you—power—an in with the European Summit. But that's an assumption, nothing concrete."

"I understand. Have you tried talking to Jonah?"

He nodded. "Many times."

"Okay, I'll talk to him."

WE HAD JUST PULLED up to my parents' small house when my cell phone rang. Roman's name appeared on the screen. He was worried, and I'd given him every reason to be. I declined the call again, telling myself to call him as soon as I made it back to the city and had some time alone.

"Mackenzie?" I heard my name as my mother's mouth fell open and tears fell down her cheeks. She was standing in front of the kitchen window that faced the front lawn, and then she disappeared as she ran through the house and outside. "Thomas!" she screamed. "Oh, my baby!" She ran to me and engulfed me in a hug that no longer felt warm.

My father came out of the garage in his signature fishing shirt and Levi's. "What's all that—*Mackenzie?*"

"Hey," was all I could say as they both held onto me with a death grip. "Can we go inside?"

My father's gaze turned to Sebastian, and unlike there had been with Jonah, there was no warm welcome. "Thomas Grey." My dad extended a hand to Bash and they shook. "You look familiar. Weren't you here two Christmases ago?"

"Yes sir," Sebastian answered.

"Are you the reason why my daughter disappeared?" my father accused.

I stepped between them before anything happened. "Dad," I choked. "No he's not. Can we please go inside?"

He nodded reluctantly and we followed my parents inside my childhood home. The small brick house hadn't changed, but it no longer felt like it was mine. Every school picture and family portrait that filled the walls of the living room felt like a lie.

"Where have you been, Kenzie?" my dad asked as he held my mother's hands. She was still crying.

"I was out west," I answered vaguely as I glanced at Sebastian. I didn't know why, but there was something in me—maybe the wolf—that told me I could trust him. "I needed some space."

"Space from what, dear? Us?" my mom said and I nodded. I couldn't tell them the truth. They'd lock me up in a mental institute unless I showed them what I was, and then they'd disown me. "But why?" she asked.

I raised my gaze toward them, trying to keep my own tears at bay. "Because I found out I'm adopted." It was the excuse I thought up while on our way to Cold Springs.

They paled, and that was all the confirmation I needed.

"How...?" my mother stammered.

Sebastian cleared his throat. "Mackenzie's biological parents gave her away to keep her safe. Her identity was compromised, and now she's in danger. It's why she had to leave." Once again, Bash came up with an excellent cover story. Good thing, because I couldn't seem to find my voice.

"I'm so sorry, Kenzie," my mother cried. "We didn't know." My father pulled her into his arms and held her.

"It was a closed adoption; how did they—whoever they are— find her?" my dad asked.

"We're still trying to figure that out," Bash answered.

"Why?" I mumbled. "Why didn't you ever tell me? Does Ollie know? Is he adopted too?"

My dad shook his dead. "He doesn't know...and he's our biological son."

"But—but we *look* alike!" I sputtered. "How is this even possible?" I was trying to find reason within all this madness. Oliver and I shared the same eyes. How could we not be related?

"Coincidence," my dad explained. "Pure coincidence."

"Were you ever planning to tell me the truth?" I didn't even know who I was anymore.

"Someday," he said. "We just never found the right time. I'm so sorry, Mackenzie. This doesn't mean we love you any less. You're still our daughter."

I wanted to be mad. I wanted to scream and throw things at them. Blame them for what was happening. But I couldn't. None of this was their fault, not entirely. If anything, I was blessed that they chose me. Who knows where I could have ended up? The real perpetrators of this web were my biological parents. They abandoned me in a world that wasn't meant for me. They left me with humans who I could have injured because I didn't know what I was. It was pure luck that I never hurt anyone.

"It's okay," I said, shedding the last bit of anger like a second skin. "*Parent* doesn't always mean blood. It's the ones who raised me that count. The ones who made sure I had a roof over my head and a hot meal every day. The ones who took care of me when I was hurt, and who were proud of me during my greatest accomplishments. You were both there...no one else. You're my parents."

9

I arrived in Cold Springs furious but returned to the city bearing a much lighter load. What I needed most was confirmation that what I suspected for the past year, since Charles first told me, was true. I wished there was another reason why I was a wolf, but I realized more than most that life wasn't fair.

We informed my parents of my situation as best we could, and I promised to stay in contact until the whole ordeal was over. I didn't want them to get caught in the crossfire of whatever was about to happen.

Since we were closer to the city than Little Falls, Sebastian dropped me off at the warehouse before making the trek back to the estate to pick up Jonah.

"Stay in the warehouse. I'll be back tonight. Until we know what threats are out there, I'd rather keep you safe with us," Sebastian said as he parked outside the building in Dumbo, Brooklyn.

"Roger that." I saluted and got out of the car.

"I mean it, Mackenzie. This isn't a joke."

I leaned into the open window of the passenger side and rolled my eyes. "I know, Bash. Chill."

As promised, I went inside the home of the Brooklyn Pack, but I wouldn't be staying there all day—it was only three in the afternoon. To be fair, Sebastian was right to be wary of me. While he was road tripping, I planned to start putting my plan into action.

"Hey, have you seen Blu?" I asked the first Luna I could find. She was a petite little thing, cleaning up a table where others had eaten. The whole situation made me grind my teeth.

"She's in the laundry room," she responded.

I was about to leave when I turned to her again. "Do you like cleaning up after others? Is this what you wanted to be when you grew up?" I knew I was being cruel, but they needed to face the harsh reality.

"This is all I know," she said and walked away.

THE LAUNDRY ROOM door was ajar, and I heard the yelling loud and clear. I busted in there like the police and found Blu cowering in a corner as another Luna tossed clothes from a basket all over the room.

"Vivian told you to do her load first before anyone else's. Why are her clothes still dirty?" yelled the Luna.

"Maybe because she should be doing it herself," I suggested as I strolled in.

Blu's frown flipped to a huge grin when she saw me, and I knew she was itching to tackle me into one of those Amy-hugs.

"Mackenzie!" she exclaimed.

I brushed past the Luna I didn't recognize and gave Blu a crushing hug. She gripped me something fierce. "Finally, someone who actually missed me!" I joked.

"Excuse me," the Luna behind me interrupted, "but we were in the middle of something."

"I know, but I take priority at the moment. Go on, shoo." I waved her off.

The Luna scoffed, "Wait until *Vivian* hears about this. She'll have both your heads!"

I whirled around on the girl, my gray eyes flashing silver. "I dare you," I growled. "Try me, because I'm the *last* person you want to mess with." I was in no mood to have my buttons pushed.

She stumbled backwards and diverted her eyes to the ground submissively, then left me alone with Blu.

"Oh my gosh, Kenzie, you can't do that!" Blu complained with a smile. "It was great, don't get me wrong, but Lunas aren't allowed to establish dominance."

"What if I told you I wanted to change that?" Her eyes sparkled. I remembered Blu as a very curvy woman, but since I'd been gone she'd lost weight, and not in a good way.

"I'd say you were asking for a death sentence," she replied dryly, crossing her arms over her chest.

"Possibly," I conceded. "But it seems like I'm already knocking on hell's door."

Her smile fell. "You know?"

"Well, shit, did everyone know but me?"

She shook her head. "Everyone found out after you ran away."

"Whatever, I don't want to talk about that. What I *do* want to chat about is the future of Lunas." I paused. "Look at me getting all political and shit. Can we say *Mackenzie for President in 2020?*"

Blu laughed. "You never change, Kenz, and that's good. But why this sudden interest in the plight of the Lunas?"

"Charles gave me my freedom," I said, and her eyes rounded. "But it came with a price. He told me that other Packs can come and pretty much force me into submission if they want to. And according to Bash, they want to ... because of, you know ... " I trailed off.

"I know," she said. "What are you planning?"

I straightened and my smile grew, excited about what I was about to share. I felt like I could finally do some good. "Okay, so Lunas have been taught to be mild and complacent all their lives, right?"

She nodded.

"Look at me, Blu. I'm the complete opposite. It's not a genetic defect; Lunas are just afraid to go against the grain. We need to learn to speak up and fight back. I can't be the only one who feels that way."

Blu shifted on her feet uncomfortably and scanned the empty room in case someone was eavesdropping on our conversation. She walked over to the laundry room door and shut it all the way, locking it from any intruders.

"What you're suggesting, Kenz, is treason. You might get special privileges because of who you are, but that doesn't mean it applies to the rest of us. I don't know ..."

"Answer me this," I started. "Are there other Lunas out there who want more? Who want to be free?"

She suddenly looked sick to her stomach. I understood her apprehension. She was going against everything she had been raised to believe in, and I knew my proposal wasn't ideal. I was no longer the underprivileged lone wolf; now I knew I came from some pretty important people. I might not be the best person to cry injustice, but no one else was doing it.

"Yes," she relented. "There is a group of Lunas who want things to change. They're from all over the Northeastern Pack. During the full moon, they shift together."

"A group has already formed?" I asked in shock.

She nodded. "But Lunas are scared to speak up, Kenz. They might agree on wanting change, but they won't do anything about it. We're very comfortable with our way of life. We would have to give up a lot in hopes of success. This could turn out badly for us."

"I understand, Blu, but if we don't try, we'll never know if it was possible. Don't you want to try?"

She stared at me for a long moment, debating whether I was right or wrong—whether fighting was even worth it.

She sighed. "I'll contact Rachel and let her know you want to talk, but that's all I can do—for now."

I wrapped my arm around Blu. "You know I missed ya, right?"

"Yeah, yeah." She swatted me away. "Of course you did."

ON MY WAY HOME, I received another call from Roman. When I tried to answer, I lost reception when heading toward the train. I reminded myself again to call him as soon as possible.

When I walked into the apartment in Alphabet City, Amy was lounging on the couch watching TV while working on her laptop.

Her flaming red hair was pulled into a messy top knot, and I was pretty sure she was still wearing pajamas.

"Whoa, now that's a fashion statement," I said as I shut the door and eyed her Harry Potter sweatpants and t-shirt. "Everything okay?"

She sighed, "I miss Jackson."

I snorted. "Oh, good Lord, scoot over." I knocked her feet off the couch and sat down. "It hasn't even been twelve hours, Amy! What is there to miss?"

"You have *no idea*, Kenz." She wiggled her eyebrows. "He does this thing with his tongue like ..."

She stuck out her tongue to show me, but I smashed the palm of my hand into her face. "No, Amy, please don't scar me more than I already have been today. Boundaries, please." I grimaced.

She pouted. "Bad day?"

I turned to her in anguish. "Horrible! I've been Jon Snow'd!" I exclaimed and she raised a brow.

"Explain." She reached for a box of Girl Scout cookies. "Thin mint?"

"No, you know I like Samoas."

She shrugged and grabbed one for herself. "Alright, what do you mean you've been Jon Snow'd? I have a million scenarios running through my head, and I'm praying it has nothing to do with White Walkers."

"Charles spilled the beans on my bio dad," I said.

Amy choked on a cookie and I patted her back as she coughed. "What? Like your *real* Pops?"

"The one and only. And get this, he's no regular Joe."

"Well, obviously. You're a total badass wolfey." She reached for my hand. "Who is he?"

I took a deep breath. "The King."

IT WAS nightfall by the time I finished telling Amy everything that had happened today. Beginning with Charles, to visiting my parents, and ending with my conversation with Blu. And of course, Amy took my side on everything because she was the greatest friend ever. Even after I ran off without her, she still stood by me when it counted. I vowed not to take our friendship for granted ever again.

"Do you know what he looks like? If not, we can get a picture of a wolf and pretend it's the sperm donor." She launched to her feet. "Oh! And we can dig up that dart board we have somewhere around here and stick his picture on it!"

I chuckled. "That's a great idea. While you look for it, I'm gonna go down to the bodega and get us something to eat. I'm starved." I stood from the couch and stretched.

"Ask Mrs. Mejia if she's serving breakfast sandwiches. I could really go for one at this time of the night."

"Oh my gosh, yes! A bacon, egg, and cheese on a hoagie sounds like heaven right now. You, my friend, are a genius." I bent down and gave her a loud kiss on the cheek.

Amy headed into the spare bedroom where my cage used to be, which had since been converted into a storage room. I grabbed my cell phone and ear buds and headed out of the apartment, figuring it was the perfect time to call Roman.

When I hit the second-floor landing, he answered on the first ring.

"Ace! Where the hell have you been? I've been worried sick!"

I plugged in my ear buds. "Sorry," I squeaked. "It's been crazy out here. But you'll be glad to know that I am now a free lone wolf!"

"What? How?"

"Charles, the Northeastern Alpha, gave it to me. I can officially stay in New York without any trouble from the Pack." The phone line went silent. "Hello?"

"I'm here," he said after a while. "What did you have to do for it?"

I swallowed the lump forming in my throat. There was no point keeping this a secret, at least not from Roman. It seemed like everyone else either already knew or would find out about it real soon. He might as well hear it from me.

"I didn't have to do anything. My father is King Alexander MacCoinnich," I muttered.

"WHAT?" Roman screamed into my ear.

"Holy shit, Rome, want to say that any louder? I think they heard you down in Florida."

"How come you never told me, Ace? This isn't the type of shit you keep from your lover," he barked, sounding hurt.

"Your *lover*?" I laughed. "I need you to come back to the twenty-first century, Rome. And for your information, I only found out today, so calm your tits."

The chime above the bodega door rang as I walked in. I looked over at the counter but didn't recognize the boy behind the register.

"You *just* found out? Holy shit, Ace! That's insane! What—" Roman rambled on while I muted the call.

"Hey, is Mr. or Mrs. Mejia around?" I asked the boy. He appeared to be no more than eighteen years old.

"They're on vacation. My mom and I are running the bodega while they're gone." By his accent, I pegged him as either Puerto Rican or Dominican. He spilled the beans about the owners' whereabouts as if I were harmless. I wanted to laugh. I was the most dangerous person here.

"Oh, that's nice. They deserve it."

"Ace? Ace, are you still there?" I heard Roman call out.

"Yes, I'm still here." I smiled at the boy and held up a finger so he would give me a second. I was roaming the aisles for snacks and listening to Roman when the smell of wet dog hit me. Except it was mixed with something else—I just couldn't put my finger on it. I wrinkled my nose and ignored it.

"Rome, it's no big deal. He's not my father, and I have no interest in meeting the bastard," I said as I grabbed a bag of jalapeño Cheetos.

"How can you not care, Ace? He—"

"Mackenzie Grey," a deep baritone voice said behind me.

I whirled around, not expecting my face to connect with a big, fat fist. The force behind it sent me crashing into the stand that carried all the potato chips, and my head slammed on the linoleum floor and bounced.

"What the fuck?" I shouted, blinking away the stars clouding my vision and trying to stand.

"Ace? Ace, what's going on?" Roman yelled, but I couldn't find my voice to answer. I needed to know where that hit came from.

The same hands pulled me up by the lapels of my jacket and dragged me across the store, my feet gliding over bags of chips that now littered the ground.

"It is so damn good to finally get my hands on you," rumbled the deep voice. "Hey Larry, come take a look at her. The boss will be *real* happy about this one."

My hands scrabbled at the wrist that held me and I extended my claws, digging them into his flesh.

"Oh, that's not how a pretty Luna like you is supposed to behave," he chastised as he backhanded me.

The stars were back, and I had to shake my head a few times to see. My breathing became erratic as I wondered who the hell these guys were. He flung me to the ground and I slid across the dirty floor, stopping when my back slammed underneath the counter.

"Sorry to disappoint, boys," I slurred, "but I think you've got the wrong girl." I attempted to stand, but my legs gave way and I fell on my ass again. My sight was blurred and I could only make out two very distinct body types: a scrawny guy, and the big guy who had dragged me around the bodega like a rag doll.

They both laughed. "She thinks we made a mistake," said the guy I assumed was Larry, the scrawny guy. His voice was nasally and high pitched; I imagined him as Gollum from *The Lord of the Rings*.

What's wrong with me? This was *not* the time for side commentary.

"Listen –" I was finally able to make my legs work and I stood. "I'm sure we can come to some sort of an understanding." I was never one to back down from confrontation, but that big guy knew how to pack a punch. I still wasn't seeing straight.

"The only *understanding* we have is bringing you to our Alpha," said Big Guy. He moved to reach for me again, but this time I was prepared. I roared and accommodated my wolf into a half-shift.

I turned to the boy who was frozen in shock behind the register. "Run," I growled before I pounced on the other werewolf. My claws extended and I aimed for the first person in my way. They slashed Larry right in the face, as Big Guy kicked me from behind. My vision cleared a bit and I saw the scrawny wolf cowering in a corner as he clutched the scraps of his bloody face.

"One down, one to go," I snarled. I scrambled to my feet as the big guy stomped toward me. With my sight in better shape, I got a good look and realized how massive he was, like a freakin' giant. His meaty hands aimed for my head again, but this time I ducked and slid across the floor like I was running to home plate. I swirled and hopped to my feet, striking him in the back of his knees. I kicked with all the force I could muster and he barely wobbled. I scanned the bodega and saw an old-fashioned wooden broom. I snapped it in half above my thigh and jammed the sharp ends into the back of his calves.

When Big Guy dropped to his knees, I could have sworn the floor shook like an earthquake. He howled in pain, but I didn't wait to see if he was incapacitated or not. I jumped on him, flinging the cord of my headphones out and wrapping it around his neck—pulling on opposite ends. He choked and flung his head back against my chest, the force almost knocking me down. I held on for dear life.

"Die, motherfucker!" I screamed and pulled even harder. I felt the cord ripping. "Come on!" I shrieked in anguish. Finally, his body fell limp, and I had to move out of the way before he pinned me to the floor.

Number eight.

I was dripping both blood and sweat, all my own. My legs

shook like Jell-O and I felt as if I would pass out at any moment. The asshole had rattled my brain.

"You!" I pointed to Larry and staggered over to him. "Who the fuck sent you?" I grabbed the collar of his shirt and hauled him to his feet.

"L-Logan," he stuttered. "T-The Alpha of the Ch-Chicago P-Pack."

I gripped him tighter. "And what the fuck does he want with me?"

He cried, "H-He wants you as h-his ma-mate."

I scoffed, "And *this* is how he courts a lady? He should watch a Nicholas Sparks movie and up his game," I said as I eyed Larry. He was shivering as if I'd poured a bucket of ice water on him. I didn't know what he feared most—me or his Alpha. "Are you a wolf?" I asked in shock.

"I'm an O-Omega," he stuttered.

"Whatever. Tell you what, Larry. You seem like a coward, so I'll let you live, unlike Big Guy over there." I jabbed my thumb behind me. "But I have a message for your Alpha."

I shifted back to human form and instantly felt the bruises and cuts on my face. Only adrenaline kept me going. "Tell him to come and get me."

10

I ran.

I ran like ice cream was my dying wish and the truck was five blocks away. I pumped my weary arms, raising my knees to my chest as I raced back to my apartment. Amy wasn't safe. They tracked me close to home, which meant they already knew where I lived. And my best friend wouldn't be able to protect herself.

My shoulder rammed into our apartment door, once again breaking off the hinges. "Amy!" I shouted. I barged into her room like the SWAT team and found her lying in bed watching something on her laptop.

"What took you so long? I'm hungry over—" She didn't finish. Her green eyes nearly popped out as she took in my current state.

My heavy breaths pumped in and out of me like a five-pack-a-day smoker. "We have to go—now!" I demanded, and for once, she didn't bombard me with a million questions. Amy took a moment to gather herself and then moved about her room to collect a few things while I did the same. Luckily, I'd never unpacked my duffle bag from Los Angeles, so I grabbed it and pulled my cell phone from my back pocket. The screen was so shattered, it wouldn't turn on. It was useless. I dumped it in my bag and waited for Amy at the front door.

We took a taxi to the only place I could think of where I felt safe—St. Paul's Cathedral. I needed to see Lucian.

I threw more money than charged at the cab driver and jumped out of the car as soon as we pulled up to St. Paul's. Amy's tiny feet tried to keep up and I had to stop, grab her wrist, and drag her behind me. We blazed up the steps of the cathedral as I pushed open the heavy doors and strode into the church.

We speed-walked between the pews as I called out, "Lucian! Lucian, I need your help!"

The vampire's porcelain skin and dark eyes were frozen in time, never to age a day as he came out of the sanctuary beside the altar. "Pet?"

I let go of Amy and ran to him. Never in a million years did I ever think I'd run to a vampire. "I need your help," I gasped as I collapsed to the ground. I no longer had the strength to hold myself together. I was somewhere safe, so I relaxed my guard and the pain came rushing toward the surface.

Lucian knelt beside me and managed to keep me upright. "What happened? Who did this to you?" Amy fell to her knees and gripped my hand.

"The Chicago Pack. They ambushed me inside the bodega down the street from my apartment," I sighed in exhaustion. "They must know where I live, Lucian. We're not safe there."

"You aren't safe anywhere, Pet," he murmured as he lifted me and carried me in his arms. "Come on, let's get you cleaned up."

THE SLOSHING SOUND of water as Amy re-dipped the bloody rag, squeezed, and dabbed it on my face captivated my attention. I tried to remain as still as possible while Lucian stitched up a cut on my arm, even though I wasn't a fan of needles. A few superficial cuts were scattered across my face, and the skin was held by medical tape. The bruising, on the other hand, would be rather noticeable.

"You should have listened when I told you to head to South America," Lucian complained. "We could have avoided all of this."

"Could we?" I challenged. "They would have found me sooner or later."

He huffed. "I would have made sure they didn't, but now? You're putting me in quite a pickle, Pet."

"I have no one else to turn to, Lucian. The next time they come for me, I might not be able to fight them off."

He finished stitching me up and sat on the stool beside me. We were in some type of infirmary or nurse's station. "You don't understand. There's not much I can do unless I want to start a war with the Lycan. And while you've grown on me, you haven't grown on me *that* much, Pet. I have to think about my people too, and if I put them on the line for you—well, that won't bode well."

"So, what are my options?"

"South America or ..." He paused. His dark eyes narrowed, made more pronounced by his blond hair slicked away from his face into a ponytail at the nape of his neck. "... or join the Pack."

"What?" I exclaimed. "Are you high? There's no way I'm joining a Pack!"

"Kenz," Amy called out. "You might not have a choice. It's for your safety."

"No, I'll die before I give up my free will." I climbed off the infirmary bed and walked over to the full-length mirror across the room, taking a good look at myself. I looked like I'd been run over—repeatedly. "You know," I started, "I wouldn't be surprised if this was all Charles' doing. He probably set this up when I rejected his offer."

Lucian froze. "What offer?"

"Nothing," I shook my head. "It's pointless now."

Lucian was at my side in two strides. An icy hand gripped my upper arm. "What. Offer?"

I arched an eyebrow. "I met with him this morning. He told me some stuff about who I am, but it's nothing important." I tried to downplay it, but he wouldn't let me.

"About your parents?" he inquired.

I shouldn't have been surprised that Lucian already knew. I was the last one in on the joke. "Seriously? Am I the only idiot who didn't know?"

"I didn't," Amy interrupted.

"Of course you didn't Aims," I said. "They know you would have told me."

"And you didn't think to tell me, Pet?" He frowned. "My feelings are hurt. However shall I move on?" He put the back of his hand on his forehead, pretending to feel faint. "I thought we were the bestest of friends."

"Really?" I deadpanned.

"Well, I should have been at least the second person you called upon hearing the news." He rolled his eyes. "At the *very* least."

"And why's that?" I smirked. He was always so theatrical.

"Because *now* I might have a way to help you." When he offered a secretive grin, I felt a sense of dread for what he had hidden up his sleeve.

I BEGGED Lucian to let us stay at the church, but even Amy wasn't having it. The vampires wouldn't be happy to have a wolf hanging around, and my best friend was uncomfortable by the whole arrangement. I attempted to bribe Amy with staying at a hotel, but she was afraid for me. Funny enough, I was afraid for her.

So there we were, standing in front of the warehouse in Brooklyn, waiting for me to grow some balls and go inside. I wasn't pretty at the moment, not that it mattered, but I knew Sebastian and Jonah would wig out. I needed to prepare myself for their reaction to my fucked-up face and the impending speech I was sure Bash would give me for not staying with the Pack as he recommended.

I took a deep breath. "Alright, let's go." I pushed the double doors open.

Sebastian and the captains were seated at one of the cafeteria tables eating. Blu and another Luna were picking up their discarded dishes when she looked over at us and dropped them with a clatter. The clanking of ceramic plates echoed throughout the vast room. The wolves all turned to her and then followed her shocked gaze to me.

She shuddered her shock away and started barking orders. "Get a bath started in the spare room," she instructed the other Luna. Then she turned to another one standing two tables away.

"Get me the first aid kit and some clean clothes." Blu hustled over to me and inspected my face, tilting my head toward the light so she could see better. "Kenz, what happened?"

"It's nothing." I tried to brush her off, but her hold on me was firm. "I've already had someone patch me up, Blu. Don't worry."

"Don't worry?" she scoffed. "You look like a battered plum!"

I gave her a sly smile. "A sweet plum?"

"Mackenzie," she chided. "This is not the time for your jokes."

Heavy boots resonated against the warehouse floor. I didn't need to look to know who they belonged to.

"What happened?" Sebastian barked. "Who did this?"

"Listen," I raised my palms up in defense, "let's not go overboard. It's no big deal. Just a few scratches—"

"*A few scratches?*" Bash yelled. "I'll ask once more, and then my patience is up. Who did this?"

"The Chicago Pack," Amy tattled. "She was attacked at the bodega by our apartment. We think they know where we live."

Sebastian's blue eyes turned fierce and I imagined smoke coming out of his ears as his nostrils flared. *These damn wolves and their short tempers*, I mused. Bash stomped over to the nearest table, not worrying who was seated there, and flipped it over. Everything came crashing down, the sound so much louder in the quietness of the warehouse.

"Maybe I should come back another time," I said, inching backwards.

"NO!" he roared, pointing a finger at me. "You're not going anywhere! I told you to stay in the warehouse and you didn't listen!"

And *there* was the 'I told you so' I was expecting.

I geared up for battle. "When are you going to get it through that thick skull of yours that I don't have to do everything you say? I am *not* part of the Pack!"

His eyes went wild. "Pack or not, you're only safe here! Other Packs cannot attack on our property. Do you get it now?"

I looked away. "Maybe you should have said something about that earlier," I mumbled, hearing him groan impatiently.

"Just ..." he paused as he ran a hand over his pitch-black hair. "Just stay here!"

"Roger that." I saluted and swerved around him. "How about that bubble bath?" I waggled my brows at Blu and she led me to the second floor. Halfway up the stairs, I heard a name I never thought I'd hear in New York.

"Ace?" a small voice asked from the main floor. I whirled around and my eyes landed on a little girl with strawberry blonde hair and blue eyes.

"Emma!" I ran down the steps toward her. She met me halfway and wrapped her frail arms around me.

"Did you come for me?" she said with such excitement, I almost wanted to lie and say I had.

I squatted down in front of her, groaning when I felt something snap in my right knee. "Holy cheese balls," I grumbled.

"Are you okay? You look like shit," Emma remarked as she touched a blossoming bruise on my face.

Jonah was standing behind her, and I wasn't sure if his face was shocked because of my appearance or because she cursed. Could be both.

"Always so eloquent," I deadpanned. "What are you doing here?"

She shrugged and jerked her thumb at Jonah. "This dude told

me I was going to see some chick named Mackenzie Grey. You know her?"

I couldn't resist the laugh that bubbled up, though it caused some serious pain in my ribs. "Yeah, I know her. She's the greatest werewolf in the whole world. And beautiful, don't forget that. She is one hot tamale."

"Doubt it." Emma rolled her eyes.

"Kenz, stop lying to the girl," Amy said as she extended her hand. "Hi! I'm Amy."

Emma looked at the offered hand, then at Amy, and then at me. "Is she for real?"

"What's wrong?" I asked.

"She's human."

"Yup, and she's my best friend, so be nice."

Emma did a double-take. "Wait, she called you Kenz ... are *you* Mackenzie?"

"In the flesh." I grinned. "Ace is an alias."

"Doesn't matter to me," she said. "Why am I here?"

"Good question, kid." I turned to Jonah. "Why is she here?"

I could tell by the firm line of his mouth that Jonah was dying to ask me questions about what happened to me. By this point, I was sick and tired of retelling it, so he'd have to get the scoop from Bash.

"You said you wanted to see her and make sure she was okay," he admitted.

I did, though I'd forgotten my request after finding out who my bio dad was.

"My father said she could stay with us for as long as either of you wanted. He hasn't found a suitable Pack for her yet," he continued.

"Well then, kid, what do you say? Want to hang out here for a while?"

Her gaze traveled over the warehouse and the assembled wolves who watched the exchange with wide eyes.

"As long as I get my own room and nix the curfew—I'm game."

EVERYONE WENT TO SLEEP, but since my night schedule was still wonky, I was wide awake. I was also afraid I might have a concussion, so I stayed up just in case. When the silence of my room was too much for my ADD-ridden self to bear, I slipped out to the main floor. In all my times coming here, I'd never asked where the kitchen was. In this moment, I regretted my lack of foresight. My stomach grumbled and I froze mid-step, afraid my belly would wake someone.

Amy was sleeping with Jackson—*ew*—and I had no clue where Jonah slept, but I did have an idea where Sebastian might be. I crept down to the basement and to his office. Sure enough, the light was still on and I heard his strong heartbeat through the door.

I knocked twice and peeked through the crack of the door. "Can I come in?"

He looked up from an open book and nodded. "What are you doing up?"

"I can't sleep."

He grunted. "Same." He waved me over to one of the chairs in front of his desk. "How are you feeling?"

"Like a ninety-year old woman who needs a hip replacement," I admitted as I slid into the seat.

"You should shift. The wolf will heal you quicker," he suggested.

I shook my head. "I'm hoping my ugly mug will deter any other potential suiters."

Bash watched me carefully for a moment. "With those eyes —unlikely."

I splayed my hands over my heart. "Aw! Did Sebastian Steel just compliment *moi?*"

He grinned. "Don't let it go to your head, Grey."

"It already has." I winked, and even that small gesture made my head throb. Maybe shifting wouldn't be such a bad idea.

"You don't look well, Mackenzie," Bash said as he came around and leaned against his desk in front of me. "Let's go out. I'll shift with you."

He extended a hand and I reluctantly took it. Not because I didn't want to, but because every time I moved, I hurt. Sebastian's blue eyes were impossibly bright under the florescent lighting; they always looked so much more pigmented in contrast to his black hair. His square jaw and Roman nose made him look like a Greek god. It was really unfair that he was that good looking. Especially compared to the state of disarray in which I currently found myself.

I was on my feet when my knees wobbled. I wasn't going to fall, but Bash wrapped an arm around me anyway, smashing me against his chest.

"Bash ..." I warned as his heart beat in tandem with my own.

I had always assumed that Sebastian Steel only wanted me because I was hard to get—just to say he had me. And that what I felt for him was purely physical, an insatiable lust demanded by my wolf. Whenever we were in the same room I gravitated toward him like a magnet, but that spark could also be due to our similarities; we were both stubborn control freaks. It was no wonder I felt this pull. He wasn't perfect—far from it—but I was starting to realize that no matter what, I could count on him. Even if he was a short-tempered, domineering wolf.

"Just listen to what I have to say, Mackenzie," he whispered, only a hair's breath away from me. "I plan to do things much differently this time around. If you're here to stay, I won't let you slip away again."

"I can't," I protested. "Nothing's changed, Bash."

"Why?" A cool smile curled his lips. "Name one thing standing in our way."

"I can give you a grocery list of things in our way. Don't you have any consideration for Jonah? I promised I wouldn't get between you two, and I still stand by that decision."

With his arm encircling me, I shuddered with his touch. His gaze flared with desire and I had to look away. My body betrayed my words, keeping me rooted firmly in place. My wolf awoke and clawed inside me, demanding to take control, but I couldn't let her.

He exhaled. "You're right. My apologies." The moment he stepped away, I felt an emptiness that made me reach for the desk to stay upright. "It's not easy being around you, Mackenzie."

"Ditto," I muttered as I tried to get my bearings. I might have been able to move on from James with Roman, but I couldn't be a floozy, either. I'd just slept with Roman the other day. *Boundaries, Kenzie,* I thought. Being around all these wolves would be the death of me.

Sebastian squared his shoulders. "We should still go out for a run. If I'm attracted to you with a bruised face, so will any other wolf. Let's go." He reached in a drawer for a set of keys.

With a blank look, I only nodded and followed him out. I was doomed.

11

We were in Central Park in the middle of the night, yet all I heard was the squealing of brakes a far distance away. I expected to find people milling around no matter the hour. I kept an eye open for the fae, remembering this was their territory that the wolves helped to protect, but didn't see anyone.

Trekking further into the woods, Sebastian stopped and pulled off his shirt in one fell swoop. I gulped as I traced the curves and indents of taut muscle on his back with my eyes. I attempted to memorize every inch of him in case this was our last time together. At least that was the reason I used to try to convince myself.

"You're staring," he said, his back to me. "I can feel your eyes, Mackenzie."

"Right," I mumbled and began to undress. Taking a hair tie from my pocket, I pulled my dark brown hair into a high ponytail. "Will the fae mind that we're here?"

"As long as we don't disturb them, it's okay," he said as he watched me pull down my jeans. I felt dizzy as he ensnared me in his gaze, those blue eyes following my every move.

"So how does this work?" I asked, my voice sounding like sandpaper. "The healing part," I clarified.

An idle smile played over Sebastian's lips and I was positive he knew what his presence did to me. So unfair. He had a perfect poker face.

"We are Lycans, a strain of the wolf, mixed with magical properties that allow us to shift from human to wolf and vice versa. Within those magical properties, we have the ability to heal quicker. It does not fix us right away, but it speeds up the process. What takes humans weeks to recover from, takes us no more than twenty-four hours."

"Well, damn, I wish I would have known that sooner," I snorted. While working with the SIU, this would have been a nice tidbit to have that time I was chasing a fire fae. I'd spent a month trying to regrow my eyebrows.

"You've been hurt like this before?" He squinted.

"Uh, yeah, but it's no biggie," I said. Without thinking, my gaze glided down his body and stopped right at his package. *Holy mother of—!* My eyes snapped back up to his face before he caught me. "Ready?" I squeaked.

"Yes, let's go," he said and started to run further into the woods. I followed behind him as we sprinted, jumped over rocks and logs, and avoided getting smacked in the face with branches. We ducked and swerved with the swiftness of a wolf as my shoulders arched back and I felt the ripple of my bones shifting. I felt no pain amidst my human body being damaged. On the contrary, the pain in my ribs receded and I exhaled in relief. Before, it hurt just to breathe. I craned my neck from side to side and let out a deep howl as I dropped on all fours. The wolf was out.

"HOLY SHIT, Bash! I thought you were going to run into the lake chasing that damn squirrel," I laughed as we jogged back to where our clothes were hidden.

"It was a chipmunk, and of course I wasn't going in the water. I'm not daft, Mackenzie." He rolled his eyes.

"Well, *excuse* me." I pushed him, teasing. Sebastian's head snapped to me when he almost fell.

"Did you just push me?"

"Ohhh, is the big, bad wolf angry?" I goaded as I jogged backwards. I clamped an arm over my breasts to prevent them from bouncing all over the place—not that I had much to bounce.

"I don't think you want to play this game, Mackenzie." Sebastian stalked me like prey and my stomach tightened—in a good way.

"Oh yeah?" I baited.

"I like a good chase." When he grinned, I almost stumbled on my own feet. His eyes narrowed as he ran a hand through his ink-like hair. "Run," he growled.

"Crap." I turned around and took off at a sprint. Sebastian's loud steps thudded behind me and my body shuddered with excitement. The anticipation of being caught was both terrifying and thrilling. I couldn't wipe the goofy smile off my face as I felt him get closer. I wanted him to catch me.

His hand snaked around my middle and lifted me off the

ground. A fit of giggles erupted from me as Bash flipped me and threw me over his shoulder, then smacked my bare ass.

"Did you really think I wouldn't catch you, Mackenzie?" He paused. "I'll always catch you."

I was face-to-face with Sebastian's well-sculpted behind, my ponytail swinging as he walked back to our clearing. I wiggled my ass, feeling too exposed, when his palm resonated against my skin.

"Keep still," he growled.

"Okay, Bash," I gasped, the blood rushing to my head. "You caught me, now put me down!"

"Oh, no," he chuckled. "You wanted to play, now we're going to play."

I felt my skin warm and my face turn red at his words as I awaited what he would do next. Once he stopped walking, he slid me down the front of his body and I could feel his hardness against my stomach.

"Bash," I warned.

"Mackenzie," he said, a sly smile crawling over his face. He dug his fingers into my side and tickled me.

"Shit, shit!" I cackled as he brought me to the ground on my back with him above me—a position that was too dangerous for two people who were way too attracted to one another to be in. "Okay, I surrender!" I called out.

He rolled off and laid on the ground beside me with a loud thud. We were nestled on a patch of grass, dry leaves rustling beneath us with every move. Sebastian's scent engulfed me, and for a moment it was all I could smell—the familiar smell of the woods after it rained, along with a hint of peppermint. My head turned to face him, not expecting to see him staring back.

"Did you have a good run?" he asked, his voice hoarse.

"Yes."

"How does your body feel?"

I wanted to hump him like a freakin' dog, but I couldn't say that. *Get it together, Kenz.*

"Better. My ribs no longer hurt," I said. "Thank you, I needed this. Aside from the physical healing, it helped clear my mind."

He nodded. "I understand. It's not easy to find out you were abandoned."

I stilled. My jaw opened and closed as I tried to figure out a response. *What is he talking about? I don't feel abandoned ... do I?*

"I don't—"

"I recognize the sadness in your gaze, Mackenzie," he said. "It's the same one I had when my father dropped me off at the Cadwell Estate."

I jerked up to a sitting position. "What?"

He shifted to his side and rested his head on his propped-up hand. He quieted for a moment and observed me as if contemplating whether to share something about himself. I didn't know anything about his past—unlike Jonah.

"If you don't want to tell me, it's okay, Bash. We're all entitled to our secrets."

He cleared his throat before he said, "My mother was human ... and I was the product of rape."

A small gasp escaped my lips. I wanted to reach out and comfort him, but Sebastian always had this tough, cold wall around him that stopped me. He spoke without a hint of vulnerability, in such a clinical way, with no emotion laced in his words. It was both disarming and sad.

"You see, not all wolves are good, Mackenzie, but they're not all bad, either. Like humans, there are always bad apples in the bunch." He paused. "My father was a bad apple.

"I was born in Providence, Rhode Island to Margaret Pierce and Gregory Steel. According to Charles, Greg was visiting a friend in Providence when he decided to have a night out on the town."

"Bash ..." I reached for him. "You don't have to tell me if you don't want to."

"I do—I have to. You need to understand," he said. "Wolves have a hard time when they don't get their way—especially from Lunas, but even worse when it comes from humans. We consider humans less than us, so when Margaret turned down his advances, his pride wouldn't allow it. He left town shortly after, never realizing he'd impregnated the woman he forced himself on. Eleven years after his visit, I had a similar run-in to the one you had, but with the local Pack. They caught Gregory's scent on me and informed him that I was his son."

Nothing but the sound of Sebastian's voice and the hard winds of winter were heard in the dead quiet of the night. My heart pounded in my ears as I processed Bash's story. It made my own family issues seem miniscule in comparison.

"He came back. He slaughtered my mother and then dropped me off on the front steps of his Alpha's home, pawning me off. Not once did he speak to me, and I was too scared to try. Anytime I looked at him, he would flash his wolf eyes and I nearly pissed myself. I didn't know what he was or that this world even existed, but he got what he deserved in the end. Charles made sure of it when he found out the truth."

"Is he ... dead?"

"Very much so," he replied. "This is why I will never force you to join the Pack, and why I need you to understand how much danger you're in, Mackenzie. While I wish you would reconsider, I accept your decision, but there are still many bad apples out in the world. I would lose my mind if they ever got ahold of you."

I gulped. A lot of things started to make sense and I had a newfound respect for the Alpha. Things were unfair for the Lunas in his Pack, but it could have been a lot worse if another leader had found me. Even if he didn't realize it, he was changing things within their system as well. Starting with me.

"Thanks," I whispered. "You've been a jerk at times, but I get that it could have been worse."

He nodded. "How about we head back? I think you're getting a little cold," he smirked as his gaze fell to my breasts.

I looked down and then slapped my arm over them. "Bash!"

"*Now* you want to be modest?" He chuckled, and suddenly it was like we hadn't finished such a heavy conversation. I couldn't understand how he was able to do that, open himself up and then shut down. If he had a method, I wanted the secret. After learning the truth of where I came from, I wasn't sure how much longer I could last before I snapped. With me, it could go either way: either I cried like when I watched the movie *P.S. I Love You*, or I could get angry and revert to my aggressive ways. Only time would tell.

We found our spot where we had hidden our clothes, and I had just put on my bra and underwear when we heard twigs snap a few feet to our left. It wouldn't have been that big a deal except it was loud—which meant a person was headed our way.

We jumped to attention in our undergarments as Sebastian lifted his nose in the air and sniffed. His rigid body relaxed once he caught the scent. "It's ..."

"Well, look who we have here," a feminine voice purred from between the trees. "It's been *so* long, Mackenzie Grey."

Her paper-white hair was like a beacon of light. The Fae Queen walked into the clearing in her sheer pink dress, her long hair trailing on the ground behind her. Two strands of hair on either side were twisted and pulled back, keeping her hair away from her face—her pointy elf-like ears on full display.

"Drusilla," I murmured. "How lovely."

"Yes," she smirked. "Lovely indeed. Sebastian? Is that you, love?"

I growled.

"Oh, simmer down, Mackenzie, I've only slept with Jonah." She waved off my ire flippantly. "He's a hard habit to kick. While you were gone, we—"

"What do you want, Drusilla?" Sebastian said, his voice gruff with impatience. He moved closer and stood between me and the Queen, protecting me. All I could think was, *Her and Jonah?*

"Always to the point and no foreplay," she giggled. Her pale gray eyes shifted to me. "Well, then, I'll just grab what I came for and be on my way. Gentlemen?" She signaled.

Three male fae stepped into the clearing wearing nothing but fitted, forest green pants. Each one held a bow and arrow nocked and aimed at us. Their shoulder-length hair and pointed ears made me think of Tinkerbell for some reason.

"What is the meaning of this, Drusilla?" Sebastian barked.

"This is of no concern to you, Alpha. We just want the girl."

He growled, "If you want Mackenzie, then yes, it *is* my concern. You will not go near her."

"What he said." I jabbed my thumb toward Bash. "I'm not good company anyways, Queen Bee. I tend to talk a lot."

Her grin stiffened. "Trust me, lone wolf, you're the last person I'd go to for entertainment. But alas, you aren't for me."

"For who, then?" Sebastian demanded. "With this act, you're breaking our treaty."

"I am breaking *nothing*, Alpha. I'd advise you to remember that our agreement protects *Pack* members *only*," she said. "We were hired by the Toronto Pack for the retrieval of this lone wolf. If you stand in our way, *you* will be the one breaking our treaty."

Sebastian's chest rose in rapid motions, his breathing coming out heavy. He was aggravated with the mire of wolf politics. He couldn't protect me here.

"Just because *he* can't do anything, doesn't mean *I* won't." I twisted my mouth to the side. "How dumb do you think I am?" I paused and shook my head. "Wait, don't answer that."

"You cannot fight us, Mackenzie. You don't know our magic," Drusilla boasted with the over-confidence common to every asshole.

"Mackenzie," Sebastian warned. "She's right, just let me think."

"Clock's ticking, Alpha," the Fae Queen chided.

I smiled. "Don't worry, Bash, I got this." I pushed him out of the way, still only in my undergarments, and faced the three bow-wielding fae. "Alright, boys, give me your best shot," I beckoned.

One of the henchmen dropped his bow and ran toward me, his platinum hair tucked behind his ears. He swung and I ducked and rolled out of the way, coming face to face with his buddy, this one with bright green eyes that blazed with fury as he began speaking an incantation.

"Nice try, buddy," I jeered as I rammed my knee against his sternum and drop-kicked his ass. The one behind me grabbed my arms and pulled them back while the third fae readied his arrow. I stopped.

"Not so swift, now," Drusilla giggled.

"I'd bet all fifty-seven dollars in my bank account that you guys need me alive, so let that arrow fly," I smirked. I hadn't noticed Sebastian was on his knees, claws digging into the earth and growling as he restrained himself from helping me. His glowing sapphire orbs stared at me with anger and frustration. There was nothing he could do to help unless he wanted to break the treaty, and I saw the pain behind his eyes. I wouldn't be surprised if he threw it all away for me and started a war, but I couldn't let that happen.

"You might not be killed, but nothing can stop us from hurting you," the fae behind me whispered. The arrow was released and I slammed my head backward, hearing the satisfying crunch of cartilage.

"AH!" the fae yelled. I swerved, and the arrow missed and struck his shoulder instead.

"Thanks." I grinned and stalked toward the one in front of me. He began whispering another incantation, but what they didn't know was that the tattoo on my hip bone protected me from their magic. It was a gift from Roman when I first began working with the SIU. A small Celtic triquetra was inked on my skin—a Celtic three corner infinity knot within a circle—which protected me from all malicious magic.

I grabbed some soil from the ground and threw it into the fae's face, breaking his concentration, then rammed my palm up his nose, making it spurt blood like a fountain.

"Sorry, Fae-man, I'm sort of bullet-proof," I joked as I grabbed him from the back of his neck and flung him to the ground. "And

I didn't even have to shift. Did you underestimate me? Because I feel like they went easy on me," I taunted, turning my steely gaze to Drusilla.

"That's impossible," she whispered, taking a step back. "You are not just a wolf, then."

I sighed, "Bash, what restrictions does a lone wolf have if they want to attack a certain queen?"

"None," he growled.

My grin widened. "Perfect."

Drusilla didn't lose her decorum. She was poised to perfection, with clear distaste in her scowl. Her pale eyes roamed my body up and down, searching for whatever was protecting me. Unfortunately for her, it was hidden beneath my underwear.

"You lay one finger on *me*, Mackenzie Grey, and I will kill *him*." She pointed to Sebastian. "Want to gamble his life?"

I stopped mid-step. My teeth grinded as I clenched my fists. "Let me make myself clear, Drusilla. This is the last time you attempt to do me any harm, or I promise next time, I'll gamble everyone's life to end yours."

"Understood," she sneered.

"And Dru?" I said. "I'd be careful who I make deals with next time. You might live to regret them."

SEBASTIAN and I raced out of Central Park so fast, we were still holding our clothes in our hands when we made it to his car. I kept my mouth shut on the ride back to the warehouse. His anger radiated out of his pores and I feared awakening the beast. I'd seen it before, and it wasn't a very happy wolf. He parked the car across the street but didn't move to leave the vehicle. I sat with him in utter silence until his breathing slowed to a calmer cadence.

"How were you able to repel the fae's magic? Those incantations are as old as time. No one is capable of deflecting them without some sort of assistance." His voice was low, but it resonated in the quiet night.

I pushed my hip up and pulled down the top of my panties until my tattoo was revealed. It was small and gold, easy to miss. The color blended well with my tan skin.

He exhaled. "For once, I'm glad you didn't risk your life on pure stupidity."

"You thought I'd bring a knife to a gun fight?" I asked with mock horror.

"Yes, Mackenzie. You have a tendency to speak before you think—at least you used to," he retracted. "What the hell were you up to in the last year? Ninja training?"

"Wouldn't you like to know?" I teased.

I unlocked my passenger door and stepped outside. Bash followed behind me as we crossed the street to the warehouse and entered. The captains hovered over a map on one of the cafeteria tables when I heard Amy yelp.

"They're here!"

"What's happening?" Sebastian barked.

Jonah stepped forward as his eyes ran over our bodies and flashed gold. Sebastian was in his boxer briefs, while I wore my sports bra and panties. This wasn't the attire I wanted everyone to see me in.

"Awkward ..." Amy muttered as she turned to Jackson, who was barely holding back a laugh.

"We heard your cry, Bash," Jonah gritted between his teeth. "We should be asking *you* what happened."

"His cry?" I asked. "You were crying?" I arched a brow at Bash.

"I wasn't *crying*, Mackenzie." He rolled his eyes. "I howled. The Pack must have heard me."

Jonah scoffed, "Of course we did. I've never heard you in such pain."

"Enough," Sebastian clipped out. "Everyone can return to their rooms."

"What happened?" Jonah pushed. "You can't just dismiss us after calling out to us. This is *not* how things work, Sebastian!"

"Jonah ... learn your place," Sebastian growled.

"I was attacked again tonight." I stepped between the Alpha and Beta. "The Toronto Pack hired the fae to capture me. We went for a run, and they took a shot at me in Central Park. That's all that happened."

"Oh my gosh, Kenz." Amy came toward me and gripped my hand. "Are you okay? You don't look hurt ... Whoa, you look much better now than you did after your first attack."

I nodded. "It's why we were out there, so I could shift and heal."

"You couldn't help her, could you?" Jonah asked Sebastian, although it seemed he already knew the answer.

Sebastian shook his head. "She's not Pack, which means it would have broken our accords with the fae."

"Fuck the treaty, Bash! How could you let her fend for herself?" Jonah tried to push past me, but Jackson was there to hold him back.

"Easy, brother," he said. "Remember who the real enemy is."

"It's okay, Jonah. I was prepared to handle them," I said,

raising my hands to stop him. "And I'm not worth starting a war over. I understand my place in this fucked-up caste system."

"You? Prepared?"

I rolled my eyes. "Yes, me. Now drop your hissy fit and let's all go back to sleep. I feel weird standing before you all in my underoos."

The captains laughed while Sebastian and Jonah glared at me.

"What are we going to do about the Packs?" Jonah asked. "She won't stay locked up in the warehouse, and even if she did, we cannot keep her here forever."

"I second that," I said as I slipped on my t-shirt. "And I can't keep asking for your help, either. I don't want to put the Pack in a situation that could bring conflict."

"What do you suggest?" Sebastian asked.

I scrunched my mouth to the side. "I haven't thought that far ahead," I admitted.

Bash sighed. "Until then, stay in the warehouse. If you need to go anywhere, take me or Jonah with you ... clear?"

"Crystal." I winked.

"Good," he said, his voice weary. I wouldn't believe me either, if I were him. "Now, let's all get to bed. My apologies for waking everyone."

The captains all muttered their responses of support for their Alpha and left the main floor. Amy squeezed my hand before slinking with Jackson back to his room.

"Night, Kenz," she said.

I smiled. "Night, Amy."

Jonah stood still for a moment, watching me with those milk chocolate eyes that used to melt me into a pool of teenage hormones. Since I arrived, things had been wonky between us. Tomorrow, I needed to have a sit-down with him. I needed both him and Bash in my corner, and although I knew Jonah would never do a thing to harm me—it didn't mean he wouldn't unintentionally sabotage my plans.

"Goodnight, Jonah. We'll talk tomorrow?"

"Count on it." He gave me a small smile, his one dimple playing on his cheek.

I was about to leave when Sebastian caught my wrist. "About tonight ..." he started. "I hope it stays between us."

"Of course, Bash," I said, stunned that he would even think I'd share something so personal with anyone. I wouldn't even tell Amy.

"Good," he said. The wall between us clicked back into place as he returned to the basement and I was left alone.

12

My hair did not want to cooperate. It was a bird's nest as a result of all my tossing and turning in my sleep. Shifting last night might have healed me, but my emotions were catching up to all the turmoil of recent events. In less than twenty-four hours I'd been attacked by two Packs, but none of that plagued my mind as much as King Alexander MacCoinnich. My dreams were filled with self-conscious musings about what he looked like, if he ever thought of me, or if he even knew I existed. A small voice in the back of my mind kept asking the same question: *Will he help me?* I shook my head. No, he wouldn't. Lunas wouldn't be considered second-class citizens if he cared.

A knock came at my door and I was pulled out of my head and back to the real world. "Come in," I called out.

Blu's head popped in and she bit her lip. "Kenz ... uh ... someone wants to talk to you."

"Who?"

"J-Just come up to the attic," she said.

I stopped fiddling with my hair in the mirror. "What's going on, Blu?"

She slipped into my room and shut the door with her back. "Rachel is in the attic waiting for you," she whispered. "No one goes up there. It's the perfect place to talk when you don't want to be overheard."

"Oh, okay! But you could have just said so, Blu. Stop wiggin' out." I laughed and pulled my hair into a ponytail. "Ugh, my hair is being a pain in the ass."

"It looks beautiful, Kenz, but I have to go. I cannot be involved. There's a door at the end of the hall on the third floor. It will take you to the attic."

I nodded. "Alright, Blu, thanks for everything you've done." I meant it. I knew it was hard for her to go against the traditions of the Pack and I hadn't expected her to go this far. She'd already been burned once by the Pack for rebelling, which was a story I still needed her to tell me someday.

She smiled and left my room. I slid my feet into my Nike Air Max's and pulled on a hoodie. I was too tired to care what I looked like. I needed coffee and food before I withered away. Dramatic, I know.

I headed to the third floor, searching for the door she mentioned when I found it at the south end of the warehouse. No one was up there, and I prayed no one would see me on the balcony. I pulled the hood over my head and tucked my hands into the front pockets of my sweatshirt.

I twisted the handle of the door that led to the attic and it revealed ... a closet.

"What the ...?" I slid my hand up the wall, looking for the light switch. I flicked it on and the closet brightened, revealing a single string hanging from the ceiling. I tugged on the string and a folded ladder came down. "Ah, the attic. Cool," I murmured to myself as I shut the door behind me and started to climb.

Natural sunlight filtered through the dusty windows in the attic. A few dusty boxes cluttered the space, but not much else. I sneezed a few times as I swatted away dust bunnies. The floorboards creaked with every step I took. At the end of the room, by the window overlooking the street, a Luna stood with her back to me.

"Rachel?" I asked. She turned around and I had to swallow the gasp that threatened to come out. Half of her hair was shaved off, and four claw marks raked down her face and over her scalp. One of her eyes was sealed shut by scar tissue.

"Mackenzie Grey," she said, her lips moving with an unnatural twist as she spoke. "It's a pleasure to meet you."

"Likewise," I mumbled.

She laughed. "Let's get the questions out of the way. I know I'm not what you were expecting."

"Definitely not," I whispered.

"It's okay. I was already warned of your lack of filter—it's refreshing."

I nodded. "So what happened to you?"

She waved me over to the window and I walked up to her. She pulled two boxes over and we sat down. "I'm from the Chicago Pack," she started. "I heard you already had a run-in with them, eh?"

"Yeah." I scrunched my eyebrows together and curled my lip. "They were a real piece of work."

She laughed. "Yes, well, when I refused to mate with one of

their captains, they did this to my face. Real piece of work," she repeated as she pointed to her disfiguration.

"Fuck," I gasped. "Isn't that illegal?" I wanted to jump out of my seat in outrage. How could they let something like this happen? It was against all human rights laws—then I remembered we weren't human.

"No. Logan, the Alpha, was the one who carried out the order of my punishment."

"Couldn't you shift to heal?" I asked, thinking back to how much it helped me last night.

She shook her head. "These weren't superficial wounds that would heal with time, even for a human. They ripped apart my skin and took one of my eyes. I can heal, but the scars will never disappear."

"This is bullshit!" I raged. "How could anyone let this happen? Something has to be done about it!"

Her hand rested atop my right knee as it bounced wildly. "It has been over a decade since it happened. What's done is done," she exhaled. "But enough about me. Blu told me you were interested in speaking. What of?"

The fury within me was a forest fire that wouldn't die down anytime soon. Rachel's testimony only further motivated me to action. I would find justice for all victims like her, and for the future Lunas like Emma. This sort of barbaric treatment had to end.

"I want freedom—but not just for myself—for all of us. And I need your help."

Rachel leaned back and straightened. She obviously hadn't expected my call for war.

"What exactly are you proposing, Mackenzie? I'm sure it's not an uprising, because that would be treason," she chided.

I swallowed the lump that formed in my throat. "That's exactly what I'm proposing."

She stilled.

"Just hear me out, Rachel. I'm sure what's happened to you has happened to many others. Right now, there is an eleven-year-old Luna in the warehouse and Charles has no idea where to place her. What if she lands in a Pack similar to Chicago's? Is that the future you envision for any child you plan to have? To raise girls who will become slaves and boys who will become monsters?" I took a breath and eased my racing pulse. "We can do something about it. We have to stand up for ourselves! We are more than capable. I'm living proof that we are."

"You are the exception, Mackenzie Grey. You're not one of us, and you never will be." She gave me a sad smile. "Count your lucky stars that you are privileged enough to avoid this lifestyle. We appreciate your desire to help us, but no Luna will risk their lives for this foolish venture. We have everything to lose, while you have nothing." Rachel leaned forward again and reached for my hand. "Thank you, Mackenzie. You have a beautiful soul and a courageous heart filled with compassion for others. You proved it when you defeated the Skinwalker last year, but I urge you to forget about this life and enjoy your freedom. Do it for those of us who don't have the luxury."

"Are you serious?" I was taken aback. "You think I'm privileged?"

She nodded. "You're King Alexander's heir, are you not?"

"Biologically yes, but that's it!" I exclaimed. "You don't see him going up in arms about what's happening with me, do you? I want to change that!"

"I understand," she said soothingly, "but you don't know what it's like to be one of us, and we would never wish that upon you. Please, Mackenzie, go live your life. We're all rooting for you."

WELL, that was a dud.

I left the attic feeling like a total failure. My initial feelings were right; I was the wrong person to be yelling '*Viva la revolution!*' when my sperm donor was the King. I sounded like a spoiled brat with daddy issues who just wanted to rebel because he wouldn't extend my curfew. I was such an idiot. That damn vision quest was a crock of shit, and I was gullible for feeding into La Loba's crazy ramblings. There was nothing I could do if the Lunas weren't willing to fight beside me.

I headed back down to the main floor where I found Jackson sitting alone. "What's up, Cadwell?" I said as I plopped myself in the seat across from him.

He looked around us. "Oh, *now* you're talking to me?"

"Don't be a smart ass," I deadpanned.

"I make no promises," he said. "Why you slumming it with me? Where's my brother? If you're here, he must not be too far behind."

"Very funny, ass-hat. He's not here—at least I don't think so."

Jackson snorted. "Right."

"Where's Amy? You know, *my* best friend whom you failed to protect."

He sighed. "She's taking a shower, and I did protect her, Kenz ... just in a different way." When he smirked, I wanted to barf.

I blanched. "Do *not* go into detail about your protection methods, or I promise you a permanent disability."

"I wasn't planning to share the glorious details with you anyway," he scoffed.

I rolled my eyes at his absurdity. At first glance, Jackson seemed so serious he wouldn't crack a smile, but his dry humor was entertaining, and I'd like to think he at least tolerated me. It was his way of showing he cared. I mean, I *did* save his life.

Now that you mention it ... "You know, I never got a thank you for—"

"And you never will," he cut me off. "Don't hold your breath."

I chuckled. "Aw, you're so sweet, Jackson." I reached over to pinch his bearded cheek when he brushed me off.

"Mackenzie," he cautioned.

"Fine," I grumbled. "You're no fun."

"Never said I was."

"Right." I nodded and tried to think of something to talk about. "So, when did you decide to grow the peach fuzz?" I scratched at my own face.

He gave me a blank look and I bit my lip to hold back a laugh. "I got tired of shaving."

"Hey!" I exclaimed. "Where's my other bearded friend? I haven't seen Bernard since I arrived!"

Jackson glanced down at me with boredom. "First, we're not friends. Second, he's in South America."

"What? Why?" I sputtered.

"For you. He joined the Tracking Pack to be the one to find you, so no harm would come to the precious Mackenzie Grey."

My mouth fell open. Bernard, the big ole' lumberjack-lookin' werewolf was protecting me? I didn't think he cared that much about me.

"Does he know I returned?"

"Yes. Sebastian called him the day you showed up. However, members pledge a year of fealty, so he won't be released from duty for another three months."

I slumped in my seat. "I feel like even more of an asshole than I already did."

"You should," Jackson grunted.

"Not helping," I growled.

"Wasn't trying to."

"Fine, be a butthole." I stood. "I'll go look for Bash. I'm sure he'll be better company than your grumpy ass."

"I'm sure he will," Jackson smirked, "but you might not want to go to his office right now."

"Why?"

"Because he's busy."

"So?"

"Don't bother him, Mackenzie. Trust me, I'm doing it for your own good, believe it or not."

I should have listened to Jackson, but I was a masochist. At this point I was just a glutton for punishment, and anything I saw or heard was my own doing because Jackson warned me. But of course, I, Mackenzie Grey, never listened to reason. Never have, and I probably never will.

I made my way down to the basement toward Sebastian's office. My mind screamed in a dull roar, clogging my ears from any potential hints as to what I was about to witness. If I believed it was nothing, it would be nothing. He was just doing boring Pack paperwork and nothing else.

My knuckles rapped on the door and I didn't wait to hear his response. I twisted the doorknob and walked right in.

"Hey Bash, I was wonder—" My voice cut out as I saw Sebastian standing behind Vivian as she was bent over his desk. One hand was wrapped around her blonde hair and the other was on her hip to keep her still as he pumped behind her.

The sounds of slapping skin and her moans grew louder when she saw me. A malicious grin spread across her face as she slid back and forth, and I wanted to rip out those fake hair extensions.

"Mackenzie," Bash grunted, a guilty look sliding over his face.

I felt sick. "Sorry," I muttered, suddenly finding the strength to move my feet.

It was déjà vu. I stumbled out of his office, slamming the door behind me hard enough that I heard some of the picture frames that lined the hallway crash to the ground. I didn't bother picking them up. I was pissed, though I didn't understand why. I had no right to be. Our outing to Central Park didn't mean anything. Once again, I read into stuff that was no more than two friends hanging out. I allowed myself to get sucked back into this stupid game Bash played. Nothing had changed—he just wanted a challenge. That's all I was to him.

I sprinted out of the basement and up the stairs to the second floor. I heard Amy call my name from downstairs, but I ignored her. I ripped my bedroom door open and banged it shut—surprised it didn't fall off its hinges.

"I will not freak out, I will not freak out," I repeated into my empty room—at least I thought it was empty. My racing heart screeched to a stop.

Emma was strewn in the middle of my bed, her legs crossed at the ankles and her hands resting behind her head casually. "Hey Ace," she said. "I was looking for you, so I decided to wait in your room. You still look like shit."

"You're too kind." I flung myself on the bed face-first, burying the panicky emotions that wanted to be released in a swirling fit of jealousy.

"Bad day?"

"*Very* bad day," I mumbled against the mattress.

Emma scooted further down beside me. "Want to tell me about it?"

I lifted my head up. "Sorry, kid, it's grown-up issues. Anyway, what brings you to my humble abode?" I waved my hand around the room.

She scrunched her mouth to the side. "Well, you see ... Ugh, whatever, I'm just going to spit it out. These Lunas are nuts! They have me folding laundry! Are they serious? I don't want to touch someone else's nasty clothing." She shivered in disgust and I chuckled.

"I wouldn't either. So how did you get out of it?"

She looked around guiltily. "I didn't. I escaped, Ace. I'm now a fugitive!" She slammed her little body on the bed and huffed, "I'm on the run from the man."

"Don't worry, kid, you can hide out in here as long as you want. I'm sort of on the run from the man, too." Images of Bash and V together brought on another bout of nausea. *Seriously, the office again? Doesn't he have a bedroom? That desk needs to get disinfected ...*

My door suddenly flung open. I was afraid it was Sebastian, but Amy's red mane poked inside.

"Kenz, are you okay?" she asked. I figured Jackson must have told her what happened.

"Yeah, I'm good."

She stepped inside and quietly closed the door. "Oh, hey, Emma, how's it going?" Amy said as she noticed the little person lying beside me.

"Just gravy," Emma answered with a thumbs up.

"We haven't had much time to talk, Kenz." Amy sat on the edge of the bed.

I sat up. "I know. Shit's just been nuts, I'm sorry. I promise as soon as this blows over, I'll tell you all about L.A., okay?"

Emma jerked up and said, "Ohhhh, I want to know too! Roman is so dreamy," she sighed.

"Roman?" Amy questioned. "Who's that?"

I cleared my throat and glared at Emma. "He's a friend."

"A friend? Yeah, right, Ace. You guys are like, together and stuff." Emma giggled. "Roman and Ace, sittin' in a tree. K-I-S-S-I-N-G!" she sang as she jumped on the bed.

"Oh, yeah?" Amy laughed, her curiosity fully piqued.

"She has a very wild imagination," I refuted, pulling Emma down before she hurt herself. "Roman is—"

"He's a vampire!" Emma exclaimed as she positioned her two pointer fingers in front of her teeth to mimic fangs.

"A *vampire*?" Amy shrieked. "Are you crazy, Kenzie? Getting involved with them will *not* end well."

"Oh, come on, Aims. You don't even know him. You've been spending way too much time with the Pack if you're already starting to think like them."

"That's not what I mean, Kenz. It's because I know how the Pack *thinks* that worries me. I don't want them to say anything bad about you."

I hardened. "They can think what they want. I don't give a damn anymore."

13
___

I snuck out of my room in search of Blu. Emma, Amy, and I were having girl time and we wanted her to hang with us. It would feel just like old times. The second-floor balcony was empty, so I peered over to see if I'd catch her downstairs. Running into Sebastian was the last thing I wanted to do, but who I should have been avoiding was Vivian.

My feet shuffled across the main floor to the laundry room where Blu usually was, when I turned the corner and ran smack into Vivian. Her hair was smoothed neatly in place as was her clothing, which irked me. She didn't even look like shit after her wild romp, which would have done loads to ease this rage-filled ball of envy that was currently eating up my insides. All while I was having a horrible hair day, and my lack of sleep left dark circles ringing my eyes. The universe was officially against me.

"Walking in on people is your specialty," V sneered. "Did you get a good look at what you'll never have?"

"You're seriously bragging about being the side chick?" I laughed, refusing to let her see how rattled I was.

"That's where you're wrong." She pronounced every word as if I were illiterate. "We'll be mating soon, and then who will you be left with—Jonah? No, he's been getting hot and heavy with the Fae Queen. That leaves you with ... Logan, maybe?" she giggled.

"Excuse me?" I growled, enraged to hear her utter the Chicago Pack Alpha's name after just learning what he did to Rachel.

"I hear he likes it rough. Right up your alley, eh?"

I didn't hold back. My fist aimed straight for that pore-less face of hers. She crumpled to the ground with one loud thud, but it wasn't enough to knock her out. But that wasn't my intention in the first place. I didn't care about anything she said besides the name *Logan*. After what he did to Rachel, the audacity she had to even joke about him made me sick to my stomach.

I squatted down to her level. "You disgusting, petty-ass bitch," I gritted out. "If you ever say some shit like that to me again, I'll make sure Sebastian never wants your dirty snatch again. Because let's be honest, I have sway in matters around here," I bragged.

V clutched her already bruising face, her eyes wide with an unknown fear. "It's only a matter of time before Logan comes for you. He always gets his way."

"He already failed. I'm not worth the trouble."

She shook her head. "You don't get it, you dumb bitch. Whoever you mate with could be the next king. He won't stop."

My eyes narrowed to slits. Was that why all these Packs were after me? Why Charles wanted Jonah to mate with me? Her words made sense, but believing anything V said felt stupid.

"Thanks for caring." I rolled my eyes and stood up. I was done entertaining this dimwit.

She snarled, "Watch your back, Mackenzie Grey."

AMY, Emma, and I were having a late lunch when we heard growls and snarls coming from the entrance of the warehouse. I was in the process of destroying my second foot-long sub when I paused mid-chew. I sniffed the air and recognized a familiar, unexpected scent. Lucian and Roman had entered the territory of the Brooklyn Pack, and the wolves were not happy.

"What are you doing here?" one of the men called out. He was already popping his neck back and forth, preparing for a fight.

Lucian glided forward in his funeral-like attire and his blond hair in the never-changing ponytail tied at the nape of his neck. "Easy there, Wolf-Man," he chided. "I'm only here to see a friend." His eyes searched the room until they landed on me. "Pet, will you please call off the dogs?"

"Dogs?" the wolf cried out.

"Hey, hey!" I ran over before things escalated, sandwich still in hand. "Let's not lose our heads over this. Lucian, please apologize. That was disrespectful," I urged, nodding my head toward the wolf who was ready to start a brawl.

"Fine," Lucian huffed, "but only for you, Pet." He turned to the raging werewolf and apologized.

Roman stepped around the Head Vampire and pulled me into a hug. "Shit, Ace, I've been so worried. What happened? The call cut out, and I haven't been able to get ahold of you since. Why weren't you answering?"

Gasps from all around the warehouse floated around and my body stiffened. Roman pulled away and arched a brow in confusion. When he noticed everyone staring at us, he caught on.

"Oh, yeah, my bad. Forgot you guys have beef here on the East Coast." He pulled away and took a measured step back. His tousled dirty blond hair was messier than usual, and his dark grey V-neck shirt was wrinkled beyond repair.

"Are you okay?" I sized him up.

"Now that I've seen you, yeah. Why didn't you call me back?"

I glanced around the warehouse and noticed we were the sole object of everyone's rapt attention.

"Uh ... how about we go somewhere more private?" I suggested. "Amy, can you watch Emma for me?" My best friend nodded wordlessly and pulled Emma away. Amy waggled her eyebrows after getting a good look at Roman.

"He's hot," she mouthed.

Emma ran to Roman and he scooped her up in his arms. "Hey there, missy! I see you found our girl."

She nodded. "Ace came to get me. It's been really boring out here. Do you know they had me doing *laundry*? It's inhumane!"

Roman chuckled. "The horror!"

"I know!"

"Alright, kid." I took her from Roman and deposited her in front of Amy. "Go with Aims and I'll come get you in a bit." She nodded and they both went up to Jackson's room. "And you two," I pointed to Roman and Lucian, "follow me."

The whispers grew louder as I led the two vampires up to my room. Someone must have notified Sebastian, because half-way up the stairs, both he and Jonah stood at the mouth of the basement.

"Lucian!" Bash barked out. His arms were crossed over his chest, his bare feet planted wide as he stood in only a pair of low-rise jeans. Why couldn't he be hideously ugly? It would make things infinitely easier.

"Ah, Sebastian Steel, what a pleasant surprise. It's been far too long, *friend*," Lucian replied smoothly as he walked back down toward the Alpha. "I was just here to see Mackenzie. Is there a problem?"

Those blue eyes drilled holes of pure hatred at me and I drilled them right back at him. I guess we were back to how things were when we first met. Fine by me. "The three of you, in my office," Bash growled. Without waiting to see if we followed his directive, he turned and headed down the stairs.

"Somebody's in trouble," Vivian taunted in her sing-song voice as we passed, her left eye already blossoming into lovely shades of black and blue.

"Nice shiner," I ridiculed.

She flipped her middle finger at me.

"Stick it where the sun don't shine, V," I sneered before we disappeared into Sebastian's office.

"WHAT IS THE MEANING OF THIS?" Sebastian yelled, his deep voice bouncing off the walls of the small room. "If you're upset with me, Mackenzie, fine, but *this*? Bringing vampires into our territory is crossing the line!"

"Whoa!" I stopped him. "You think they're here because I'm pissed at you? First off, I'm not upset, I have no reason to be. And secondly, I might be immature, but I would've hoped you wouldn't think so low of me to think I would stoop to something like this. But thanks, asshole. I guess I know where I stand."

I paced the small office as much as I could with the five of us standing around. "You know what? This was just a bad fuckin' idea from the start. I don't know why I thought coming back here was worth my time." I turned to Roman. "Let's go home."

"Home? You know this clown?" Jonah asked, taken aback.

"Hey mate, no need for name calling," Roman said.

Jonah laughed. "Mate? Is he serious?"

"Yeah, Jonah, he has more class than all of you combined. Where he's from, wolves and vampires aren't at each other's throats like idiots."

"You're not leaving!" Sebastian roared as he slammed his fists on his desk.

"Watch me," I threatened. I swung open the office door, but was halted as I ran into a barrel chest. "Damn it, Jackson! You just ruined my very dramatic storm out!"

"We have other issues at the moment besides two vampires."

"What is it?" Sebastian demanded.

"Duke, the Alpha from the Nashville Pack—he's here."

We all froze for a beat before the six of us rushed out of the basement and up to the main floor. Like children running for the first piece of cake at a birthday party, we all came to a halt when we came face-to-face with three unknown wolves in jeans and boots—though I was disappointed they weren't also wearing cowboy hats and spurs. The man in the middle, Duke, I assumed, wore a tucked-in denim shirt and appeared to be in his forties.

"Sebastian Steel, long time no—*vampires*?" The stranger jerked to a stop once he saw Lucian and Roman standing beside me.

"Duke." Bash walked over to him. "It's been a while. How are things going?" They greeted each other with a man hug-slash-handshake, and I had to tame the eye roll. Men were so darn predictable.

"Things are good down south; you should pay us a visit some time," Duke said.

"Will do." Bash nodded. "So, what brings you to Brooklyn?"

"Well, I heard through the grapevine y'all know where I can find that lone wolf, the Luna."

No one moved or said a word—we all waited for what Sebastian would say. I could hear everyone collectively hold their breaths. The situation was almost laughable.

"Why?" Bash asked.

"Why not?" Duke chuckled. "You know how rough it could get. I want to offer her a place in my Pack."

"She won't join," Bash said. "She will refuse you."

"I'll be the judge of that." Duke winked and looked around the warehouse. "Now, which one of these lovely Lunas is Mackenzie Grey?"

When the Nashville wolves weren't looking, both Jonah and Roman pulled me behind them to shield me from their line of sight.

"Don't let them see your eyes, Kenz," Jonah whispered so low, I barely heard him. I didn't answer him for fear they would hear me, so I lowered my head and didn't look up.

What do my eyes have to do with anything?

"Aw, come on, don't be shy. Where ya at, girly?" Duke bellowed out.

"Fuck it," I muttered as I pushed past my bodyguards and

went to stand beside Sebastian. "I'm Mackenzie, what do you want?"

Duke swiveled around and met my gaze. His dark brown eyes sparkled with excitement while mine stared back, bored as hell.

"My, oh my, aren't you a spitting image of your father? Look at them eyes, boys!" he called out to his friends. "Mesmerizing."

Sebastian let out a loud whistle, simultaneously breaking the attention of Duke and alerting all the Brooklyn Pack to disperse. Some of them left the warehouse entirely, while others returned to their rooms. Most everyone cleared out, and the ones who remained were the usual suspects. I searched for Amy, knowing damn well she wouldn't have left, and found her standing with Emma and Jackson. *Good.*

"Alright, let's cut to the chase," I started. "I'm not buying what you're selling, so you might as well head on home. You wasted a trip."

"Darling, it was worth it," Duke grinned, "but why don't you hear my pitch before you start making decisions? You might like what you hear."

"Doubt it." I fake yawned.

Duke walked toward me, his boots loud on the concrete floor as he approached. He extended his arm for me to take, playing the part of a genteel suitor. I looked down at it and then at him, unmoving.

"What?" I asked.

"Take my arm, Mackenzie, I promise I won't bite."

After a growl from Sebastian, I interloped my arm with Duke's and let him lead me to a cafeteria table away from the earshot of my friends. He set me down in a seat and sat across from me.

"Now that we have a semblance of privacy, I want to formally introduce myself. My name is Duke Davenport of the Nashville Pack." He lifted my hand and kissed the top of it.

"Well, aren't you a southern gentleman?" I smarted.

"Momma taught me well," he admitted. "And you, Mackenzie Grey, are all the rage down south. No one can seem to stop talking about you. What's your secret?" he asked as if mystified.

"My secret?" I laughed. "There is none. Spend a day with me and you'll be wondering what all the fuss is about."

"Oh, I find that hard to believe." He looked taken aback. "A beauty such as yours is rare. You are quite the lady."

I snorted. "Dude, open up them eyes and take a good look. You got the wrong idea about me. I have the mouth of a sailor, the temper of a toddler, and my most lovable trait is that I lack a filter when I speak. Does that really make me a lady?"

He tsked. "But surely that's not your fault. You were raised in the wild, by humans. Had you been at your rightful place by your father, you'd be different."

I thought about his comment for a moment. "You know Duke, you might be right, but thank fuck I wasn't, because the last thing I ever want to be in life is a goddamn Luna."

He chuckled. "I'll be damned. Aren't you a little spitfire? I hadn't heard that."

"Duke, your intel is all kinds of whacked. Let me school you real quick." I beckoned him further. "I'm not joining anyone's Pack, no matter what I'm offered or threatened with. I'd rather gouge out my own eyeballs; my hatred for the system is that intense."

"Nothing I can say will change your mind?"

I shook my head.

"Have you been threatened by other Packs?"

"Twice now," I said and waved it off. "But it's all good. I'd like to think it's because I'm so darn lovable."

Duke laughed. "I can attest to that. You have spunk, Little Girl. I like it."

"Why, thank you, Duke." I smiled and did an awkward curtsey in my seat.

He reached into his back pocket and pulled out a business card, sliding it over the table to me. "If you ever change your mind, Mackenzie Grey, or find yourself in a pickle, you give me a call," he offered. "My Pack is similar to Sebastian's; we treat our girls with respect. And if I were you, I'd stay as far away from Chicago as you can. I've heard the whispers, and they aren't good."

My smile stiffened. "Don't you worry. I can take care of myself."

As soon as Duke and his Pack-mates left, everyone started asking me a million and one questions.

"What did he say?"

"Is he coming back?"

"Did he really roll up in here in some cowboy boots?" Of course that was Amy.

All I wanted to do was take a nap for a few days ... or maybe a week. That whole conversation was exhausting, but the Alpha wasn't so bad. He was kind enough to come to the warehouse and ask me to join his Pack instead of hiring someone to snatch me or send his minions to rough me up. It was classy, but no matter how generous he was, there was no way I was joining his Pack—not in this lifetime, at least.

"What did he want?" Sebastian demanded.

"What do you think, Sherlock? What all these Alphas want— a piece of my ass," I smirked. "But no worries, I'd rather sell it on a corner than give it away for free."

"Mackenzie," he warned. "This is not a joking matter. For once, be serious!"

Roman chuckled behind me. "Oh, Ace, your sarcasm is a novelty."

"Her name is Mackenzie, not Ace!" Jonah exclaimed.

"I only know her as Ace, so until she gets tired of it, that's who she'll be," Roman argued.

"Alright," I interjected, "let's all call this one a win since I wasn't beaten to a bloody pulp. I needed a victory after yesterday. What I'd appreciate now is if everyone got along. I don't have the strength to fight and deal with all your supernatural issues plus my own. I'm going to take a nap." I turned and pointed at Amy. "Wake me in two hours, please." I ignored everyone's protests as I dragged my feet upstairs and shut myself in my room. No one, and I meant *no one*, was going to matter to me for the next few hours.

14

Calloused hands slid from my shoulder down my arm, making the hair on my skin tingle from the roughness. Soft lips kissed between my shoulder blades and I shivered. Collapsing onto my back, I saw who had been lying behind me: Jonah. His milk chocolate eyes brightened when he caught my eye. His bare chest, well defined and groomed, was at eye level with me.

"Hey there, Sleeping Beauty. Did you have a nice nap?"

I gulped. "Y-Yes. What are you doing here?"

"We're here to make sure you're well rested," Bash's deep voice answered. My neck snapped to the other side, where he, too, lay shirtless under the covers.

"W-What?" I stuttered. "What are you guys doing here? Are you naked? Did we ...?"

Jonah kissed the crook of my neck while Sebastian's blue eyes traveled down my body as he bit his bottom lip. Leaning down,

Bash whispered sweet nothings in my ear as the tip of his tongue teased me.

I clutched my sheets as the overwhelming sensations burst out of me, unable to stop a moan. My lower body grew cold as the covers fell from my chest and a mop of dirty blond hair emerged from down below.

"Need me to keep you warm, Ace?" Roman taunted with a grin as he came out from under the blankets and rested his chin on my belly.

"Where the hell did *you* come from?" I gasped. *For the love of God, what is going on?*

Roman kissed his way up my bare stomach in meandering trails until he reached between my breasts, his cold breath hardening my nipples.

"I'm perfect for you, Kenz. I have been from the very beginning," Jonah whispered.

"But I challenge you, Mackenzie. I make you a better person," Sebastian growled.

"You can be who you want to be with me, Ace, no strings attached," Roman promised.

All three of them stared longingly at me, waiting for an answer. My throat closed up and I groaned as I searched for a response to give them. The room started to grow fuzzy around the edges and something crinkled nearby. Panicked, I realized someone else was with us and I shot up to a sitting position.

"What was that?" I gasped, opening my eyes to see Amy sitting at the foot of my bed, eating from a bag of jalapeño Cheetos. I wiped the trail of drool matted on my left cheek and blinked as I glanced around the room. Only Amy and I were here.

. . .

"I COULDN'T TELL if you were having a sex dream or getting your wisdom teeth pulled. I'm still debating," she mused as she merrily munched on Cheetos.

"What time is it?" I croaked. I tried to run my fingers through my hair, but it was a knotted beehive.

"It's time for you to get up."

"Then why didn't you wake me?"

She shrugged. "You were entertaining. Also, I'd rather be in *here* than out *there*."

"What's going on?" I rolled out of bed and searched for my robe in my duffle bag.

"Here." Amy handed it to me. "It's pandemonium out there. The vampires are still here, and all you can hear is Bash and Jonah yelling from the office. Jackson comes out once in a while, but it's mainly to grab aspirin."

I walked into the en suite bathroom and attempted to comb my hair. Upon visual inspection, I determined it was a disaster. "I don't know what to do, Amy."

"You can start off by dishing about who you were dreaming about ... unless it was the wisdom teeth, then forget it, I don't care."

I popped out of the bathroom with the brush stuck in my hair. "Amy, it wasn't just *one* of them," I answered sheepishly. "Shit, I'm a dream-slut. My subconscious is a dirty, dirty girl!"

Amy giggled. "Hell, yes! I've only ever had one of those kind of dreams before, and it was short lived," she sighed wistfully. "The Hemsworth brothers are so skilled."

"You need help." I rolled my eyes. "But was it the three brothers or just two?"

"Just Chris and Liam, why?"

I groaned. "Because mine was three! I'm going to hell."

She gasped. "Shit, no way!"

"Way."

"That's ... awesome!"

"You're a freak," I deadpanned.

Amy herded me back into the bathroom and sat me on the closed toilet lid. "I know I am. Now sit still while I detangle this mane. You look like Hermione Granger in her first year at Hogwarts."

MY BEST FRIEND wouldn't let me hide out in my room for the day, no matter how much I attempted to bribe her. She was right; I couldn't pretend shit hadn't hit the fan. Since the Lunas didn't want to fight for their freedom, I had to make sure I kept mine. That meant finding a way to not get abducted by a Pack—particularly Chicago's. Rachel's story sealed the deal, but there was something about those guys at the bodega that made my skin crawl. If I thought the Brooklyn Pack were assholes, then Chicago was downright abusive.

I knocked on Sebastian's office door, this time waiting until I was told I could enter. When I slipped inside, Roman and Lucian were seated in the chairs across from Sebastian's desk. Sebastian sat behind it, flanked by Jonah and Jackson. It was staged like a scene out of *The Godfather*. I had to hold back a million quips that sat poised at the tip of my tongue. Particularly a Vito Corleone impression. I inwardly sighed. My brain really needed to focus on the issue at hand.

"Finally, Sleeping Beauty awakens," Jonah said.

My face turned fifty shades of red as I remembered him calling me that name in my dream. "Why'd you call me that? I wasn't asleep *that* long," I muttered as I avoided staring into anyone's eyes. "So why are we here? I'm getting antsy. I need to get out of the warehouse." I couldn't stand being in such close quarters with these guys after having that damn dream. It screwed me all up inside. I came back from L.A. feeling confident and secure, just to revert to a puddle of hormones again in a matter of days. Damn assholes.

"That won't be possible, Mackenzie," Sebastian said. "I just spoke with Charles, and he refuses to call a Summit to discuss your situation." Jonah's nostrils flared. I supposed he wasn't too happy with daddy dearest.

"Why does that matter?"

Bash sighed. "We were hoping to speak on your behalf with the American Summit to call off all the Packs, but Charles," he glared up at Jonah, "believes you've made your bed and now must lie in it. Don't worry, we'll figure something else out."

"Right. Something else," I mumbled. "Look, I appreciate everyone wanting to help me and all, but maybe Cadwell's on to something." The reason I never backed down from the Pack when I first met them was because I wanted to prove that as a Luna, I was capable of defending myself without the aid of a penis. How could I forget what I stood for?

"Pet, you can't be serious!" Lucian said, shocked.

"I said he was on to something, not that he was right," I said. "I can't ask for freedom and then expect the Pack to help me. It doesn't make sense."

"What do you propose?" Roman asked.

Once again, I hadn't thought that far ahead. "Right now, I

propose that I get a new cell phone because mine was smashed by some beefed-up meathead from Chicago. I'm going out into the wild to get one. I won't be a victim and hide inside anymore. Also, I'm getting cabin fever."

"I swear, it's like you have a death wish!" Sebastian yelled.

"Maybe I do," I replied, exasperated. "If it'll keep everyone's undies out of a twist, Jonah, do you want to come with?" It would keep my protectors happy, plus it would be the perfect opportunity to talk to him.

"Yeah, I'll go." He perked up.

"Ace ..." Roman stood. "We can go home. You don't have to deal with this," he whispered to me.

But running off to California didn't feel right. I would just be putting off the inevitable. "That's the easy way out. When have you known me to take that route?"

"Never. Doesn't mean I can't warn you of the potential dangers."

"Why do you care?" I grinned as we repeated our interaction from my first night in the Mojave Desert.

"I don't." He gave me a sly smile. "Just be careful."

I nodded.

Lucian cleared his throat. "I've also been working on a Plan B in case the wolves can't come up with anything—which might be the case." He leered at Sebastian. "Nothing concrete, but I'll inform you when I hear something. Stay alive, Pet. I'd miss you dearly if no one were around to stir up trouble."

I laughed as the two vampires left, escorted sullenly by Jackson. I turned to Bash and Jonah, still unable to look them in the eyes. I could feel the ghost of their lips on my skin. Being around them was proving to be maddening.

"Is a cell phone that important? Who do you need to call?" Bash inquired.

"My therapist," I snapped. "After dealing with you all, I'm pretty sure I'm going to need a Xanax prescription."

"Your *what*?" Jonah asked.

I rolled my eyes. "Nevermind. Come on, let's go."

Jonah looked to Sebastian for permission, which made me want to rip my hair out. Bash nodded and Jonah led the way out.

"And Mackenzie?" Bash said. I didn't turn around. "She means nothing—"

I didn't wait to hear him finish. Without a word, I slammed the door behind me. I was done caring. We were never anything to begin with.

THE WALK to the bus stop wasn't far, so I needed to take the opportunity to clear the air with Jonah. I didn't like hearing how Charles was manipulating his son, and I needed him to understand that it wasn't going to fly with me. If only I knew where to begin.

It was early in the evening, the sun just starting to set as we walked to the corner of Sands and Pearls Street. Horns blaring, brakes squealing, and the everlasting smog that filled the air; I felt nostalgic being back in my city.

Jonah started. "About these vampires ..."

I pushed him. "Oh, don't start with that. They're good guys, Jonah. Roman was there for me when no one else was."

He stuffed his hands in his coat pockets. "You wouldn't *let* us be there for you. There's a difference."

I shook my head. "You guys couldn't be. It was impossible."

Jonah latched onto my arm and pulled me to a halt. "No it's not, Kenz," he exploded with pent-up emotion. "If only you had just stayed and not run away, I'd already found a way to help you."

I arched a brow. "What? By mating with me?"

His smile slipped. "Would that be such a bad thing?"

"Of course it would!" I yelled and had to look around to make sure we didn't attract attention. Like most New Yorkers, no one cared about our squabble. "Do you listen to anything I say? Absolutely *nothing* is worth giving up my freedom—the very essence of who I am. I would no longer be Mackenzie."

"You think I would own you? I wouldn't do that to you, Kenz." His brown eyes were sad.

"Essentially you would. At some point in our mate-whatever-matrimony, you would put your foot down on something you were against me doing. It would be irresponsible of me to think you could change."

He opened and closed his mouth as if trying to figure out what to say. That last bit was harsh, but I had to stick by my guns and show no weakness. I had hope that the wolves would change in the future; I'd seen some slight improvement—particularly from Bash—but they still had a long way to go.

"I also don't trust your father, Jonah. The way he told me about the King being my father wasn't right and you know it. He tried to manipulate me, and now because his plan backfired, he's playing with my life by not calling a Summit," I continued. If I stopped now, I would lose my nerve. "Look at me! I can't leave the warehouse without a damn bodyguard! You know I won't last living like this. It's only a matter of time before I pack up and leave again."

I wasn't sure if that was an empty threat. The idea had crossed my mind a few times, but I didn't think I could really leave Amy again, and I wasn't sure if she'd leave Jackson behind. In the midst of all my drama, I'd seen the way they looked at each other. The last thing I wanted to do was mess up their relationship. Amy deserved some happiness.

WE WERE AT ATLANTIC TERMINAL, the shopping mall on Atlantic Avenue across the street from the Barclays Center. We had exited the store and I was thanking the heavens above that I had remembered to back up my last iPhone.

"You have no idea how good it feels to have my phone safe and sound," I said as we swerved through the cluttered streets. "And it also doesn't hurt that I got to upgrade to a 6s Plus." I grinned.

"I don't understand people's fascinations with those little computers." Jonah waved a finger at my device. "It seems complicated."

"You haven't lived, my friend," I sighed as I hugged my new phone. "Now let's go get some ice cream. I'm in a cake-batter-with-rainbow-sprinkles kind of mood."

Jonah laughed. "Kenzie, when are you *not* thinking about food?"

I snorted. "The day I'm not, I've been abducted by aliens, FYI."

"Good to know." He elbowed me. "And ... I'm sorry about my father."

When I peered up at him, those sad eyes undid me. "You don't have to apologize for him, and I know your intentions were good. Water under the bridge, Jonah," I said, trying to cheer him up.

He nodded. "Do you remember our conversation before you left?"

My heart skipped a beat. His declaration of love that I never responded to? Yes, of course I remembered.

"What about it?"

"It still stands, you know. No matter if it's not reciprocated, you and I—"

An unmarked, navy blue police car swerved across the street and jumped the sidewalk, stopping before us. Pedestrians darted out of its way to avoid getting hit. Two more cop cars pulled to the side and within seconds, the officers aimed their guns in our direction. Both Jonah and I looked around to see if we were in the way of the real perpetrator, but then I heard my name.

"Mackenzie Grey!" I heard through the bull horn. "Put your hands up where we can see them!"

My pulse raced and I almost dropped my brand-new cell phone. I attempted to hand my phone to Jonah, but flinched when they yelled, "Put your hands up!"

"Okay, okay!" I screamed as I put my hands up in surrender and fell to my knees. I knew the drill.

Armed officers ran up to us and escorted Jonah out of the way. I could hear his growls as he fought them and was impressed that it took five officers to tame him. He called out to me with so much pain I felt it in my bones, down to the very core. I couldn't look at him.

Detective Garrett Michaels walked up, yanked my wrists behind me, and clipped on a set of handcuffs as he read me my Miranda Rights.

"Never thought I'd be seeing you again," Michaels grumbled. "At least not in these circumstances." He hauled me to my feet and dragged me to his car.

"What the hell is going on, Michaels? There has to be a mistake!"

"No mistake, we have you on video." He ducked my head none too gently and eased me into the backseat. "This is an open and shut case, Grey, and you just bought yourself a one-way ticket to Rikers."

AFTER THAT, everything happened in a blur. I was booked and processed—my fingerprints and mug shot taken, yet I barely noticed. After two hours, they placed me in an interrogation room with detectives I didn't recognize, each one playing the standard role of good cop/bad cop. I was zoned out, too rattled to even answer them. All I could think about was the colossal amount of bad luck I had. The minute I stepped back on the East Coast, everything went to shit. Not only was I being hunted by wolves, but now humans, too.

A hand slammed on the table, snatching me from my self-pity. A man in a cheap suit stood above me while his partner pretended to be the cool one and told him to back off. I'd witnessed too many of these interrogations by Michaels to be rattled. And to be honest, anyone who'd seen any crime show could pick up this trick.

"We have it all on camera, Grey. You can't hide the truth. Just tell us what happened and you'll feel better," Good Cop said.

I peered up at him and raised an eyebrow. "I'd like to know what I did before I confess to it."

"What do you think?" Bad Cop barked.

I shrugged. "I don't know, did I leave the toilet seat up? Do I have an unpaid parking ticket from my imaginary car? Or did you catch me picking my nose on camera?"

Bad Cop fumed with anger. "You're a real comedian."

"I can go on forever, so someone better tell me what I did, or I'll say the magic words that will shut this whole conversation down," I threatened. "I want a—"

"Okay!" Good Cop stopped me. "The Mejia's bodega, the one by your apartment."

My heart skipped a beat, and I had to school my expression so I didn't seem suspicious. I didn't do anything wrong. If anything, *I* was the victim. What video did they have?

"Okay?" I said. "But I don't understand. I was attacked, and *I'm* the one who gets arrested? Welcome to 2016." I rolled my eyes.

"You were attacked?" Bad Cop snorted. "Yeah, right. So why didn't you call the cops? You used to intern at IPP, you had the connections. Why not give your old supervisor a call?"

Talking about my supervisor, why wasn't Garrett the one interrogating me? We weren't family, and I wouldn't say we were friends. It couldn't have been considered a conflict of interest if he did.

"It was no big deal. The guy tried to rob me, but I fought back. I didn't call Garrett because I know how this stuff works. The robber wouldn't have been found, and it would have been pointless."

Good Cop sat in the chair across from me. "What about the body, Mackenzie?" he asked as if we were friends. "Where did you take the body?"

"The body? What are you talking about?"

"We caught you on film, dragging his body out of the bodega."

I couldn't stop the laugh that broke out of me. "Now I *know* that's not true, because I hauled ass out of there the moment I got the chance."

Both detectives shook their heads. Bad Cop was back. "We have you on video! You killed him and then you dragged him out to God knows where! So tell us, where is the body?" he screamed at the side of my face and I felt his spittle on my cheek.

I didn't flinch. I sat there staring at the detective in front of me and took a moment to analyze my current situation. Something wasn't right. If they had irrefutable evidence, why did they need a confession?

"No." I shook my head. "Nice try, but if you had any proof that I did anything, I'd already be halfway to Rikers by now. Either something's wrong with your video, or you have no other suspects. In which case, I'm going to have to ask for a lawyer, please." I grinned.

The tension skyrocketed as both detectives left the interrogation room without a single shred of proof—and they weren't going to get it from me.

I was facing the one-way mirror and was pretty sure Detective Garrett Michaels was watching the whole exchange. I closed my eyes and channeled my wolf, letting my sensitive hearing stretch to the outside of the interrogation room.

"She's not going to tell us anything. Even with just an internship under her belt, she already knows the tricks to the trade."

"Not just an internship, Davis, she's been working with the LAPD for the past year as part of an undercover unit. She's more skilled than we're giving her credit for."

"Grey?" I recognized Michaels' voice. "*Grey* has been part of a top-secret group? I don't buy it. She was good, but she wasn't *that* good."

"Well, she is, and she just lawyered up. We've got nothing. Any rookie attorney could waltz in here and set her free with the piece of shit video we have."

"What if she's telling the truth? We couldn't see who dragged the body out; only a hand. She could be innocent."

"Then why didn't she call me? She should have called me!" Michaels argued.

I tuned out my hearing and opened my eyes. The video was wonky, which was why they were pressuring me for a confession. The real question was, who the hell came back for the wolf's body? Was it Larry? It certainly wasn't anyone who was looking out for me. If there are time lapses, then the video footage was tampered with, or else I'm just one unlucky girl.

The interrogation room door flung open and Michaels charged in. I noticed the peppering of gray hair that hadn't been there before. He was pudgier than he was last time I saw him, but same ole' cranky Garrett. The sleeves of his buttoned-up shirt were rolled up and his badge was clipped on his belt.

"Stop bullshitting us, Grey." He dropped a manila folder on the desk and spread out pictures of the crime scene. "Do you see all that blood? Some of it's yours, but not a lot. The rest belonged to a Joey DeLuca of Chicago, Illinois, who is currently missing."

Hmm. The guy's name was Joey. Good to know.

"Now I don't know how you did it, but at this point I

couldn't give a rat's ass. You're a resourceful girl, and it's completely possible in my mind that you are capable of this type of crime."

I leaned forward. "Do you truly believe that? Think, Garrett, *really* think about what you're saying."

His eyes hardened. "Fine. Why don't you tell me what you did with the LAPD?"

"You'll have to speak with my captain," I said.

"Bullshit!" He slammed his hands on the table. "The only person I've been able to speak with is a joker named Lou Horowitz, and all he tells me is that it's classified. I'm asking *you*, Grey, what exactly are you involved in?"

"I don't understand what that has to do with the incident at the bodega. Go touch your nose, Michaels. I called for a lawyer, now give me my one phone call, please."

He stormed out of the room and I exhaled the breath I didn't realize I was holding. I always imagined myself in this position, bragging about how I wouldn't break, but sitting here was intimidating.

I racked my brain for someone to call, but hello, it was the twenty first century—no one memorized phone numbers anymore. The only one I knew was my own, and Amy's. When a uniformed officer finally came to escort me to a phone desk, I plopped down and dialed the only number I knew.

"Hello?" Amy's normally cheery voice sounded anguished and I could imagine why. I swear, I would be paying for many years of therapy for my dear friend.

"Amy?" I exhaled. "Oh, thank God you answered! I thought you'd ignore it since you wouldn't recognize—"

"Of course, I'm going to answer!" she cried out. "Hey! She's on the phone!" she called out to someone. "Are you okay, Kenzie? What's going on?"

"I'm fine. It's about the attack at the bodega. I'm being accused of murder."

"How?" she asked.

I sighed. "They have a chopped-up surveillance video with me in it. It's all good, though. It's worthless. Can I speak with Bash?"

"Sure. He's hovering over me anyway. Stay safe, Kenz. Love you," she said before Sebastian's gruff voice came on the line.

"Mackenzie, what's going on?"

I glanced around the room and caught Garrett watching me, but other than him, everyone else was minding their own business.

"The bodega – someone is making it out to be like I'm the one to blame. But don't worry about it, they have nothing. What I need now is a lawyer to bail me out. I'm at IPP; can you get someone for me?"

"Of course, Mackenzie, but—"

"They're listening, Bash," I whispered. I wasn't stupid, I knew they were tapped in on my phone call. They needed probable cause to keep me here, so until they had it, I was a free woman. It seemed I couldn't be free with the Pack *or* with humans. What a conundrum.

"Right," he said. "I'll contact our attorney and we'll be on our way. Just ... be careful. This would be a perfect time for them to get to you."

"I know. That's why you need to hurry."

I hung up and stared at the phone, my mind blanking on my current predicament. The last thing I wanted was to go back to the interrogation room alone. I needed to be around people where it was safest.

"On your feet, Grey." Michaels hauled me out of the chair and started dragging me back into the room.

"Let's play a guessing game, yeah?" I grinned. "You thought you were golden with that surveillance footage, but the D.A. tossed it, am I right? It obviously didn't show me doing the deed, so it's not enough to convict. That's why I'm in an interrogation room and not on a bus to Rikers Island. I mean, did you guys think you had enough? You processed me and everything. How clueless could you be?"

"Shut it, Grey," he clipped out. "Keep playing games, I can play all day long." He deposited me back in the interrogation room chair.

"Well ... not all day. My lawyer is on the way so you only have until then, but nice try, partner." I smiled.

"We are *not* partners!"

"We were," I corrected, "and if you remembered that little tidbit, you wouldn't believe in a million years that I would be capable of committing cold blooded murder."

He winced.

Not enough time had elapsed for me to process what happened at the bodega, but now that I knew his name, Joey DeLuca would haunt me like the rest of the souls on my kill list. It didn't matter that the blood on my hands was justified, it still didn't make me God. The empty feeling inside of me never went away. It just sat there, taunting me like a constant reminder of the monster I could become.

"Don't go!" I called out to Garrett as he started to leave the room. "Just stay here with me."

"Why?"

"Please stay," I repeated.

His glare drilled into me as he huffed and took a seat across the table. "Say for argument's sake that you didn't do it. Are you in some kind of trouble?"

I shook my head but didn't dare speak.

We sat in silence for several long minutes before the door opened and a man in a tailored suit walked in, his greasy brown hair slicked back. A gold ring with a square black stone the size of a small Lego glinted off his right ring finger. Alligator shoes shuffled toward us and he smiled—a gold tooth glinting between his lips.

I growled.

"And you are?" Michaels questioned. He stood up and hid me from the stranger's view.

"Detective Garrett Michaels, I presume?" He extended a hand to shake. "My name is Tom Martin, and I am representing Miss Grey."

"You are?" both Michaels and I said at the same time. *This was the Pack's attorney?*

"Yes, and I think you're done here, Detective. My client is ready to go." Tom waved for me to follow him.

I stood hesitantly, my metal chair screeching against the tile floor. I wasn't sure if I should go with him or not. Tom looked more like a loan shark than a lawyer.

"Sebastian sent you?" I questioned.

"Yes." Tom nodded. "Mr. Steel wanted to come, but was unavoidably held up. He sends his regards."

"Yeah, okay," I replied, more confused than ever. I grabbed my coat and followed my attorney out of the room.

Before I left, Garrett latched onto my arm. "I don't know what kind of shit you're into, but if you need help, you know where to find me," he muttered and let me go.

"Thank you." I turned and left the squad room.

Tom and I went out through the back exit of IPP. He was speed walking in his shiny alligator shoes, and I was having a hard time keeping up.

"Hey, thanks for the bail, but if you're in a rush I can just take the bus." I slowed and then stopped, about to head back around to the front of the building.

He gripped the sleeve of my jacket. "No, our ride is waiting out back."

"Dude, get off," I snarled. "I left my cell phone." I pulled my arm back, but his hold on me didn't loosen. My stomach fell and my face turned up a few degrees. Something was definitely off with this guy.

"I said," he gritted, "we're going through the back." He released my arm and grabbed a chunk of my hair. "Now let's go, bitch."

Someone pulled the fire alarm in the building and a cacophony of sirens blared around us. Tom yanked me harder down the back street toward an idling van. The sliding door opened and before I had a chance to see inside, someone tossed a hood over my head and knocked me out.

15

LUCIAN

Everything was falling apart.

Mackenzie Grey was never supposed to be found—much less be a wolf. She was meant to live a normal human life. *Where did it go wrong?*

The blasted witch gave me the formula. It should have worked. *Why didn't it bloody work?* I'd been burying myself in the past, retracing all our steps to figure out what I missed.

"Lucian!" Roman yelled as he snapped his fingers in front of my face.

"What, boy? Can't you see I'm busy?"

He snorted. "Yeah, busy staring into space."

"Fine." I waved him off. "What do you want?"

"The human friend and one of the wolves are here. They say it is urgent they speak with you."

I remembered when I first found Roman a few centuries ago, a savage feeding off the deaths of many on the battlefield. He'd come a long way since then.

"If they must," I sighed. "Bring them in."

Roman escorted the human girl and Jackson Cadwell into the library and I plastered on a wan smile. They were the last people I wanted to see. I had better things to do.

"Amelia, Jackson, what a lovely—not so much—surprise." I smiled.

"Trust me, the feeling is mutual," Jackson grumbled, "but she made me bring her." He jabbed his thumb toward the little human girl. She was a spunky one. It intrigued me how much loyalty she had for her friend. Her bright red hair hung loose in beautiful curls and all her body art was covered up by winter clothing. The weather in March was harsh, and I could only imagine how cold she must be. I hadn't felt it in so long, I'd forgotten the sensation. When you were no longer human, it was hard to remember, much less maintain, your humanity.

"Lucian, it's Mackenzie. She's been taken!" she cried out.

That was when I noticed those enchanting green eyes were blotched red and her lips trembled, on the brink of further tears. I stood in one fluid movement. "Excuse me?" My gaze flickered over to the wolf. "Explain."

"The Chicago Pack took her, and we have no clue where she is," he replied grimly.

"How in the bloody hell is that possible?" I yelled. "Didn't she leave the warehouse with the *other* Cadwell?"

"The humans arrested her while she was with Jonah. They were trying to pin the incident at the bodega on her," Jackson said. "Someone pretended to be her lawyer and snatched her from the precinct."

"Fuck!" Roman screamed as he ran his fingers through his

hair. "This is just wonderful, Lucian. You didn't tell me the Brooklyn Pack was filled with a bunch of geniuses."

"Hey, asshole!" Jackson stepped forward. "This is not our fault. You know Mackenzie just as well as we do; she makes her own rules. If she wanted to leave her only sanctuary, no one would be able to stop her."

"He's right, Roman," I chided. "Makes no sense to point fingers." I turned to Jackson. "I assume you sniffed around the precinct. Did you find a trail?"

He shook his head. "We lost it in Times Square. It's hard to track a single scent in the city."

"Very well." I turned away. "Go back to your home."

"What?" Amelia exclaimed. "You're not going to help us?"

"Go home, Amelia Fitzgerald," I said. "There is nothing you can do, hovering over my shoulder. Let me work my magic."

LEFT TO MY OWN DEVICES, I rushed to the bookshelf hidden in a far corner of the library. I scanned the spines in a rush until I found the one I was looking for. Sliding out my copy of *The Oracle of Delphi,* I opened it gingerly. A square had been cut out to house an empty vial and a ripped sheet of paper. On the paper was a set of numbers I never thought I'd have to call. Throughout the years it had changed, but he never failed to update me with it. It hadn't changed in the last ten years.

I sat in my reading nook, dragged the black rotary phone closer to me, and dialed the number.

"'Ello?" he answered.

"Alexander ... it's Lucian. We need to talk."

16

With my wrists bound behind me and a hood draped over my head, someone threw me to the ground. When I landed on my left arm I heard my shoulder dislocate from its socket, and I cringed to keep from screaming. It didn't take a genius to figure out what was going on. If I was a betting woman, I'd say this was the Chicago Pack's second attempt.

My eyes strained to see through the woven fabric of the hood, but not even the wolf had that superpower. The smell of mold and rat droppings filled my nose as I inventoried the scents around me. I scooted my palm on the ground and dug my nails into the soil. *Outside, maybe?*

Someone grabbed my right arm and tugged me up to a sitting position. The hood was lifted from my head and my hair dropped back into my face. I squinted and waited for my eyes to adjust, although my surroundings weren't all that bright. I was in a cramped space reminiscent of a jail cell. *Did that mean I was underground?* The only light came from a utility work lamp that was positioned on the opposite wall.

"Have a good nap?" said the man who stood before me. He was of average height, about six feet tall and stocky. His shaved head reflected the brightness from the single lamp. Dark eyes that glassed over like orbs slid over my disheveled body like I was dessert. He licked his lips and I gagged. I trembled with fear at the thought of what could happen if I didn't find a way out of here.

"Who are you?" I asked, my throat dry and rough.

"I'll be whoever you want me to be," he smirked. "But most people call me Logan."

My stomach twisted into knots and I felt icy pins prick my skin as I realized who had abducted me: the same monster who disfigured Rachel—the Alpha of the Chicago Pack.

"Speechless? Yeah, I have that effect on Lunas, but don't worry." He squatted in front of me and dragged a finger down my cheek in a crude caress. "I'll take good care of you. Quid pro quo, that is."

I flinched away. "I'd rather go down in a plane crash."

He chuckled. "Oh! Snarky, I like it! Makes the chase all the more entertaining."

"Entertain *this!*" I slammed my head against his and attempted to crawl away—as far away as my bound hands could take me, at least, which wasn't far. The beating pulse in my forehead made my attempts to flee sloppy.

He growled. "You're turning me on, Mackenzie Grey." He caught my leg and I kicked, hoping I'd get a good hit in, but all I caught was air.

I screamed, I cried, I prayed.

"Touch me and I swear I'll kill you!" I yelled.

He laughed as he dragged me away from the corner of the room by my ankle. The zip tie-handcuffs sliced the skin of my wrists with every movement.

"Darling, you can try, but you're just a Luna. Your place is either on your back or on your knees." He grinned maliciously. "So choose. What's it going to be?"

"Neither, you piece of shit!" I spit in his face. "Wait until King Alexander hears about this," I threatened.

He back handed me and I tumbled to the ground, my cheek bouncing off the dirt. I bit my inner cheek and a metallic taste filled my mouth.

"What? You think I don't know every single detail about you, Mackenzie Grey? I know *everything!*" He cupped my face and squeezed my cheeks, bringing me face-to-face with him. "Down to the detail of you not wanting to know a goddamn thing about your father. I doubt he'll be hearing about my fun times with dear ole' Princess Mackenzie any time soon, eh?"

His grin was that of a mad man, a maniac. It scared me to my core.

"Find a better source of fun, dipshit," I grumbled through the hand that held my face roughly. If he knew that much about me, someone was tipping him off. No amount of recon could give him that much information.

He grinned and flung me to the ground. "You've put me off for tonight, but you should get some rest. Tomorrow's going to be a *long* day," he promised as he touched himself.

Logan opened the cell door and shut it behind him with a loud clang, clicking the lock shut. Once he was out of eyesight, I leaned to the side and vomited.

I DIDN'T GET any sleep that night. My mind tortured me through the interminable hours, showing imagined scenes of dark places. I feared a visit from Logan in the middle of the night.

When I first learned of my heritage, I imagined many scenarios, but this wasn't one of them. Even after Sebastian warned me, I didn't listen. I wanted to slap myself for being so willfully ignorant. I remembered what Rachel said about me; that I was privileged, and as such, thought I was exempt from this outcome. This was proof that no matter who I was or how I carried myself, I wasn't invincible. I was getting a first-hand lesson on that.

My stomach rumbled with hunger and my mouth tasted like it was stuffed with cotton balls. I had to come up with a plan; anything to get myself out of here, or at least send word to Bash and Jonah. But from the looks of my surroundings, that would be an impossible task. I was surrounded by darkness.

"There's nowhere for you to go, Princess," Logan's sinister voice came through my muddled thoughts. "You can scream, and not a single soul will hear it."

"Why are you doing this?" I croaked. He unlocked the cell and sauntered inside. "I'm not important. This is pointless."

"For someone who is so outwardly confident, you sure have low self-esteem," he taunted as he laid next to me on his side. I couldn't move away—my body was too weak.

"I'm merely stating facts. If you want the throne, you won't get it through me."

"Not yet, but soon." He stretched his hand out and tucked a stray hair behind my ear. "You're so pretty, Princess. Even with all that dirt and filth, your eyes shine like a diamond in the rough. You're quite captivating."

I swallowed the bile rising in my throat. "They're just eyes. I'll rip them out before I let you near me."

He sighed. "That would be a shame, Princess."

I built up enough strength to turn my head and face the devil incarnate. "What made you the monster you are today? You must have some serious mommy issues if *this* is what you do to get your kicks," I muttered.

Logan smiled. "Look at us bonding already." He traced the outline of my body with his finger, sending unwanted shivers through my body. "You respond well."

"And you're avoiding my question, Ted Bundy."

His grin faltered. "Your sarcasm will only get you so far, Princess. The more you fight me, the longer you'll be down here. I like my girls scared. It makes things more exciting."

A cold sweat dripped down my spine. I *was* scared—but I wouldn't give him the satisfaction of knowing it.

"Then I guess we'll be here for a while."

When he stood to leave, I was suddenly gripped by desperation.

"Where are you going?" I demanded, swiveling my head in his direction.

"I'm going to have lunch," he answered flippantly, closing the cell door.

"Water," I begged. "I need water."

Logan shook his head. "Not today."

As the metal clanked into the quiet underground, my heart sank.

I TRIED to lick my chapped lips, but my mouth was so dry all I did was feel the ridges of cut skin. As the minutes ticked by, I learned that the less I moved, the less I felt the pain of my dislocated shoulder. I was losing track of time and the hunger within me gave me a second wind. I couldn't take another day of this. I didn't know how much longer I would last with no sleep, food, or water.

"Did you dream about me?" Logan said, startling me from my thoughts. He was leaning against the metal bars from the outside. "I dreamt about you, Princess."

"You could say I dreamed about you," I grumbled. "Skinning you alive brought me to my happy place."

"I was told you had a tendency to talk a lot, but they made you sound like such a drag," he smirked.

"Hmm. I wonder who that could be," I mused. "I have such a long list of people I've annoyed in my lifetime. It could be anyone."

"I can't imagine why," he chuckled. "Riddle me this, Mackenzie Grey: how did you manage to take down one of my boys? A small thing like you cannot possibly have killed Big Joe."

Small? I was five feet-nine inches tall. I was the farthest thing from petite. I raised my bound wrists. "Untie me, and I'll show you."

"Tempting, but no," he replied dryly.

"Worth a shot." I shrugged. "Although it's comforting to know you fear me."

"*Fear* you?" he howled. "Not in the slightest, but you do seem like a sneaky little minx."

"I aim to please."

He watched me for a moment. His dark gaze followed my

every move as if analyzing how I worked, like I was some strange species. I found it impossible to think I was the first Luna who was a lone wolf that he'd come across. Why was I so intriguing to these idiots? It had to be the royal blood.

"Take a picture, it lasts longer," I said with a bored tone. Sure, it wasn't my best material, but lack of food and water made me groggy.

"You're magnificent, you know," he said, enthralled. "You have your father's eyes, a rare color in our world. Only those born of royal blood are silver. It would be impossible for him not to acknowledge you."

"Dude, I don't care. Can you bring me a hamburger?"

He ignored me. "Do you know who your mother is? That is still a mystery. Everyone has been speculating, but no one knows for sure."

"Good for you guys." I faked excitement. "Can I at least have some water?"

"I heard you were a late bloomer. Didn't shift until you were eighteen—"

"Logan!" I exclaimed. "We can talk about my estranged family members and your obsession *after* you feed my ass, okay? I'm still a living, breathing being. I need something to eat and drink!" I awkwardly shuffled to my feet and walked up to the bars.

"Fine!" he barked. Logan unlocked my cell and wrapped his hand in my hair, tugging it like a leash. "Let's get the princess some food," he snarled as he drew me out of the cage. When I tried to jerk away, my scalp burned as strands of hair were pulled from the roots.

"Let me go! I can walk on my own!"

"Oh yeah?"

He pushed my head down and I fell, then he dragged me down the hallway by my hair. I dug my heels in the ground to stop him, but he was too strong. The bumpy ground was filled with rocks that dug painfully into my skin. I felt my flesh being cut and ripped by the roughness, my dislocated shoulder barely hanging on.

"Motherfucker!" I screamed.

"If only I knew who she was," he growled, throwing me to the ground like I weighed nothing.

I winced from the pain in my shoulder and glanced at my surroundings. Now that we were out in the open, I could tell we were definitely underground in what looked like an abandoned train tunnel. It was dark, but with the wolf's night vision I was able to see the other four men sitting around. They were on over-turned wooden crates, eating out of cans. I recognized my fake attorney among them.

I'd been thrown in the middle of the group and I scrambled to stand. "What, no one could spring for some Taco Bell?" I muttered when I smelled baked beans.

"What'd you say, bitch?" my fake attorney demanded.

"Easy, Tommy Boy," Logan scolded. "Mackenzie is a little different. We'll have to teach her how to be a Luna."

Another one of his Pack members chuckled. "You mean break her? Nice. That'll be fun."

I snorted. "Not if I break you first."

They all laughed at me. "She's funny," one of them said.

"She sure is," Logan agreed, "but the princess is hungry. Any of you care to share?"

Tommy stood up and started to unbuckle his pants. "I'll share ... for a price." He grinned lasciviously.

I rolled my eyes and looked away. "I'd rather starve, so put your little guy away."

"Bitch!" he growled and charged toward me.

Surprisingly, Logan came between us before Tommy could reach me. "Heel!" he ordered. "Control yourselves. You're only feeding into her nonsense."

"Nonsense? Well, *that's* a first," I joked. I was becoming delirious.

Logan gave me a sideways glance as if warning me to be quiet, which was impossible. If I was going to die down here, I was going out without a filter.

"You still hungry, Princess?" Logan asked.

"Duh," I deadpanned.

He nodded. "Since you're so keen on threatening us with physical violence, let's give you the opportunity." He looked around at his Pack members. They smiled like they were in on an inside joke. "You want a can of beans? Then fight for it. You take down one of my boys, and then you can eat. If not ... well, you know your other option." He winked and unbuttoned his pants.

My stomach churned. How disgusting could these wolves be? When the Brooklyn Pack told me I was in danger, this was the farthest thing from my mind. I thought maybe I'd be held up at gunpoint or something of that nature. But not rape. It made me wonder why the Brooklyn Pack even associated with their kind.

"I don't get it. Why are we down here? Shouldn't you be taking me out of Brooklyn Pack territory?" The thought had crossed my mind many times during my confinement. I could feel it in my bones that we were still in New York—but why?

"How do you know we aren't in Chicago?"

"Oh, please. If we were, we wouldn't be slumming it down in

the sewers. You look like the bragging type. You'd be flaunting me around your Pack like a brand-new car," I smirked.

Logan's eyes narrowed to slits. "Your *boyfriends* have blocked all exits out of the city. We can't leave until things cool down. We're working on it."

I sighed with relief. *They're looking for me. Thank heavens. That means there's still hope for a rescue.* And if I knew my people, they would move heaven and earth to find me. I might not be part of the Brooklyn Pack, but I'd created my own dysfunctional Pack with some wolves, vampires, and even a human thrown in for good measure. It was unconventional, but they'd become family. They would find me; I was sure of it.

"Don't get your hopes up, Princess." Logan came up to me and rubbed his thumb over my lower lip, dipping it sensually in my mouth. "Our scents are completely masked. It will be impossible for them to find us down here."

I flinched away from his touch, my stomach bottoming out with his words.

"Aw, no longer confident?" he pouted.

"Fuck off," I growled.

"Very well," he sneered. "Shall we commence *The Hunger Games*? See what I did there?"

I rolled my eyes. "Oh, get over yourself."

"And since Tommy Boy was deeply hurt by your insults, I think he'll volunteer as tribute," Logan smirked. "How about it?" he asked the wolf.

"With pleasure." Tommy grinned.

I sized him up, taking in his frame. He was stockier than the others, but that would make him slower. I was counting on that. Tommy placed his can of beans on top of the crate he had been sitting on and peeled off his shirt, revealing six-pack abs. He pounded a fist against his chest like a warrior in an attempt to intimidate me, but it wasn't working. I had something to live for, and that was all the motivation I needed. All I had to do was hold on until they found me.

I brought my tied wrists toward Logan. "Do the honors?" He eyed me warily but cut the restraints with a clawed finger. Once I was released, I stretched my wrists and placed a hand on my injured shoulder—it drooped lower than the other. I gritted my teeth and pulled my arm as hard as I could without support, and after a few attempts, was able to put my shoulder back in its socket. I bit down a cry. I didn't know if I'd done it right or only ended up hurting myself further, but I needed both of my arms.

"Ouch, that sounded painful," one of the wolves commented.

My face was streaked with silent tears. I licked my chapped lips and tasted the saltiness. I didn't care what they thought, all I cared about was that can of beans. Without an estimated time of rescue, I needed fuel, and that meant I needed to stay alert. I didn't trust these assholes to leave me alone while I slept if I was going to be holed up down there for another night.

"I'm ready," I clipped out.

The wolves lit up their lighters and flashlights from their cell phones, brightening the tunnel. I tapped into my wolf, satisfied that she woke up pissed. I knew the feeling. I roared at Tommy as I went into a half-shift. My canines extended, and the wolf was released.

"Whoa!" Logan shrieked. "We were told you were moon bound!"

"Like I said, get a better source, dipshit."

I didn't wait for Tommy to attack first—I went on the offense. I ran toward him and slid between his legs, aiming a fist to his crown jewels. Too late, he sensed my goal and tried to move out of the way, but not fast enough. After a successful first attack, I jumped up behind him and elbowed him in his lower back. He howled in pain and dropped to one knee. My good arm wrapped around his neck in a chokehold and I squeezed. My limbs felt weak, like rubber, but I knew I had to push through the pain and exhaustion.

"That can is *mine!*" I cried out. The cheers of the wolves around us were drowned out as I concentrated on Tommy's breathing until I couldn't hear it any longer.

Suddenly he growled with renewed strength, gripping my forearm and flinging me over his shoulder. My back slammed onto the ground and I gasped as the wind was knocked out of me. Tommy grabbed my bad arm and twisted, eliciting a howl that I felt down to my toes.

"Not so tough now, are you, Princess?" he snarled.

My claws dug into the dirt and I gritted my teeth, but the pain was too much to bear as I felt my shoulder dislocate again. Taking a deep breath and ignoring the pain, I swung my body around and swept my foot behind his, knocking him to the ground, and wrapped my legs around his torso when he attempted to sit up. Compressing my thighs on his abdomen, I gripped his arm with my good hand and held him still. We both screamed; me from the exertion of holding on, and him in pain. I felt my resolve leaving me, so in a last ditch effort, I twisted my hips to one side and then slammed him to the ground. The crack of his skull was music to my ears.

Number nine.

I relaxed and sagged to the ground as complete silence encompassed me. No one moved, and no one said a word.

"Now," I panted, my breathing wild, "where are my beans?"

I WAS AN ANIMAL, and not the cute kind, either. I was straight-up savage as I demolished the disgusting, chemical-infused beans I earned. I was never a fan of this barbeque favorite, but I wasn't going to complain when I was hungry. With only one functioning arm, I tilted my head back and shook the can with my lips on the edge to get the last few stragglers in the back. I didn't care that the others were watching me with sick fascination. The jury was out on whether they were angry or not.

When I was done, I sighed contentedly. Slouching on the crate that once belonged to Tommy Boy, I dropped the empty can on the ground and tapped my belly.

"Got another one?" I asked as four sets of eyes stared at me. "What?"

"What you just did," Logan started, "is treason. Do you understand that?"

I shrugged. "I'm damned if I do and damned if I don't. That's why I make my own rules; it's just easier." I sniffed over my shoulder and blanched. The lack of a shower plus sweat and dirt was *not* a good mix on me.

"Logan," one of the wolves called out. "What are you going to do? She can't get away with this."

"I know," the Alpha replied.

I stilled. "What are you talking about? You made me fight him!"

"But you weren't supposed to win," Logan argued.

"Then you should have specified that before we got started!" I yelled, flailing my one good arm in the air.

"She needs to be punished, boss!"

"I know," Logan growled. "I'm thinking. She can't be killed, regardless of what she's done. But—"

"But nothing," I scoffed.

"But there are other ways to extract punishment." He gave a wicked grin and the sinking feeling in my gut returned. "Get up."

"No," I snapped.

Logan grabbed my arm and hauled me to my feet. I tried to stop him by pulling the opposite way, but with only one good arm and in my weakened state, there wasn't much I could do to resist his momentum.

"Stop, please!" I begged. "Don't let him do this. It's not right!" I pleaded to the others. But none of them seemed to care. On the contrary, they looked excited. One by one, they stood and followed us.

I was thrown back in the cell, landing face-first. I flipped over and scooted back until I hit the wall. This was every woman's worst nightmare, and I was powerless to do anything about it. For all my bluster and bravado, I could not talk my way out of this.

"Alright, boys, who wants to go first?" Logan cheered as he leaned against the cell bars, his forearm resting above him casually.

One of the wolves started cracking his knuckles as he stalked toward me. He was lean, but short. I measured whether I could fight him off, but quickly deduced I wouldn't be able to take all four of them.

When he dropped to his knees before me, I kicked and

clawed with every ounce of strength I had. The wolves on the sideline came in and held me down. The one before me unbuttoned my jeans and pulled down the zipper with a taunting slowness. He spread my legs apart and pulled me closer to him by my hips. The sound of my skin slapping the ground was vulgar and crude, and angry tears streaked from the corners of my eyes. My heart felt like it would slam out of my chest with every filthy touch, every rancid breath blown in my direction, and every nasty grin aimed for me.

His eyes flashed red when he ripped my t-shirt straight down the middle, exposing my plain sports bra to the jeers of the spectators. I thrashed against their hold, refusing to give up, to fight harder. But the more their hands wandered over my exposed skin, the less fight I had left in me. I felt dirty and unsanitary, and my flesh pebbled with goosebumps as the temperature dropped inside my personal hell.

"No!" My nails extended and the wolf inside me roared with unbridled anger. I clawed and snapped my canines at the air but they only laughed, swimming in the ecstasy of my terror.

Logan growled, "Move out of the way! Let me show you how it's done." With one fluid movement, he ripped the wolf off me and took his place. The sinister gleam of his eyes hovered over me, his eyes wide and wild as he licked his lips.

My wolf began to tear at my insides, her anger bubbling within me like a volcano ready to erupt. Her slow prowl to the surface disconnected me from reality—leaving me exposed and vulnerable, a feeling I despised. I no longer had control of myself as something built up within me and stalked to the outside. A bundle of pressure felt trapped in my throat. I swallowed multiple times, thinking I was going to throw up like I did the night before, but the wolf pushed the lump further up until I couldn't keep it down any longer.

I howled.

My body froze as my chin lifted and my mouth formed an O-shape toward the moon, a howl ripping from my throat like never before. The pain, fear, and desperation curdled out of me like a battle cry. I called out to *my* Pack.

When the wolf's cry died out, my body slumped against the ground. That single action stole the last shred of energy from me. My mind no longer present, I went somewhere far away, giving up on the world around me. I failed, and the only person I could blame was myself. If I had just listened and kept running, I wouldn't be in this situation. Something visceral cracked inside me as I contemplated my fate and stared at the cracked, dirty concrete ceiling, and I didn't know if I could ever fix it.

I was tired, so tired. My eyelids fluttered and threatened to close. I vainly fought the sleep that wanted to take me under, stealing me away someplace safe in my mind, until I could no longer stay alert. My vision fogged up like the inside of a car in the middle of a New York winter. I dimly heard shuffling nearby, followed by multiple feet running. Then I heard nothing at all as I drowned in the darkness of my subconscious.

Only God could save me now.

17

My body floated in a waterless sea without destination, carried by a strong current that wrapped its arms around me and whispered sweet nothings in my ear. I reached out for its comfort, exhaling the bad and inhaling the good—the safe. I was home.

In a flash, I shot up to a seated position in the bed I was in and scrambled back until I hit the headboard. Realizing my left arm was in a sling, I rummaged around with my free hand, searching for something to fight them off. I still felt the imprints of their filthy hands on my skin like a blistering rash.

"No!" I cried out. "Don't," I whispered, orienting myself and realizing I was in the Brooklyn Pack's warehouse.

"Kenz? It's okay, you're safe," Amy soothed as she startled and came over to the side of the bed. "You're okay," she assured me.

"Amy?" I trembled, unable to stop shaking.

My best friend climbed in the bed with me and pulled me into her small arms. I hid my face in shame in the crook of her neck as all the suppressed emotions came bubbling to the surface. I grasped her shirt, making sure she was real and not a figment of my tortured imagination.

"It's okay, Kenz," she whispered over and over again. "It's okay."

But I knew I would never get enough reassurance.

"What happened?" I choked out. "How did you find me?" I pulled away and wiped my face with the back of my hand.

Amy's face twisted in confusion. "You called for us, Kenz, don't you remember?"

I shook my head. "I-I can't remember anything after ... Did they ...?" I gulped. I couldn't finish the thought. I had no memory of what had happened, though my stomach churned with the memories I did have. I held my breath as I waited for her to fill in the blanks. The anticipation was too much. "Oh, God, I need a shower!" I cried, trying to rip off my shirt one-handed and scratch their touch off my flesh.

Amy's cheeks blazed and her green eyes brimmed with tears. "No, Kenz, they didn't," she whispered as she stopped my hand.

I exhaled loudly. *I wasn't ... They didn't ... Oh, God, they didn't.*

"How long have I been out?"

"Just a few hours. Jackson said your energy had been depleted and that it would take some time for you to recover," she said as she softly stroked my hair. "They fixed your shoulder, but you'll need to shift to fully heal."

I took deep, calming breaths to steady the trembles that wracked my body. I was okay. They didn't do anything to me, I was fine. I needed to chill out.

"What happened to Logan and the Pack?" I asked, sounding a bit stronger, more secure of myself.

"Bash said he'd talk to you about everything. Do you want me to get him?" she offered.

"No, I need *you* to tell me, Amy. I don't want to hear it from any of them," I demanded. The last thing I wanted to do right now was speak to another man. I didn't know what I was feeling, since I had no other experiences from which to draw. The only thing I knew was that I wanted to be near someone I felt safe with, and away from everything supernatural. Coming back to New York was a bad idea. I regretted every minute of it.

Amy shifted uncomfortably as her eyes wandered around the room. "They caught the Pack members ... but Logan escaped."

"What?" I shrieked. "How could they let him get away?"

"They didn't, Kenz!" Amy rebutted. "Please, just talk to Bash."

"No." I yanked the covers off and tumbled out of bed on shaky legs, grabbing my jeans and starting to get dressed. I wanted to go home, I wanted a shower to wash away the grime, and I needed time to figure things out. Logan couldn't still be out there. I would never sleep again if he was still breathing.

"Kenz, please wait," Amy pleaded as she stood in front of the door. "You're not thinking rationally. It's been a hard few days since you've been back in New York, and you need to rest!"

Somewhere deep down I knew she was right, but in that moment, I didn't care. Logan had to be taken care of, and if Bash wouldn't handle it, I would.

"I will move you, Amy. Don't make me," I growled as we faced off.

Her wild green eyes looked everywhere for a reason for me to stay, but I was too riled up to change my course of action.

"I'll scream," she threatened. "I will scream bloody murder, I swear."

"You wouldn't." I squinted my eyes.

"Try me, Kenz."

"Why are you doing this? You should be on *my* side, Amy!"

She deflated, but I had to get out of there at whatever cost.

"I *am* on your side, Kenzie. I'm *always* on your side. Even when I'm mad because you left me behind, I'm still here, protecting you." She exhaled in frustration. "You know what? Fuck you, Mackenzie!" She pushed off the bedroom door and stormed toward me, aiming a manicured finger at my chest.

"Amy—"

"No! You listen to *me* for a change! When you left, *I* was the one who kept my mouth shut, even when Ollie found you in Los Angeles! *I* was the one who convinced him to cancel his flight and let you stay when all he wanted to do was drag you home. *I* was the one who dealt with the Pack's million and one questions and kept them away from your secret location. *I* did that. No one else! So you owe me, Mackenzie Grey. I know you're hurting and you want revenge, but I want my best friend alive. I didn't protect you all this time just so you could get yourself killed!"

I was rooted in place, my feet glued to the ground by wet cement. *Ollie found me?*

"I'm sorry, I didn't mean—"

"I know you didn't," she sighed, "but you owe me, and I'm calling it in. Talk to Bash—for me."

What had she been up to while I was gone?

I nodded. "Fine."

WHILE SHE WENT to look for everyone, I went ahead and showered. I scrubbed my skin with scalding water, intent on erasing the bad memories. My flesh reddened to the point I thought I'd break the skin, but I didn't care. Once I finished, I scrounged around for some clean clothes. The only items of clothing that survived the underground train tunnels were my Nike Air Max's. I held onto them for a second before deciding to throw them away.

A knock on my door startled me and I shot up from the bed as Amy, Sebastian, Jonah, and Jackson came in. Like a deer caught in headlights I watched them silently filter in, and I shook out my hands to release the tension. I was overreacting. I had to get it together. Plastering on a fake smile, I waited.

"Mackenzie," Sebastian started, his cold demeanor never changing. "How are you feeling?"

My smile strained and my cheeks felt like rubber bands being stretched beyond their limits. "I'm great! I just took a shower and freshened up, and now I'm ready to, you know ... do stuff." I gave an awkward, high-pitched chuckle. No one laughed with me.

Sebastian nodded. "Amy said you planned on leaving."

"Yup! I want to see Roman, and maybe head back to the apartment. I haven't had a chance to watch that new Netflix show — oh, man, what's it called? Oh, yeah! Marvel's *Jessica Jones*."

"That's a bad idea," Jonah gently interjected. "You should stay here, Kenzie."

I laughed. "Don't be silly, Jonah. Everything's good now. I can go home."

As they looked at one another with dubious expressions, I wanted the ground to swallow me whole. I was starting to sound as airheaded as Diana Stone.

"He's right, Mackenzie. You're staying here. It's for the best,"

Bash ordered. "The full moon is coming soon, so there's no point in you leaving."

"No, I'm not, and I'll be fine on my own. Thank you anyway." I attempted to swerve between them and leave the room, but Sebastian's arm snaked out and pulled me back.

"Let go of me!" I shrieked. A cold sweat broke out and I felt my muscles seize up. I didn't want to cause a scene, but the tension in my shoulders was a dead giveaway—they were scrunched up to my ears. He slowly released me, his eyes clouding with an unknown emotion.

"I'm not part of this Pack, which means I can come and go as I please. If you would excuse me." I glared at them with as much dignity as I could muster, waiting to be allowed out of my personal prison.

Sebastian nodded, but Jonah nearly had an aneurysm. "What? You can't—"

"Quiet!" Bash barked, and then turned to face me. "You are free to go, Mackenzie."

———

MY CELL PHONE was once again MIA, so I couldn't call in advance. I left everything but my Metro Card, some cash, and my identification back at the warehouse. I didn't need anything where I was headed, but first, I needed to make a pit stop.

The cathedral steps loomed above me as I took them two at a time. I opened the ancient doors, their hinges squealing and protesting my intrusion, and walked into the church like I owned it. I whistled into the quiet sanctuary, waiting for someone to show themselves. This was a hub for vampires, but I never saw anyone but Lucian. I wondered where they were. My gaze traveled all over the pews and altar, but nothing. Then I looked up at the ceiling and halted mid-step. Hundreds of bats covered the church's ceiling, their wings hugging their small bodies as they hung upside down. The hairs on my arm prickled with static and I found myself trying to cover my neck. I was sure it was just a silly superstition, but after what I'd seen, I didn't want to take any chances.

"Ace?" Roman called out from the altar.

I sighed with relief. "Oh, thank God."

Roman chuckled. "I don't think God would appreciate it if I did."

I rolled my eyes. "Shut up." He met me halfway but kept his distance, keeping me at arm's length. "So ... what are you up to?"

His hazel eyes narrowed as he ruffled his hair. "Helping Luce with some stuff. How are you? Still in that sling, I see." He flicked the suspension that held my shoulder in place.

I flinched away. "How'd you know I was in a sling?"

His face scrunched up in confusion. "Because I put it on you ..."

"You did?"

He nodded. "Yeah, we brought you back here after we raided the tunnels. It was closer than going to Brooklyn."

I took a step back. "You were with the Pack when they came for me?"

"Ace, are you okay? Didn't Twiddle Dee and Twiddle Dum tell you what you did?"

I shook my head.

Roman's mouth fell open. "Come on, let's go find Lucian. He can explain it better than I can."

We walked through the entryway at the side of the altar that led to another building connected to the cathedral. It used to house the priests and nuns, but the vampires now used it as their sleeping quarters and home base in the city.

As soon as we walked into the converted library that he practically lived in, Lucian was the only one so far who smiled at me with joy. I didn't know if I should be offended or relieved.

"Pet!" he exclaimed. "Glad to see you up and running! You look absolutely ravishing, by the way. The sling looks very fashionable, if you ask me."

"I didn't, but thank you." When he came forward and took my hand in his I cringed from his cold touch, but either Lucian ignored me or he didn't notice.

"Come along, Pet, we have much to discuss."

"We do?"

"Why yes!" He startled me. "Much has happened and you're, goodness, Pet, you're magnificent!" He directed me to his reading nook, picking up books that had been scattered around. I tried to catch some of the titles, but he quickly re-shelved them. "Sit, sit," he urged.

"Okay, Lucian, you're acting weirder than normal. What gives?"

He gave me a toothy smile. It would have grossed me out, but living with Roman had weaned me off that discomfort.

"Quick lesson: Alphas have a marvelous ability to communicate with their Pack whenever they're hurt, in need of help, or over-the-moon with joy; but it is mostly used when they're in peril, and only Pack members can hear the call," Lucian started.

"Oh, yeah, Sebastian did that the other day."

"Fantastic! Then you already know what I speak of, yes?"

"Yeah. It's their own personal bat signal." I laughed and Roman snickered beside me.

"Well, Pet, congratulations, because you have your own bat signal as well."

I was still laughing with Rome when his words caught up to my brain and I almost choked. "What?"

Lucian's dark eyes gleamed with mischief. "The night of your captivity, you called out to us. To Sebastian, the Cadwells, Roman and I— even Amy heard your howl. The last time I felt that sense of fear was many centuries ago, when I was still human. You projected your emotions to us and we felt it down to our bones, Pet. No one other than an Alpha has that ability, and no other species besides wolves have ever heard it."

That revelation coincided with the few fragmented memories I did have. I remembered howling in pain, desperate, but I didn't think I was calling out to my friends. I wasn't even an Alpha.

"That has to be a mistake. I don't have the ability to do that," I said, reassuring myself more than anything.

"No mistake, Pet. Do not underestimate your abilities. You're far more gifted than you give yourself credit for."

"So what? Let's say I *did* pull it off, it doesn't matter. It was probably a one-time deal, because that situation won't ever happen again." I shrugged as best I could with one arm.

"But if you could? Do it again, I mean," he said, leaning forward in his chair.

"What are you talking about?" Roman asked. "I get that this is a cool discovery and all, but why do I get the feeling you're planning something?"

"Excusez moi." Lucian blanched as he put a hand to his chest in mock horror. "I merely ask, because this would be an excellent ability to hone. Especially if you could reach out to anybody, not just your loved ones."

"Loved ones?" I smirked. "Is that what you're calling yourself?"

"Of course," he deadpanned. "I'm like your British Uncle Lucian," he suggested. "Yes, I rather like the ring of that."

"More like that weird uncle at family reunions you try to avoid," I countered.

He scoffed, "Why must you always rain on my parade, Pet?"

"My bad." I laughed as I took stock of the library and its overflowing bookshelves. "Hey, do you have a lighter?"

"A lighter?" Lucian gasped. "I'm a vampire! Do you really think I'd have such a deadly weapon in my possession?"

I nodded. "Yes, I do."

He sighed. "Second drawer to the left in my desk."

I chuckled. "You vamps have a weird obsession with death. It's predictable." It was exactly what I needed for what had to be done next. I stood and opened the drawer where the lighter was housed, revealing a Zippo lighter that was heavy in my hand. "Thanks!" I yelled to him.

He waved me off. "Go. I do not wish to speak to you anymore." Lucian shooed us away.

18

"What's on your mind, Ace?" Roman asked as he rested his chin on the back of the pew I was reclining on. "Surely you didn't come here to take a nap on the most uncomfortable benches known to man."

"How do you know I didn't? This could be—"

"From the girl who got pissed when I didn't buy a pillowtop mattress? Yeah, try again, Ace," he smirked.

I sat up. "Seriously, though, who in their right mind doesn't buy pillowtop?"

He sighed. "A lot of people! Okay, we're getting off track, but nice try. Now tell me why you're here."

"I just needed a break, that's all," I murmured as I laid back down and continued to watch the bats that hung from the ceiling. "Aren't you happy to see me?"

"Of course I am, but you've had an eventful few days. You should be resting."

"Isn't that what I'm doing?"

"Don't be a smartass, Ace."

"Fine. You want to know why I'm here? It's because of them." I pointed to the ceiling with my good arm. "Are those vampires?"

Roman looked up at the cathedral and broke into a fit of laughter. "Are you serious? You think we turn into *bats*?"

"I've come to realize that anything is possible."

"Well, no, we don't. Stop watching crappy vampire movies. Now will you tell me why you're *really* here?"

I peered up at Rome with a sly smile. "I need a favor, partner."

"Anything, Ace."

I nodded and sat up. "I want to go after Logan. Tonight."

Roman's face reminded me of the time he ran out of A-positive blood bags, his favorite—like the Anti-Christ had come and it was the end of the world. If he could have gotten paler than he already was, I wouldn't have been surprised.

"Are you insane?"

"No more than usual, no." I played with the strands of my hair, checking for split ends. If I pretended to be cool, calm, and collected, maybe he wouldn't notice my desperate need for revenge.

"You can't go after him, Ace. He's long gone by now, anyway." His hazel eyes pleaded with me to see reason, but all I saw was red.

"Am I supposed to let him go," I snapped my fingers, "just like that? The man who ... who attacked me? Just let him get away with it? That doesn't even sound like something I'm capable of."

"You have to be. He'll kill you, and if by some miracle he doesn't, you'll start a war that the Lycans will be left to clean up," he warned, his voice as quiet as death.

"I'm a lone wolf. I'll deal with it."

He laughed. "They won't care! I'm not stupid, Ace. If I see how protective the Alpha and Beta of the Brooklyn Pack are with you, so does everyone else. Chicago will declare war on them just by their association with you. Is that what you want to do to your ... *friends*?"

The emphasis wasn't lost on me. I hadn't exactly been forthcoming with Roman about my past. I'd mentioned James, but never Bash or Jonah. That part of my life felt more private and not something to gossip about, but keeping my mouth shut made me feel like I'd kept a dirty little secret from him. That was never my intention, but then again, I never thought I'd be back here.

"They're just friends," I tried to convince him, but even I didn't believe it.

"Friends like us?" He arched a brow and smirked. "Aren't you the friendly type?"

My face reddened, not in embarrassment but with anger. How dare he shame me in that way? We never claimed to be exclusive, and I never said a word when he flirted with other women. He wasn't my boyfriend—he'd made that clear to me more than once.

"Fuck you, Roman." I stood from the bench. "The nerve of you! I've never slept with *either* of them. And if you think so low of me, then why have you been slumming it?"

"That came out wrong, I'm—"

"Damn right it did, but you know what? Forget it. You don't have to worry about this *friend* any longer," I said as I backed out of the pew. "Why don't you head back to Cali and keep fucking your way through eternity? I don't need a babysitter."

"Ace!" he called out as I speed-walked to the exit. "Mackenzie!" He yelled my government name for the first time ever, almost making me trip over myself. Either way, I refused to turn around.

I knew my relationships with Bash and Jonah were tricky—there was obvious attraction on both spectrums, but I wouldn't let anyone shame me for those feelings. I wasn't sleeping around, and I didn't plan on it, either.

My will had been severely challenged this week, and I wouldn't allow anyone to take that away from me again. The only way I knew how to make sure it didn't was to eliminate the threat.

I ran down the cathedral steps and hailed the first cab back to Brooklyn. I knew what I needed to do, and I wouldn't do it alone.

I stood on the sidewalk across the street from the warehouse as the taxi sped away. I wouldn't be going inside. I knew if I did, someone would try to talk me out of what I needed to do. Amy's beseeching eyes couldn't dissuade me from this—and if Lucian was right, I could use my howl again if needed.

I glanced around the empty streets of Dumbo to make sure no one was around. My wolf was inside, tormented from the violation we'd endured, and I had to soothe her. I reminded her that we were strong and it would never happen again. I would make sure of it.

Transforming into a half shift was easy since my wolf was already begging to go for a run, but she'd have to wait until the full moon. We had other things to take care of. I crouched on one knee, closed my eyes, and thought of Blu, Rachel, and all the other Lunas within the warehouse that felt powerless and wanted to be set free. I reached for their presence inside as if a tether connected us all, and when I felt them hovering at my fingertips, I raised myself up at the sky and howled.

Adrenaline coursed through me, along with the anticipation of tearing into the man who had injected fear into my veins and made me doubt everything about myself. I waited as one by one, Lunas streamed out of the warehouse and searched for the one who called them. About a dozen female wolves crowded the streets of Dumbo, looking around at each other uncertainly as they tried to understand what was happening.

"Kenzie?" Blu called out from within the crowd. "What's going on?" Her wide eyes glanced around, not believing what I'd just done.

"I can't sit back any longer," I declared. "At first, I believed what I had been told—that I was privileged because of my lineage and wasn't the same as the rest of you." I paused, cataloging their captivated expressions. "But that moment passed when I discovered I wasn't any different. Who I am and where I originated from means nothing. I may have the blood of a king but I have the heart of a slave. And I refuse to be caged any longer."

The whispers in the crowd grew as realization dawned on them.

"Mackenzie, we already talked about this," Rachel whispered as she moved up to the front, her disfiguration another reminder of Logan's misogyny.

"You're right, we did." I nodded. "You told me Lunas wouldn't fight because they had too much to lose. But we have *everything* to lose if we don't! We must fight to live! We're not delicate, fragile beings who should be condemned to glass houses. We're *preda-*

tors; we are *wolves*—and it's about time we started acting like it. Doesn't your freedom mean anything to you?"

I saw the spark in their eyes as they ignited with a fire rooted deep within. The desire to speak up and speak out. The right to be considered equal.

"I am proof that every single one of you has the power to fight. The only question is, will you?"

Rachel turned to the Lunas but didn't say a word. She let them deliberate with one another and observed as each one came to the conclusion I knew they would.

"Yes." I heard the answers echoing all around me. More and more of them cheered as they realized they could be more than a maid and breeder to the Pack. They were capable of so much more; all they needed was a reminder of what they could do as a group.

Rachel turned to me when the assembled Lunas reached their consensus, though I couldn't tell if she was against their decision or not.

"What's your plan?" she asked.

"My plan is to send a message to the Lycans. We will no longer live in fear and be put down. We're going to behead the snake once and for all," I declared as I ripped off my sling—ignoring the stab of pain. "We're going to kill the Alpha of the Chicago Pack."

19

I dispatched two teams to search for a trail on Logan aboveground as I took my team back down to the subway lines. Blu was part of my group, and I felt her nervous energy crackle beside me. I reached down for the lid of a pothole that led to the labyrinth of New York City's underground. As the first one to drop down, my combat boots landed with a loud splash when I hit water, and I helped each of the Lunas climb down. While the rest of the group situated themselves, I pulled Blu to the side.

"What's going on?" I asked. She needed to be all in or nothing. I couldn't have her tagging along if she was scared shitless. That indecisiveness would get her killed.

"Are you sure we should be doing this, Kenz? There has to be a better way."

"What? You want to talk it out with the Summit and hope they'll change laws that have been in effect for centuries? Get real, Blu."

She huffed, "That's not what I meant, but it won't be easy going against the Summit."

"You'd be the one to know," one of the Lunas snickered behind us.

I stopped and whirled on her. "What is *that* supposed to mean?" Blu kept quiet beside me.

The Luna who made the remark was a petite little thing with dark hair and big doe eyes. They widened further as she took in my demeanor. I was pissed and didn't need bickering, back-stabbing girls to add to my shit list.

"I didn't mean anything by it," the Luna said hastily. "It's just, this isn't Blu's first time rebelling."

"So?" I remembered Blu mentioning when we first met that escaping the warehouse wasn't her first rodeo. But she never expanded on it and I didn't push.

"Nothing," the Luna murmured as she looked away.

"Alright then," I said. "Keep your ears open, and nose alert. If I had to guess, I'd say our friend wouldn't have left until he got what he came for. Let's bring the party to him." I growled and ran forward, deeper into the sewer.

After many twists and turns, we found ourselves in the abandoned train tracks where I'd been kept. Discarded cans of food and overturned crates littered the ground and claw marks lined the walls, making my skin crawl. There weren't any bodies, but the smell of blood was strong. I tasted the metallic odor on the air.

"Their scent is gone," Blu commented. "It would be stupid of him to stay."

I scrunched my mouth to the side. "I don't know. Logan seems like a prideful man. Leaving without his prize doesn't seem like something he would do."

"How can you be sure, Kenz?"

"I just know!" I bellowed. My gut told me I was right. I had no proof to go by, but I couldn't shake the feeling that he was still lingering around. He wouldn't slink back to Chicago in defeat. That didn't seem like his style. The toxic sewer gases masked their scents, so I didn't think he would go topside for fear of being tracked. He had to still be down here. If only ...

"Anyone have a cell phone?" I asked the group. "Who has service down here?"

They all checked their phones and shook their heads. I snatched the phone of the Luna who mouthed off earlier and went looking for another manhole nearby. The Lunas followed behind me, bewildered. I climbed up and slowly slid the lid off—making sure I wasn't opening one in the middle of the street. The late evening moonlight filtered in and I checked the phone—two bars of service.

"Yes," I whispered as I dialed the number to IPP. "Detective Garrett Michaels, please," I asked the operator. It rang and rang until the call was transferred to his cell phone. That was the beauty about Michaels—he was a workaholic. All his desk calls always transferred to his mobile device when he wasn't in the office.

"Michaels," his gruff voice answered.

I took a deep breath. "Did you mean what you said about coming to you if I ever needed help?"

"Grey?" Sirens blared in the background and I had to pull the device away for a moment.

"The one and only."

There was a pause. I almost thought he'd hung up, when I heard him clear his throat. "What do you need?"

I relaxed against the ladder. "I need you to send me the subway blueprints for Brooklyn."

"The what?"

I closed my eyes. "Please, Michaels. I wouldn't ask if this weren't a life or death situation. I *really* need them."

"I need more than that, Grey. You're asking me to break the law."

"Am I talking to Garrett, or Detective Michaels? I can't be speaking to the latter," I muttered into the phone line. If I was going to divulge my intentions, I couldn't be speaking to law enforcement, I needed to be speaking to a friend.

"Depends. Are you breaking the law?"

"Aside from roaming the tunnels, no."

He sighed. "You're talking to Garrett."

I sagged with relief. "I need to find a place that someone could be hiding down here. Some secret nook that no one is aware of."

"Do you know how many abandoned subway lines there are in New York City?" he said. "Hold on, I'm walking to my desk."

"There can't be *that* many in Brooklyn, can there?"

"We'll see," he murmured.

I heard him typing away on his computer. In the meantime, I looked down and saw the Lunas waiting for me. I covered the mouthpiece of my phone and whistled at them. "Get in contact with the others. Tell them to come down and bring a container of gasoline." Blu nodded and started to look for phone service.

"Alright, Grey, there's an unused tunnel under Nevins Street

Station—it's beneath the 4 and 5 train. There's even an abandoned cart down there."

"Can you do me one more favor?" I winced when I heard him smack his lips.

"I expect you to tell me *exactly* what you're up to, Grey, as soon as you're back," he demanded.

"Promise." I was surprised that I meant it. Would it be so bad to tell Garrett the truth? Maybe.

"Fine. What else?"

"Can you track this phone and tell me how to get there?"

He sighed, but in moments, I heard him typing again. After a few minutes, he found my location.

"Okay, head south until Fulton and make a left. It should take you straight there."

"I owe you big time, Michaels."

"No. You owe me the truth."

WE RAN the mile and a half to Nevins Street, meeting up with the rest of the girls on the way. I ordered a few to stay aboveground and watch the manhole on both ends to secure our return or escape route. With our wolf's night vision, we were able to walk the terrain easily. Rats scurried around our feet and graffiti plastered the tunnel walls. With my pointer finger at my lips, I shushed everyone into silence. A couple feet away was the abandoned train cart that Michaels mentioned.

I shut my eyes and zeroed in on the sounds up ahead. I could hear a heartbeat ... two ... three ... four? I took a step back. He had called for reinforcements. I waved my hand so they would move back. If I could hear Logan and his goons from here, they would be able to pick up on us, too. When I felt we were far enough away, I huddled us into a group.

"Okay, there are more of them than there were earlier. I caught about four heartbeats, anyone else?"

"I counted seven," said one of the Lunas.

"He's not alone, but there can't be more than ten, which means our odds are still pretty good," I said.

"Are we supposed to fight them?" one of the Lunas asked. "I've never fought someone before."

I saw their faces transform from excited to concerned in a split second. Of course they didn't know how to fight.

The light bulb in my head flickered on. "You two." I pointed to a pair of Lunas. "Head to our escape pothole and get ready to help us out of here. The rest of you start looking for a weapon. Wood or any pipes lying around. And let's be real quiet, okay?"

Everyone went off in search of a weapon while Blu, Rachel, and I stayed behind to keep an eye on the train.

"Do you think he's in there?" Rachel asked.

"I'm not sure. I hope he is."

"What are you planning?" Blu wondered.

"The girls are afraid to fight, and I don't blame them. But we don't have time to give a quick lesson on using your wolf to defend yourself." I pulled out the lighter Lucian gave me and popped the cap to light a flame. "So we'll start a fire."

TWENTY MINUTES PASSED before everyone returned. I sent a few of them up top, especially the ones who were afraid, including Blu. I wasn't heartless. I knew I was asking a lot, but their mere presence spoke volumes. They wanted change and would fight alongside me to get it.

"This is a stealth mission," I whispered to the group of six that was left. "We need to find all entrances to the train and seal it off. They typically have handles, so wedge in as many pipes as you can to bar the door. If there's not a handle, you'll need to wolf out. I have faith in you all. We're just as strong as them."

"What about the windows?" Rachel asked.

"They're practically bullet proof; it will take them a long time before they'll be able to break through. By then, they might not have the strength to do it. Are you ready?"

When they all nodded, I knew it was now or never. Like the ninja team we weren't, we navigated our way to the train without being seen, which was easier said than done. Our footfalls made too much noise as we stepped on unavoidable gravel, but we stayed in the shadows. Anytime they heard us, one of the wolves would peek out the window but they didn't see anything. We were lucky they weren't on high alert. The closer we got, the more I recognized Logan's scent. As the girls dispatched to their assigned locations, I climbed the stairs up to the roof of the train while they secured the exits. I felt a heaviness in my abdomen that I couldn't name.

Logically, I knew what I was doing was wrong, and that it would elicit unknown consequences for many involved, including myself. For the first time, I was committing cold-blooded murder. I'd always been able to use the excuse of self-defense, but not after tonight. My rational brain knew this was a purely selfish act. I was reacting to what Logan exposed me to, as well as repaying the things he'd done in the past. I was functioning on pure revenge, not solely for the trampled rights of Lunas.

Once I got the okay from everyone, I turned the wheel of the overhead latch and unlocked the door. Roughly six pairs of wolf eyes zoned in on me as I poured the gasoline down below. Their shock only gave me a few seconds to work with, and my hands shook from nerves, anticipation, and overall fear as I locked in on Logan. I reached for the lighter in my pocket and dropped it below just as growls and canines flashed. They all ran to the nearest exits, and when that didn't work, they clawed and punched the windows. The fire blossomed faster than expected, and a flame came whooshing out of the roof opening. It threw me back a few feet, bouncing my head against the metal train shell. I shook my head to straighten my vision, and then shut the ceiling door with a resounding clang.

I hopped down from the train, not bothering to take the ladder, and backtracked to help the girls. I tried to tune out the cries of pain and agony that ripped through the cart and out into the tunnel as the smell of burned flesh escaped. The Lunas' resolve was deteriorating as I watched the ones in my immediate line of sight start to let go of the doors.

"What are you doing?" I gasped.

"I-I can't," one of them stuttered as she let go and ran toward the exit.

"Shit," I muttered as the door she'd been securing burst open. Huge flames curled outward as a body emerged. His clothes were tattered to almost nothing, and his skin was covered in red, blistering welts that looked like boiling water as it sizzled. Even with all of that, I still recognized who it was—Logan.

"YOU!" He pointed to me.

The rest of the Lunas scampered away from their positions and ran to my side. I pushed them behind me as if I could protect them. Who was I kidding? I could barely protect myself.

"Run!" I yelled, but no one so much as twitched a foot. "Run!" This time, I turned to face them. If anyone deserved to die, it was me.

"No." Rachel stood firm. "We're in this together."

Though I was grateful, I didn't have time to argue. Logan came for me. Though his moves were sluggish from his injuries, he was still strong. He tackled me to the ground and landed a few blows to my face before wrapping his hands around my neck.

"You stupid bitch! I should have had your ass when I had the chance. Couldn't stay away, huh?" he growled.

I froze in his grasp. Flashbacks of my experience at his hands flitted through my mind and I was paralyzed by fear. Rachel came up behind him quietly in a half shift, slashing her clawed hand at the nape of his neck and back. His hold on me loosened a fraction and I was able to buck out of his grip. Without even looking, he swatted Rachel like a bug and she went flying back against the wall with a thud. Another Luna jumped on his back, but he pushed her away before she could strike.

I jumped to my feet and half-shifted, my wolf giving me the strength I needed. I was able to land one good punch before he snatched my wrists and pressed me against the tunnel walls. The unchecked fire within the train blazed and expanded, hungrily feeding on the air. If we didn't move soon, we'd all die.

"I am the Alpha! You will respect—"

My canines protruded from my gums as I bit down on his throat and ripped, flesh and blood filling my mouth. His hands went limp and his eyes flickered once and went still and empty before he fell to a crumpled heap at my feet.

"You will respect *me*," I growled and smashed my boot over his lifeless face.

Number ten.

20

I thought I would feel different when it was all over. Better, like a weight would be lifted from my shoulders; that I wouldn't scrub at my skin to the point of blistering redness anymore, that I wouldn't flinch or cringe when someone breathed near me. The fact that I didn't made me angry—furious. This wasn't me. My insides were knotted as I walked into the warehouse with the rest of the Lunas, the sensation pushing me to the verge of throwing up. I didn't feel any better now than when I was being held captive by Logan.

"You all know what to do," I whispered as we entered the building. The seed was planted as the Lunas fanned out, and I walked in and made a beeline for Amy. She sat at a table on her laptop while Emma was close by, drawing.

"Ace!" Emma exclaimed and waved a sheet of paper, showing me what she was doing.

"What's up, kid?" I took her drawing with shaky fingers and quirked a brow as I looked it over. "Uh ... what is this?"

"That's you, me, and Roman. See his fangs and the blood? Oh, and there's Amy!"

I chuckled nervously. "Oh. That's nice."

"You don't like it."

Her face fell and I quickly tried to recover. "What? Of course I do! You're like the next Picasso."

Emma rolled her eyes. "I'm not stupid, and you're a horrible liar."

I sighed as I sat down next to Amy and watched as Emma scrapped the drawing and started over. Gripping the pencil tightly, she pressed the tip on the paper harshly, trying to make a straight line. The tip of her tongue peeked out while she concentrated.

"She's got you there," Amy laughed as she typed. "Lying is not your forte."

"Whatever. I'm an excellent liar. I could be a politician if I wanted," I smirked, earning a laugh from them both. Watching my reflection on Amy's laptop screen, I tamed my disheveled hair and straightened my shirt. I looked a mess. I cleared my throat. "Where's the boy toy?" I asked casually, searching for Jackson's hipster ass.

Amy typed away mindlessly on her computer. "He should be back any minute now. He went for a run before the full moon tomorrow."

"Why?"

"He's going to stay with me while you're all at the estate."

"Well ..." I hummed. "I'm not going either." I held my breath and waited for Amy to unleash her wrath. I wasn't sure how she'd react, but I had to stop taking advantage of the Pack. I couldn't be half in and half out. That meant shifting on my own.

Amy shrugged.

"That's it? You're not pissed?"

She sighed and turned to me. "I agree with you on this. If you choose to be a lone wolf, then by golly, be one. Its time you start figuring out how to live without the Brooklyn Pack. Without Bash and Jonah."

I nibbled on my bottom lip. The truth sucked, but I needed to hear it. I had to practice what I preached. Especially after what I just did, I had to put some distance between me and the Pack before everyone found out. Secrets didn't stay secrets for long.

"You're right, Aims," I muttered. "And I'm sorry about before. I know you've sacrificed a lot for me, and I haven't been appreciative enough."

"You're a sucky friend," Emma blurted.

"Mind your business, short stuff." I glared at her. Amy high-fived Emma. "Really?"

"You don't suck, Kenz ... *that* much." Amy giggled and stopped suddenly as she took in my appearance. "Dude," she pointed to my jeans, "is that blood?"

I zoned in on the splotches of dried blood and chuckled. "I went out for a hot dog and made a mess." I licked the pad of my thumb and swallowed an inward cringe as I tried to scrub the stain of Logan away. It wasn't the right time or place to fill Amy in on what happened. She would freak out and cause a scene I wasn't ready to explain.

I decided to change the subject. "Earlier, you said you stopped Ollie from flying to L.A. How did he find me?"

Amy eyed me in disbelief. "Kenz, if there was anyone who would be able to find you, it's Oliver Grey. With all his government connections, I'm surprised it took him a few months."

"How is he?" I wanted to call my brother and see him, but I didn't think right now was a good time.

"Ollie misses you, Kenz." Amy reached for my hand. "I told him you needed space to work through some stuff and didn't want to be bothered. He was hurt that you didn't reach out to him, but he tried to understand and said he'd leave you alone. He's been keeping tabs on you, but kept his distance."

"I miss him too, Amy," I admitted, wiping away a stray tear. "Do you think he knows about my adoption?"

"I don't know, babe, but either way, Ollie won't love you any less."

I nodded. If there was one thing I was certain of, it was that my brother wouldn't abandon me.

"Where have you been, anyway?" Amy asked. I was about to answer when a commotion from the second floor interrupted me. All we could see was blonde hair whipping back and forth as some wolves tried to keep blondie from leaving one of the rooms. "Chick fight?" my best friend muttered.

"I hope," I answered absent-mindedly as we watched, engrossed in the scene.

"Well, aren't you anti-feminism?" she chuckled.

"I believe in equality, but any other label is irrelevant to me. And whether it's a chick fight or a dick fight, I don't care. I just wanna see a fight." Anything was a better distraction than replaying the last two hours in my head.

"I'm going to kill her!" someone screeched.

I winced from the high pitch. "Why does that voice sound familiar?" Then I groaned when I realized who was losing their shit upstairs.

"She either realized she's never going to mate with Bash,"

Amy proposed, still staring as she played with her lip ring, "or you snuck into her room and put Nair in her face wash." She paused to look at me. "Which is totally plausible."

"I would never!" I admonished. "I would have put it in her shampoo. Duh!"

Amy shook her head, resigned. "You have criminal tendencies, my friend. Why you wanted to be a cop, I'll never understand."

"Oh, stop it!" I waved her off with a grin. "You're too kind."

"MACKENZIE GREY!" Vivian shrieked as she bolted down the steps.

"Plot twist," Amy mumbled. "Although I shouldn't be surprised."

"You!" V pointed at me as she moved in my direction. "You think you have it all figured out, don't you?" she said disgustedly.

My eyebrows wanted to shoot up to the sky in shock, but I schooled my features. "I'd like to think I do, but who knows?" I shrugged.

"*I* know!" V screamed. "I fuckin' know!"

"Whoa." I put my hands up in defense and stood from the table. "Language! We have children in the vicinity." I nodded toward Emma, who looked confused and had long forgotten her drawing.

Jackson bounded up the basement stairs, his eyes going straight to Amy as if he had a GPS tracking her. "What's going on?" he demanded, standing in front of his girlfriend protectively.

"This ... this *mutt*, she broke the law!" V screeched. Her mascara streamed down her cheeks, framing her blotched, red-rimmed eyes.

"A mutt?" I smirked. "Let's try to get a little more creative, V."

"What did Mackenzie do this time?" Jackson sighed.

I was taken aback. *Why was it that I was always to blame?* "Me? She's the one who just went psycho. I'm innocent in this."

V scoffed, "The Lunas are rebelling ... because of her!" I felt like I was getting tattled on in kindergarten. I wanted to point a finger right back and yell *'Nuh uh!'* But I was an adult. At least I tried to be.

Jackson growled, "Those are serious accusations, Vivian. Do you have anything to back up your claim?"

"Yes!" she yelled. "Ask them! Ask them to do anything for you and see what they do!"

Jackson's brown eyes met mine, conflicted. I didn't understand this reaction. It was as if he didn't want to test her theory. Did he already know?

"Viv—"

"DO IT!" she screamed at him.

His eyes flashed gold and she took a step back and bowed her head in submission.

"If anyone is rebelling, it looks like it's you."

She buried her face in her hands and bawled, and for a moment, I didn't understand her reaction. Why would rebellious Lunas make her bust out in an ugly cry? I expected her to be pissed. She wanted to be the Alpha Luna, and if there were none to control, then her title would be pointless. But she was sad—devastated—as if someone had died ...

I gasped, drawing the attention of everyone who had come to gawk. "You!" I whispered. "*You* were his informant, weren't you?"

Her eyes grew round as saucers, which was all the proof I needed. Logan admitted he had an insider feeding him information about me. I figured it was Drusilla, because let's face it, the shit he had on me was sort of public knowledge. But not someone from the Pack. I never thought it would be possible.

A range of emotions crossed V's face ranging from shock, denial, anger, and then resignation—the bitchy kind.

"So what if I did? You deserve everything you got and more!" she wailed.

My wolf awoke and a roar ripped from deep within my gut. I arched my back and lunged forth in a half shift: claws extended, canines out, my face scrunched up with wolf-like features. My eyes flashed silver. I couldn't think of a single thought or insult to say. I was livid. I was lucky when it came to the Chicago Pack. If the others hadn't rescued me when they did, who knew what tune I would be singing? But for her to wish that on me —or worse — and then take pleasure from it? It made me sick. I wouldn't have wished that on my worst enemy.

"Easy," Jackson said as he came between us. "Mackenzie," he warned.

Nothing he said mattered. What she did, or intended to do, was unforgivable.

"You and your mentality are part of the reason why Lunas live the way they do," I spit. "Why they are treated as nothing more than second-class citizens. Because you don't know what it means to stick together and defend your sisters, to stand up for each other instead of the dirty backstabbing and hatefulness. Your kind of poison is why you won't leave here alive," I huffed. My chest heaved up and down rapidly, all control lost.

"Mackenzie!" Sebastian's voice boomed. The growing crowd parted for him and he strode over with calculated precision, his sapphire eyes glowing in anger. "You will not lay a finger on her," Bash warned me.

"What I did, I did for the good of the Pack!" Vivian pleaded with Bash. "I know what she came here for, and why she returned to New York. Don't let her fool you, Sebastian. She came to destroy us all!" Her whole frame shook with barely restrained anger.

She was at the brink of exploding, and I wanted to poke the bear to see what nasty truths would arise. I was too curious. "How do you know Logan?" I growled. Lunas poked their way through the crowd to watch the exchange. A hurtful expression on their faces told me V's association with Logan didn't sit well with them.

"You killed him!" V lunged for me, but Jackson was there to hold her back.

A grin stretched from ear to ear as I admitted, "You're damn right I did."

Sebastian's glare snapped to me, but I didn't care. The cat was out of the bag, and whatever happened next would just have to be. I would take the consequences like a champ because Logan got what he deserved.

"What's it to you?" I asked. "Logan your side piece?"

She blanched. "You disgusting mutt! He was my *brother!*"

This time I couldn't hold back my shocked expression. I didn't see that coming. How the hell were they related? Well ... okay, maybe I saw it in their mutual cruelness, but Logan was worse. He was demented, whereas Vivian was just a mean girl.

"If only he had the chance to do what he planned, you wouldn't be walking around here like the *bastard* princess you are! King Alexander would take one look at you and throw you out like the trash you are!"

The mention of my supposed father stirred buried emotions within me, and I was no longer able to control my fury.

With unnatural speed, I vaulted onto the table and sprinted down to the end. I hopped over to the table behind V and jumped, landing a blow to the back of her head before anyone could stop me. The male Pack members rustled toward me as I attacked one of their own, but the Lunas stood in their way, growling at anyone who tried to come near me. Their canines snapped as they crouched in defensive positions, stunning everyone into silence.

My chest swelled with pride. This was what women were— warriors. It was time they started acting like them. They just needed a little nudge. They were stronger than they knew.

"Stand down!" Sebastian ordered the Lunas, but none of them wavered. Their growls only grew louder and more aggressive.

I bypassed Jackson, who was the only one close enough to reach me. I ducked under his arms and kicked him in the back. I didn't want to hurt him, but if he stood in my way ...

My clawed hand went straight to V's neck and I lifted her a few inches off the ground. "Why?" I demanded. "Why would you do that to me? What have I ever done to deserve your hate?" I implored.

Her red manicured nails scrabbled at my hand and wrist for release. She gasped vainly for air, but I wasn't letting her go. This was one tally mark I didn't mind adding to the list. I wouldn't lose sleep over her death.

Jackson wrapped an arm around my waist to pull me away, but I dragged her with me. My claws punctured her skin possessively; holding onto Vivian was like trying to take a bone away from a dog.

Jonah appeared in my line of sight, a needle in his hand.

"Let me goooo," I slurred within seconds of him stabbing me in the neck. My fingers relaxed and my body sagged against Jackson. The last I heard were the howls of the Lunas as I succumbed to the darkness.

Not again...

21

Multiple slaps in the face stirred me awake. I was dreaming of riding a unicorn over a rainbow with a bowl of Lucky Charms cereal waiting for me at the end. Don't ask.

"What ...?" I garbled as I tried to go back to sleep. "I'm hungry, let me just grab—"

"Mackenzie!" a deep voice whisper-screamed. "Stop thinking about food for once and wake the hell up!"

"But the leprechauns ...?"

"Fuck the leprechauns! You have to go," the voice pleaded as strong hands tugged at my wrists.

My eyes fluttered open and I was met with a fuzzy vision of Jackson. The beard gave him away. We were in a dark room and I felt too weak to turn on my night vision. My eyelids felt heavy.

"W-What's going on?" I stuttered, my mouth parched. My head flopped to the side where Jackson pulled at my wrist, which

I noticed was wrapped in chains. "Are you trying to get kinky?" I gasped, out of breath. "I don't think Amy would like it."

He growled. "Shut the hell up, Mackenzie."

"I can't shut up," I said. "That would be a miracle if I did."

Jackson grunted. "For once, we agree." With a snap, he yanked the chains that held me and I was free. Now that there was nothing to keep me upright, I started to sag to the floor. Jackson caught me.

"Whoops," I giggled.

"You should go on a diet," he grumbled as he stabilized me and attempted to free my other wrist. My head fell heavily onto his shoulder, too tired to hold it up.

"That was sort of mean," I whispered. "It kinda makes me like you more."

"You're in desperate need of a psychologist if that makes you like me." He released my other wrist and scooped me up.

"I totally agree with the shrink idea. I've got daddy issues, for sure."

Jackson had only taken a few steps when he halted at the sound of a metal door sliding open. "Shit," he sighed.

"Is it the shrink?" I asked.

"Shut up, Mackenzie."

Heavy footsteps resonated toward us, but I didn't have enough strength to lift my head and check who it was. I was out of commission. If my life depended on me doing anything but sleeping, I was fucked.

"Jackson, what the hell are you doing?" I recognized Jonah's voice. "Put her back!"

"I can't, brother," Jackson said, his chest vibrating against my ear as he spoke. "How can you stand there and do nothing? You know what the Summit will do to her."

"They will do no such thing. She is the King's daughter; leniency will be given. What she did was wrong, Jack, no matter how much I wanted to be the one to kill the bastard," Jonah growled.

"Leniency? How naïve are you? You're throwing her to the wolves!"

I chuckled at his analogy but couldn't move further than that. These were some heavy drugs they doped me up with.

"We will be there to protect her. She won't have to face them alone. Bash won't allow it."

Jackson scoffed, "You think Sebastian will have a say? Dad is full of empty promises, Jo. Wake the hell up already!"

"Why do you even care? I thought you hated her," Jonah asked. "Is it because of the human? Does she already have your balls so secure that she's making you do this?"

"Amy doesn't *make* me do anything," he growled.

"Except that thing with your tongue," I mumbled.

"I swear I'll drop you, Mackenzie," Jackson said, his voice laced with irritation.

"Put her back in the cage or I'll turn you in as well, brother. Don't make me do that."

It didn't take a genius to figure out that the brothers were locked in a stand-still. Once my slow mind started putting the clues together, I realized Jackson was trying to perform a jail break. If he was caught, that meant no one would be with Amy during the full moon. I had way too many enemies floating around to keep her unprotected. The easiest way to get to me was through her, and if V was able to relay that to Logan, who knew who he'd shared it with. I couldn't risk it. Even with my fuzzy, drug-addled mind, I knew what had to be done.

"Put me back," I whispered, all jokes forgotten. "Do as he says, Jackson."

"What?" He pulled me away a little to see my face. My eyes opened and I saw those soft chocolate browns that I missed seeing in Jonah. "You can't be serious!"

"As a heart attack."

"They'll torture you. They'll force you into a Pack," Jackson sputtered.

"What I did ... comes with consequences." I patted his bulky chest and squeezed one of his boobs. "These things are bigger than mine."

"Mackenzie, focus!"

"Sorry." I shook my head. "Consequences. I need to face them."

"But—"

"I know you feel like you owe me for saving you from the Skinwalker, but you don't. The best way to repay that debt is by taking care of our girl."

His eyes hardened, but he nodded. Jackson handed me over to Jonah, and with one last, reluctant look, he left the room. My head flopped onto the other Cadwell brother's shoulder and I gripped his flannel shirt. Breathing in his scent, I drowned myself in its familiarity. Things between us were so different from before. Secretly, I believed if I ever settled down, Jonah was the one I'd do it with. But things weren't that simple. They never were.

"You know I won't let anything happen to you, right?"

"Yes," I sighed.

"But for me to do that, we have to make sure we do things the right way. It's the only way to keep you alive."

I started to play with one of the buttons on his shirt. "And what's the right way?"

"The Summit. You have to go before them so they can rule on your punishment."

"What am I getting punished for?" I had a laundry list of misdeeds. I had to make sure they got it right and I wasn't taking the fall for someone else.

Jonah walked me back to my cell and laid me on the ground. The sound of rattling chains perked me up as he started to wrap them around my wrists again.

"For one, the murder of the Chicago Pack's Alpha, Logan St. James—"

"Oh, that was his last name? I guess he didn't live up to that, am I right?" I chuckled at my corny joke, but Jonah stayed quiet.

"Two, for the uprising of the Brooklyn Pack Lunas," he added quietly. His voice was a mixture of hurt and confusion, like he didn't understand why they would want to change the way things were. Was it that hard to believe in equality?

"Guilty as charged." I grinned lazily. "What about the Lunas? Are they okay?"

I straightened as I thought of Blu and Rachel. I prayed they weren't getting punished. I never asked them to defend me with Vivian. Our plan was simpler than that. Before taking any action, they were to reach out to other Lunas in different Packs and regions and start spreading the news about the upcoming revolution and the need to stand together. The Lunas of the Brooklyn Pack wouldn't be enough. This needed to be a worldwide effort. I hoped that whatever happened next didn't deter them from wanting change and seeking it.

"They're fine. My father gave Sebastian the option to let them off with a warning if he brought you to the Summit."

I sighed in relief. "That's great to hear. He did the right thing." And it was true. Bash knew I would be furious if they went down for my decisions. I talked a big game, but my subconscious was alive and kicking, and the guilt would have driven me mad.

"That's how he said you would react." Jonah secured my other wrist. "I guess he knows you better than I do."

"Jonah, this isn't a competition," I murmured. "Sometimes you're so blinded by your need to protect me that you don't think about what *I* want."

When he was done, he squatted in front of me and tipped my chin. The pad of his thumb caressed my bottom lip as his eyes stared into mine. "I'll always put your well-being before anything else. Even what you want. I care about you too much."

I shook my head and he let go. The drugs were wearing off and I could see much clearer. We were in a basement, and the smell of pine assaulted my senses. We were near, if not in, the woods.

"I don't like what you're becoming, Jonah. You're not the same person I met over a year ago."

His face fell and his lips parted as he sucked in a breath. I knew how he felt about me, but he needed to hear the truth. His obsession with me was becoming scary. Now more than ever, I understood the amount of danger I was in by being the bastard child of the King. Jonah's obsession stemmed from that wolf need to protect the ones you love—but goddamn, I couldn't live in fear, cowering behind him and Bash the rest of my life. It was what drove me to go after Logan. I refused to be a victim.

"One day you'll understand. Until then, I can wait." Jonah stood and walked out of the cage, shutting the door and clipping the lock. "Tomorrow night is the first full moon. Someone will be back to unchain you so you can shift."

"Does that mean we're at the estate?"

He nodded sadly, then turned and disappeared.

I FELL ASLEEP SHORTLY after Jonah left. By then the drugs had worn off, but the hangover crept in and I needed to sleep it off. It was impossible to tell what time it was, so when I awoke, I didn't bother trying to figure it out. My stomach grumbled with hunger, but my pride kept me from calling out for something to eat. They had locked me up for going after my attacker. I knew that was what they were pissed about, but not a single part of me regretted it. If I could go back in time, I would do it all over again, except this time I wouldn't get caught.

I was playing with the shoelace of my boots and singing "Bad Habit" by The Kooks—badly, I might add—when someone flipped on the light switch and revealed a staircase, proving that I was, in fact, in a basement.

Blu's curvy frame came into view as she carried a tray of food. If my muzzle was any good, it smelled like honey-glazed ham. My tummy grumbled again. I patted my belly comfortingly and attempted to stand. My legs were still wobbly and my arms felt like lead from the weight of the chains. I made my way to the front of the cage and hung my arms through the bars, my chains rattling against the metal.

"Is it visiting hours already?" I joked as I pretended to check my watch.

"Oh, Kenzie," Blu cried. "I'm so sorry!"

I waved her off. "What do you have to be sorry for? This isn't your fault."

"I know, I just wish there was something I could do."

"Well, you *could* feed me ..." I shrugged as I zeroed in on the tray of food.

"Oh! Of course!" She jolted and started to pass each item through the bars. A nice, meaty, foot-long sandwich, a bag of potato chips, an apple, and two bottles of water. I wasted no time in plopping down on the ground and tearing it apart. My wolf was cranky and starved. We weren't used to this kind of diet: the "no eating" kind.

"The girls have started contacting other Lunas. Many of them are interested in following the Freedom Princess," Blu whispered conspiratorially as she popped a squat in front of me.

"Freedom Princess?" I garbled with a full mouth.

"Yes. That's what they're calling you. A lot of them are excited after hearing what you did to Logan. He hurt many Lunas during his reign."

I nodded. "There are still others out there like him. He's not the only one."

"True," Blu said, "but it's a start."

I smiled. "Are you finally joining the Luna Revolution?"

She rolled her eyes. "Of course, Kenz. I'm still scared, but I'll be by your side one hundred percent."

"Cool." I took a hearty bite of the apple. "So ... what has you so scarred that you're hesitant to go against the Summit?"

She exhaled and looked behind her to the staircase—making sure no one was coming down.

"Next month will be six years since I ran away from the Pack," she started. "I was the Luna in charge of going out to buy groceries for the kitchen. During my many trips outside the warehouse, I always stopped by Starbucks and ordered one of those caramel frappuccinos. You know what I'm talking about, with the whipped cream?"

I laughed. "Yes, I know what they are."

"Okay, so when I checked out at the grocery store, I would ask for five dollars cash back and then stop by the coffee shop on the way back to the warehouse."

"You sneaky girl. That's genius."

She gave a sad laugh. "Yeah. They never checked my receipts, so I was able to get away with it for a while. Whenever I stopped at the coffee shop, there was a human barista who always took her break when I came in and we would sit and talk. Her name was Miranda. She was this fiery, passionate Hispanic girl with long, curly hair and almond-shaped eyes that closed anytime she laughed. And her laugh ... Gosh, Kenzie, her laugh was beautiful. Whimsical, sincere, and contagious."

I stopped eating as I watched Blu's eyes twinkle in the dim light of the basement. They glassed over with unshed tears, and the smile that stretched over her face made my heart hurt.

"You loved her," I stated.

She nodded as a single tear fell down her cheek. "But we're not allowed to mate with humans, much less ones of the same sex."

"What?" I gasped. I figured falling in love with a human was a no-no, but the same sex-thing? I didn't know why I was taken aback. Their rules were antiquated, so it shouldn't have surprised me.

"I didn't tell her about me—what I was. Instead, I made it sound like I was part of a cult. I found more reasons to go on errands, then I started to sneak out in the middle of the night to meet her. After months meeting secretly, she couldn't handle it any longer. She wanted more from our relationship, but I couldn't give her what she wanted unless I left the Pack. So that's what I did."

"Blu," I whispered, reaching for her clenched hands and holding on.

"It didn't take long for them to find me. I was stupid and sloppy, and overall just a naïve girl who didn't know much about the world. In a few weeks, the Pack tracked me down and brought me back. After having a small taste of freedom, I no longer wanted to be a Luna. I refused to work and do as I was told. And when I told them I was a lesbian," she whistled, "that started a whole shit storm."

"Well, I'll be damned. Did I hear you curse, Blu?" I giggled.

"Oh, hush, you're not the only one who has a potty mouth." She rolled her eyes.

"What did they do?" I asked, redirecting the conversation.

She gulped. "I was sent to the European Summit for reeducation. I don't want to talk about what happened, Kenz, I've tried to block it out."

"You don't have to tell me. I understand." I squeezed her hand. "What about Miranda? Did you ever see her again?"

Blu shook her head. "I'm no longer allowed to leave the warehouse unless it's during a full moon."

"Are you fuckin' serious?"

"It's okay, Kenz," she said, and my eyes widened. "I mean, it's *not* okay, but it is," she corrected. "I've spoken to Bash on many occasions, and he's been trying to get my privileges back from the Summit. It just takes a while. And no one wants to mate with me after that whole incident, so I'm sort of stuck."

"This is bullshit, Blu. I can't believe you've been living like this! God, I can't wait until we get your freedom back. Then you'll be free to be with whomever you want to be with."

Her tears spilled like a waterfall and she smiled. "Thank you, Kenz. You've given me hope. If anyone can do it, it's you."

I shook my head. "No. *We* can do it."

WHEN BLU LEFT and I was given a moment to myself, everything started to take its toll on me. My ancestry, the plight of the Lunas, my experiences with Logan. I wondered if I would be sent for reeducation and finally meet this mysterious King Alexander fella. Everyone talked about the sperm donor, but I hadn't heard a peep about the lady who gave birth to me. Maybe Vivian was right, and I *was* a mutt. Since the wolf gene was stronger than any other species, my other half could be human, for all I knew. It would explain my inability to be a Luna. I was a girl from the twenty-first century, a sometimes obnoxious millennial.

I was in mid rant with a fire ant about how the series finale of *Lost* was a complete let down, when the sound of multiple boots came thudding down the stairs. You knew it was bad if I was talking to insects. My jailers could have at least given me a babysitter to annoy—I mean talk to.

"Imaginary friend?" Sebastian said as he came into view, Jonah tagging along right behind him.

"Yes." I waved to the ant beside me as I laid flat on the ground. "This is Sawyer. We were discussing how we got screwed with that shitty-ass finale of *Lost*. I mean, who the hell even knows what it meant? Did they actually die? And if so, what the hell was the point of all seven seasons? They put me through all that stress for nothing!"

"I have no idea what you're talking about," Bash admitted as he unlocked the cage.

My head jerked up. "Have I done my time, Officer? Am I free to go?" I rested on my forearms and wiggled my eyebrows.

"No," he grunted. "The full moon is in less than two hours. We're unchaining you."

"Thank fuck. My arms feel like they weigh a ton. I had an itch on my nose hours ago, and I was too lazy to scratch it."

"Now you can," Jonah said as he unchained my left arm while Bash did my right.

As soon as I had a free hand, I rubbed my nose in the most unladylike fashion, with no regard to what I looked like doing it. I stood and dusted off my jeans. "So, where we headed?"

"*You're* not going anywhere." Bash started to walk out with Jonah. "The cage is big enough for you to shift. Should be familiar," he smarted.

I felt my face pale as all the blood drained from it. Did they expect me to cage the wolf—again? "W-What?" I stuttered. "You can't be for real."

"You're not allowed out of this cage until you have met with the Summit and they decide on a suitable punishment. Didn't Jonah already go over this with you?" Bash quirked a brow.

"Yes, but I didn't know I'd spend the full moon in a *cage!* You can't do this to me—you can't do this to *her!*" I argued, worrying for the sanity of my wolf. It had taken many full moons to tame my wolf. Caging her up again could bring me back to square one.

"You'll be fine, Mackenzie. In three days, the Summit will meet with you."

"But I won't be able to run!" A vein in Sebastian's neck twitched every time I spoke. "This isn't right and you know it!"

"Well, you should have thought of that before you *killed an Alpha!*" he roared.

I had to take a step back. "You're pissed because I killed that piece of shit?" I scoffed. I thought if anyone would understand, it would've been Bash.

"I'm pissed because you got caught," he growled.

"Well, next time don't go bangin' his sister," I muttered. Bash glared at me, his eyes flashing sapphire blue. "Where is Little Miss Sunshine, anyway?"

"Vivian is also awaiting a trial with the Summit. Don't worry, her treachery will not be overlooked," Jonah responded, trying to give me a comforting smile, the ghost of a dimple peeking out.

"Well, isn't that grand?" I said, my tone laced with sarcasm.

After a tense silence, Sebastian nodded toward me. "Shift," he ordered.

"Excuse me?" I said, taken aback.

"Shift. We're not leaving until you do."

"Why? When I feel the moon rise, I will."

"You won't, Kenz," Jonah said. "The walls are laced with silver.

You won't feel anything. It's why we're asking you. If not, the full moon will come and go, and you'll never shift."

Silver didn't kill wolves, but it made us weak. *So that's what was making me feel high ...*

I laughed. "Whatever." I tugged my shirt over my head. "What is this, some kind of torture room?"

They remained quiet. I was in the middle of pulling one leg out of my jeans when I froze.

"Wait ... *Is* this a torture room?"

"We use it to hold wolves that need to be contained. That is all you need to worry about." Bash snapped his fingers for me to hurry it along.

"Will I at least have some company?"

"No," Bash said. "After the third night, you'll be released under my custody until the meeting with the Summit."

Once I stood there in my birthday suit, I craned my neck left and right and stretched my tired arms. I shut my eyes and awakened the wolf. *It's time*, I whispered to her. My spine rippled against my skin as it accommodated my upcoming form. I no longer felt the pain of bones crunching and rearranging. My shoulders hunched over and I fell to my hands and knees. Before I knew it, my head snapped up toward Bash and Jonah, eyes glowing silver, and the wolf was free.

22

I paced.

It was all I could do in this ten-by-ten-foot cage. With silver threads lacing the room, I couldn't sense if daytime had come or not, so I stayed in my wolf form. The only semblance of information filtered in with the howls of the wolves from outside. The louder they became, the more I realized it might be the second night of the full moon. No one had come to check on me, and my jet-black fur bristled with annoyance. She wanted to go out and run. I kept promising myself that when this was over, we'd go for a real run, alone.

My claws scraped against the concrete floor with every step I took, and every so often I growled at no one in particular. I imagined I'd be pretty cranky after this whole ordeal. It might not be the wisest idea to stand me in front of the Summit right away. Who knew what kind of nonsense would come out of my mouth and land me in even bigger trouble than I was already?

In the midst of my musings, the door to the basement swung

open. I inched backward into the dark corner and camouflaged myself by shutting my eyes. My muzzle twitched, but I didn't recognize the scent of whomever approached. It was only one person from the sound of the footsteps, and I smelled ... cologne? The strong, heavy scent made me sneeze, effectively blowing my cover.

I opened my eyes and found a man standing in front of my cage. He wore a dark suit, no tie, and his white shirt had a few buttons undone at the top, showing a smattering of chest hair. But what surprised me was the pin on the left lapel of his blazer. It was gold ... the same Celtic triquetra tattooed on my hip. My eyes roamed over his clothes to his face, and his wolf-like features made me wonder: friend or foe? Just what Pack did this guy come from? He was clean shaven but older, maybe in his forties, with dark hair slicked back away from his face.

His clawed hands gripped the cell bars and he began to pull them apart. The metal whined as a gaping hole formed. I growled from the intrusion and spread my front legs wide, waiting for an attack.

"Mackenzie Grey," he announced, his voice gruff, but with an accent. Irish, possibly? "In the name of King Alexander MacCoinnich, you are hereby ordered to death for murder and high treason against the Lycans."

He put one foot inside my cell and I growled, snapping my canines as spittle flew from my mouth. *Death? Ordered by my sperm donor?* My disappointment and fear took a backseat, because there was no way I was dying in this cage. Not tonight, at least.

Just then, the sounds of frenzied barks distracted us from one another. It sounded like a pack of dogs, but ... it wasn't. Almost like an echo of howling. The intruder froze mid-step as two large wolves bounded down the stairs and charged at him. One had golden, honey-brown fur with bronze highlights, and the other was a dark gray like slate, but the eyes gave them away, glowing gold and sapphire. *Jonah and Sebastian.*

Bash's canines aimed for the Lycan's forearm. He sank his teeth into his flesh, growling as he pulled, while Jonah bit into his leg. They yanked the man backwards and I ran up to the cell bars, howling at them to stop. Once the suited man fell to the ground, they sank their teeth into his neck and blood spurted everywhere. I could feel a splash land on my bristly coat, and as I licked my muzzle, I tasted the metallic saltiness. Bash and Jonah didn't stop until the man was limp and lifeless.

My heart hammered in my chest so fast, I thought it would explode. They shouldn't have done that. Somewhere deep inside my psyche I knew their actions would trigger something for which we weren't ready. I howled, barked, and cried until I was out of breath and exhausted. The silver in the room made me weak and tired.

I'd been confined in my silver-laced prison for too long, so it affected me more than the other wolves. A cacophony of voices grew louder, creeping closer by the second, but I could no longer keep myself upright. As my wolf shut her eyes, all I saw was red. Blood red everywhere.

"MACKENZIE!" I heard my name, but it sounded far away. I felt high; drunk, even. My mind was foggy and my head felt dense.

"It's the silver, Jonah. She's been down here for a while."

"We need to go before they send more. They won't stop until she's dead."

"Mackenzie!"

I rose with a start. No longer in my wolf form, I gasped in a heady amount of air, yet still felt like I was suffocating. Pennies. All I could taste were pennies as I wiped my mouth with the back of my hand, but I was only cleaning it with more ... blood. *Ugh.* I spit and gagged.

"What the fuck?"

I looked around the room, my vision spotty, but I didn't want to wipe away what I was certain was more blood with a bloody hand. Both Sebastian and Jonah were on the ground, butt-naked, watching my reaction. They were also covered in crimson.

"What the hell happened?" I growled. All I remembered was the one man who came in, but as I peered around the basement, I saw piles of dead bodies scattered everywhere. The gore made my stomach turn and I had to swallow the bile that threatened to come out. Severed body parts, faces with wide open eyes, and the stench. Goodness, the smell was so pungent, I had no idea how they were able to sit there with such ease.

"What did you guys do?" I tried to stand, but my hand slid off the slippery floor and I tumbled back down.

"We did what we had to do," Jonah answered shortly.

"Was that the Summit? I thought I didn't have to meet with them until after the third full moon?"

"You were going to meet with the *American* Summit; we were visited by the Europeans," Bash said as he palmed his eyes. The vein in his neck throbbed like it was about to pop.

"W-What?"

"How did they find out?" Jonah asked.

Sebastian shook his head. "I don't know, but it's a massacre out there."

"Wait." I froze. "They didn't just come after me?"

"No," Bash said, a single tear rolling down his grimy face. "They came for *all* the Lunas."

I jumped up, almost slipping in the blood again, but managed to hold on to the metal bars. I reached for my dirty clothes, not even bothering with undergarments. Dressed, I slid through the hole made by my would-be executioner and exited the cage. Barefoot, I skated across the wet floor to the staircase.

"Damnit, Mackenzie, don't go out there!" Bash yelled as he and Jonah rushed to catch up with me.

I took the stairs two at a time and wrenched open the door. The sunlight streamed into the living room like a freakin' laser and I squinted, covering my eyes with my arm. I felt disoriented as I walked with no clear direction to where I thought the front door of the estate was. I tripped over something and fell. When I looked back to see what it was, I came face-to-face with Vivian's lifeless body. I screamed.

"Kenzie!" Jonah whispered as he gripped my arm and hauled me to my feet. I began to shake uncontrollably as I glanced down at Vivian. Half her body was in the hallway, and the other half was inside the doorway she had tried to escape.

"No, Jonah, where are they? Where's Blu?" I gasped.

"My father told us to stay downstairs, Kenz. We have to wait."

I pushed him off me. "Fuck that," I growled and ran, secretly pleased to be making such a mess in his father's house, leaving scarlet footprints on his white, polished floors. I went through a doorway and found myself near Charles' home office. From there, I headed toward the front of the house. In less than thirty seconds, I pushed out through the front doors and emerged into complete chaos.

Wolves howled in both human and animal form. They held onto loved ones who were now dead, cradling their lifeless bodies in their arms.

I bounded down the front steps, my head swiveling in every direction as cries of agony rent the air. My heart broke into a million pieces as I ran into the woods. My feet were sliced as they caught on rocks and branches as I sprinted, raising my nose in the air to find Blu's scent.

I found Rachel first. She was in wolf-form, lying limp on the grass. Her blonde fur was matted with blood, and one eye stared back at me, empty and devoid of life. I dropped to my knees in anguish, not daring to touch her.

"Mackenzie!" Bash yelled as he reached me.

"Get off!" I cried as he gripped my shoulders and pulled me up. "I have to find Blu!" My body shook with the force of a hurricane.

In an unexpected gesture, Sebastian tucked me into his arms, smashed my face into his chest, and whispered, "I'm so sorry, Mackenzie."

I hiccupped and cried louder. *This is all my fault.*

"Oh my God, Emma!" I pulled away. "Where is she? Oh God, please don't tell me!"

He shook his head. "Don't worry, she's safe. She stayed behind with Amy and Jackson."

"Blu ... I have to find her."

"No one survived, Mackenzie."

Jonah caught up to us just as I slapped Sebastian's chest, pounding my fists onto his chest over and over again. "Why didn't you protect them? You should have been there to help them!" I screamed as I wailed on him.

The Lunas were defenseless, just starting to grow the nerve to defend themselves. How could their Alpha and Beta abandon them at a time when they were most vulnerable?

Jonah tried to pull me away. "There was nothing we could do, Kenz."

"You could have fought!" I yelled. "Just like you did for me! They were part of your Pack!"

"You were our priority!" Jonah screamed back at me. "*You* come first!"

I pushed away from them both.

"We didn't realize what was happening until it was too late," Sebastian whispered, anguish marring his chiseled features. "We came to you first when we saw them, but we didn't realize they were coming for all of you."

Just then, a whistle rang out through the woods. Bash and Jonah perked up.

"It's Charles," Sebastian stated.

We ran back toward the estate, meeting wolves from an assortment of Packs along the northeast carrying bodies to the driveway.

"Blu!" I screamed as I saw a wolf carry her out of the woods. Her head hung over his forearm and her eyes were open and fogged over. I ran to her and tried to rip her out of his arms, but he was strong. I didn't recognize him before, but up close I realized it was one of the captains from the Brooklyn Pack —Mohammad.

"She's gone," he said, his voice cold and harsh. Those black eyes drilled into me accusingly as he pushed past me with her cradled in his arms. I didn't follow. He knew it was my fault.

Someone I didn't recognize handed Bash and Jonah a pair of shorts for them to cover up. Charles descended the front steps once he saw us.

"How the hell did they find out, Charles? Who gave the order?" Sebastian demanded. His blue eyes were ablaze with fury, his muscles flexing in aggravation as he clenched and unclenched his fists.

Charles handed a folded sheet of paper to Bash as his brown eyes watched me shrewdly, with disdain. I was sure he blamed me. That was okay though, because I blamed me, too.

Sebastian closed his eyes wearily after he read the contents on the page and passed it to Jonah.

"The King?" Jonah exclaimed, looking to me.

"Your father," Charles began, "was the one who gave the direct order for your death, as well as for all the Lunas involved in your little revolution. Are you happy now? You caused the death of many innocent Lunas, which my Pack has now lost!"

Bash put out his hand to stop Charles from coming near me. The Alpha glared at him. "And you two," he spat. "What you did, going against the Summit ... not even *I* can get you out of this one. You killed a dozen of their men just to protect *her*!" Charles pointed at me with disgust.

"You expected us to let them kill her? She was in a goddamn cage, defenseless and weak because of your silver!" Sebastian roared. "You fuckin' prick!"

It was the first time I'd ever heard Sebastian curse. Jonah stepped between his best friend and his father.

"Bash!" he yelled. "This is not his fault. The *Summit* failed us, not *him*."

"He's part of the Summit!" Sebastian shouted. "This has gone too far, Jonah! I can't follow these laws anymore. They crossed the line."

"What are you saying?" Jonah asked. Like everyone else who waited with bated breath, I was curious to find out what Bash was freaking out about. I'd never seen him lose control like this. He always trained his emotions, but he was obviously at the breaking point.

"I cannot hear what comes out of your mouth next," Charles said as he pointed a finger at his Alpha-Beta.

I tuned out their argument as my mind swam with the guilt and heartbreak of losing my friend and causing the deaths of countless others. Blu didn't deserve this. She didn't even want to go against them; I made her. I forced her hand. And then to find out that the King was the one who ordered my death? How could I even begin to process that? I didn't want to meet him or have anything to do with him, but it felt like a stone dropped in my stomach as the realization that he didn't give a damn weighed me down.

"Where is the Summit meeting?" I blurted in the middle of their argument. "Where the fuck are those bastards meeting?"

23

Against Charles' wishes, the three of us rushed back into the city. Without taking time to grab clean clothes or take a shower, our skin still coated in dried blood and gore, we headed to The Plaza Hotel in Manhattan. We were just entering the city when I borrowed Jonah's phone and dialed Amy.

"Hello?" she mumbled with sleep still in her voice.

"Amy!" I screamed, my voice hoarse from all the yelling and crying.

"Oh my gosh, Kenz! Are you okay?"

"Yes, why?" I asked, confused.

She sighed. "This guy showed up at our apartment in the middle of the night! Jackson—" She paused. "Jackson took care of him," she whispered.

I closed my eyes. If they went to our apartment, it meant they were either after Emma or Amy, or both. They wouldn't get away with this if it was the last thing I did. "I'm sorry, Aims, I'm so, so sorry. Are you okay? Were you hurt?"

"No, I'm fine. Jack smelled him before he busted through the door. It was just scary."

"It was the European Summit, Amy."

"What? Jackson said your trial wasn't until tomorrow!"

"I was told the same," I said. "Is Jackson near you? Put me on speaker."

"Okay," she murmured, and I heard some rustling in the background. "Alright, you're on speaker."

"Mackenzie, are you okay?" Jackson asked. "Where's my brother?"

"He's with me, but," I paused and took a deep breath, "they came for us last night—for the Lunas. Jackson, they killed all of them."

I heard the sound of glass shattering and Amy's gasp.

"What about Blu, Kenz? Is she okay? She has to be okay!" Amy cried into the phone.

I hiccupped. "I'm so sorry, Amy."

"Where are you?" Jackson growled.

"You guys need to pack and get out of the apartment *now*. I don't have time to explain everything, but I will soon. Amy, do you remember the storage unit I used to shift in? The one in Queens?"

"Yeah," she sniffled.

"Pack whatever you can and meet us there in two hours. Take Emma to Roman. Make sure you tell him to drive to California and don't look back. I'll be in touch with him as soon as it's safe. Fill Lucian in on what's going on."

"What *is* going on, Kenz?" Amy asked.

I stared at Sebastian through the rearview mirror from the

back seat. He nodded, his eyes seething with the same anger I felt. "We're going after the King."

WE DIDN'T BOTHER to park the car anywhere since we planned to ditch it. We rolled up in front of The Plaza Hotel, leaving the engine running. Shocked gasps escaped the hotel guests and bellhops as we climbed out looking like a bunch of serial killers and rushed inside. We were drawing unwanted attention, which meant we had to hurry. Security called out to us, but Sebastian knew where to go and how we could ditch the employees. We darted up the stairs to the fourth floor, running on pure adrenaline. I couldn't even appreciate the architecture of The Plaza, a place every little girl dreamed of going because this was where the children's book character Eloise lived.

We came out of the stairwell and made an immediate right. The Summit was meeting in the Rendezvous Suite. We made a left and ran into the first set of wolves protecting the Summit leaders. We half shifted and went straight for their necks. I left Bash and Jonah to deal with those two and ran ahead, smacking into another pair just around the corner. I kneed the first one in the stomach, hunching him over to my level as I wrapped my arm around his neck and snapped it. His partner punched me in the ribs and slashed at my back, but I was already completely numb and didn't feel a thing. That was the most dangerous part. I clawed at his face and tackled him against the wall, slashing his chest over and over again until he slid down the wall in a puddle of blood. I was no longer keeping count—my kill list be damned.

Bash and Jonah caught up to me and we ran into one more

wolf, taking him down easily before we stopped in front of the French doors that led to the suite. Bash and Jonah stood on either side of me, all of us breathing hard.

"I want to know who it was!" a voice inside yelled as I kicked open the doors into the conference room.

I quickly scanned the layout as multiple eyes zeroed in on us. Fewer than ten Alphas were seated around a conference table with assorted snacks and coffee laid out. The room looked like a lame board meeting instead of an assembly of the highest-ranking leaders in the American Summit.

"What is the meaning of this?" one of them demanded. He was an older man with a round paunch and a white beard. "This is a private meeting."

I growled and flashed my silver eyes.

They gasped. Their chairs screeched as some of them stood from their seats.

"You want to come after me? That's fine. But to go after my friends? Innocent beings who didn't deserve to get slaughtered? You should have made sure you killed me, because now I'm coming after all of *you*."

Their eyes widened and shifted uncomfortably to a video screen situated at the end of the table. The logo on the corner told me it was through Skype.

A man sat there, wearing a dark suit similar to the one my hit man from last night wore. With the now-familiar gold pin on the lapel of his blazer, I didn't need an introduction. The gray eyes that pierced me in place told me who he was.

I stilled as I soaked him in. His black hair flowed in neat waves down his neck and was combed back, with a single, unruly strand curled over his forehead. Threads of white streaked his hair, but it disappeared when the light hit. His jawline was sharp, his cheek bones were high, and the wrinkles at the corners of his eyes were deep, but he was still handsome. And we also looked too much alike.

He was just as shocked to see me, though I wasn't sure if it was because of the distressed state I was in or the fact that my pale gray eyes were all the DNA testing he needed to know I was his.

The growls from the assembled Alphas in the room made me snap my attention back to them. As they stood and prepared to attack, I realized I didn't care. They could hit me with their best shot, because I knew I would make it out of there alive—not them.

I was tired of running. I was tired of fearing the faceless people who made these outrageous laws. They may have killed the Lunas from the Brooklyn Pack, but I hadn't been lying low this past year. I'd made powerful friends who owed me a lot of favors. It was time to collect.

"You!" I pointed to the screen, shaking myself out of the staring contest. "I'm coming for you next."

The shackles were off.

I won't be *caged*.

AFTERWORD

If you or someone you know has been a victim of sexual abuse, there are ways to get help. Find resources, tips, and immediate help at http://rainn.org/ or call 800.656.HOPE (4673) to be connected with a trained staff member from a sexual assault service provider in your area. International information available as well.

ABOUT THE AUTHOR

Join my Facebook group, **Karina's Kick-Ass Reads** to learn more about future projects.

Reviews are very important to authors and help readers discover our books. Please take a moment to leave a review. Thank you!

ACKNOWLEDGMENTS

They're many people to thank for the release of my fifth novel. My family and friends who have been more than supportive in my writing venture—thank you so much!

Thank you to my best friend and award-winning poet—Daniella Brooks—who wrote the poem for Mackenzie's vision quest. With very little direction, you were able to write exactly what I wanted to convey. You're a genius! And of course I owe you for all the late night phone calls, and IHOP visits every time I freaked out about this book. You're a saint.

To my cover designer, Laura Hidalgo with Beyond Def—the patience you must have to deal with me is something that not many have. I made you change the cover multiple times and even though you almost quit on me, you pulled through and continue to deal with my diva antics. Someone better give you an award!

My author besties, H.D. Gordon and Janelle Stalder—where have you ladies been all my life?! If there is anyone to thank, it has to be these two who motivated me and texted me every day to keep writing. And even when I barely wrote a few words, you both still told me what a good job I did. Your encouragement and friendship is something I have been truly blessed with. Thank you!

And last but not least, my readers. To the hardcore Mackenzie Grey fans, I hear you. I read your emails, comments, and messages. I think the hardest part about CAGED was making sure I didn't disappoint you. You're all so passionate about Kenzie and I love it! Thank you for loving her too.

READ ON FOR A SNEAK PEEK AT

ALPHA (Mackenzie Grey #3)

ALPHA

In the wise words of Eleanor Roosevelt, "You must do the things you think you cannot do."

I never thought I would be able to kill the man who gave me life, but here we were. Those words fueled my need to push forward, to aim my finger at the screen and threaten his life, because I couldn't let him get away with what he did.

"I'm coming for you next," I growled.

Gray eyes stared back at me with mixed emotions: shock, confusion, and...tenderness? His face morphed to stone as he watched my every move. The wrinkles at the corner of his eyes smoothed, and his sharp jawline ticked with unspoken words.

Sebastian, Jonah, and I were surrounded by the American Summit since we had barged in on their meeting. We were soaked in blood from head-to-toe and I didn't care that we ruined the carpet. The Plaza Hotel could bill the King—it was the least he could do for the blood that was already on his hands.

"This is a private gathering!" one of the Alphas across the

room exclaimed. He was younger than most of the other Summit leaders, average height with a beefy build—his neck red with a thick vein pulsing. "You are out of control! This is why we have laws for lone-wolves. They cannot be trusted or civilized!" he yelled. The others around him nodded in agreement.

I gave a hysterical laugh—the kind of laughter that escapes when you're at the brink of losing your goddamn mind. I was running on pure adrenaline. The moment I stepped foot in New York City, I'd been hunted by other Packs, accused of murder by the humans, and attacked in a manner that gives me nightmares. Too much happened in the past few days and I hadn't slowed down, not once.

"I'm out of control?" I said and looked to Bash and Jonah on either side of me. Their stares were full of concern for my outburst. "You're damn right I'm out of control," I glared at the Alpha who questioned me and took a step toward him. "You think you can come after me and my friends, slaughter them like cattle, then expect me to be civilized? You're crazy!"

"We didn't kill the Lunas!" the young Alpha yelled.

"Then who did?" Sebastian barked, his blue eyes ice-cold. The hurt of what had been done to his Pack was clear on his face. The flare of his nostrils, the creases on his forehead, and the trembling of his upper lip—he was attempting to keep his inner wolf at bay. His disheveled ink-black hair tainted with splotches of dried blood.

"Yer absolutely stunning," the Kings voice heavy with an accent and full of wonder. "Ye look just like her. It's uncanny," he whispered. King Alexander MacCoinnich stared in amazement and it distracted me from the real issue at hand. My relationship with my adopted father wasn't strenuous. I didn't have any

ALPHA

childhood horror stories, yet there was a distance between us that I could never pinpoint—either way, I knew he loved me— that I never doubted. But as I stood there, looking at the live video chat with King Alexander, it was the first time I'd ever felt that warm feeling in my gut I never had with my father. A strange urge took over, and I wanted him to like me—even though I was probably having the opposite effect at the moment.

"Sir, I understand she is your...spawn, but what she has done cannot be overlooked. An example needs to be made of her to keep lone-wolves *and* Lunas in check," an Alpha to my right said. He was older with such striking features, I couldn't help but stare. He had a neatly trimmed black goatee and piercing black eyes that drilled me with pure, unadulterated hatred.

"There will be. No one," the King glared at me, "will be excused from the law."

The Alpha smirked. "Death is the only punishment I see that fits the crime."

"I will decide what is fit!" the King roared.

"But—"

"Shut yer geggie, Malcolm. The only example I'll be making is of ye if ye keep at it. Yer comments have been noted."

I turned to Jonah and whispered, "Why does he sound like a leprechaun?"

He snorted. "Your father is Scottish, not Irish. Don't let him catch you saying that. They're real sensitive about it."

"Noted," I murmured and looked back at Malcolm. I could see steam coming out of his ears. "Not a fan?" I asked him, more serious than sarcastic.

"Not at all," he glared. "You're careless, crass, and everyone around you dies because of it. How many others will you infect before you realize you're an abomination?"

I was struck silent. The fierceness behind every word he spoke was a stab in the gut. Something deep within me—no matter how ridiculous it sounded—had me questioning myself. All those Lunas died because of me. It was a truth even I knew better than to bury. My rash behavior since I returned to New York City caused a chain reaction of events that could have been avoided if I had only *listened*. My desperation and fear got the better of me and I was now left to deal with the aftermath.

"Bite yer tongue, Malcolm!" the King exclaimed. "This goes for all of ye, I will nae stand for disrespect or plans for action unless I command—"

"She killed my son!" Malcolm yelled.

All the pieces fell into place.

"You're Logan's father..."

"*And* Alpha of the Mid-west," he snarled.

My chest heaved up and down in rapid motions, at the brink of an anxiety attack. I'd never had one before, but I was certain this was what it felt like. My fists clenched and unclenched at my sides, trying to keep them from wrapping around his throat.

"What your son did to me—"

"You deserved!" he slammed his fists on the conference table.

The pounding stirred me into action as I leapt onto the table, but before I had a chance to attack, Malcolm gripped me by the neck, slamming me down on the glossed oak. My head bounced against the wood and my vision dimmed. He had me pinned as I stared into obsidian eyes that now looked all too familiar. I shook. The growls cut through the hammering of my heart and I was able to recognize Bash and Jonah's snarl.

"Malcolm!" the King roared but his grip on me tightened.

"You killed him and Vivian—my only two children. They're dead because of you!" Malcolm cried, his eyes wild with hate.

"They deserved it," I choked out. If he was going to kill me, an apology wouldn't be my last words.

I gasped for air as he was ripped off me, his claws scraping the sides of my neck. I clutched my chest as I sat upright. Sebastian restrained him against the wall, his canines snapped at his face—a warning and a threat. Jonah was at my side, helping me off the table.

"You alright?" he asked as he tucked me under his arm.

I only nodded. I couldn't speak, not without my voice shaking.

"Henry," the King called out. "Escort Malcolm out of the room and seize control of his Pack until further notice."

"Sir!" Malcolm exclaimed.

"Enough! I am King—ye listen to me!" Even with thousands of miles apart, the fierceness of an Alpha—a King no less—thundered throughout the room.

Malcolm stilled, his face paled as he stopped thrashing against Sebastian. His pitiful eyes fell on The King and then to me.

"You're a cancer," he blanched.

"No, yer an eejit for defying my orders."

Henry, one of the quieter Alphas hanging in the back, took hold of Malcolm who didn't resist. He motioned another Alpha over to help escort him out of the room. I didn't give Malcolm a second glance as he passed. He spat at my feet but I didn't dare look at him. I wouldn't let another person in the St. James family affect me ever again.

"As for the rest of ye, no one lays a finger on her, unless I say so. Understood?"

"Yes sir," the Alphas murmured, giving the King a slight bow.

I glanced at the King who was once again watching me. On his dark suit sat a gold pin with the Celtic triquetra—an exact replica of the tattoo on my right hip that shields me from harmful magic. I fidgeted, confused by the rage within me and the swell of emotion from his protection. I couldn't care for him, I didn't know him. He was a stranger and a monster in my book and I needed to tread carefully.

"Now what to do with ye," he tapped two fingers on his chin as his steely eyes roamed over me. "I cannae let ye go after what ye done. Why did ye kill Malcolm's boy?"

I frowned as I looked up at Bash. He nudged me to answer but all the confidence I had when I stormed in had waned. My throat closed up and I wasn't able to speak with the man on the screen.

"Your highness," Bash began, his voice a rumble of dryness, "Mackenzie has been attacked by not only wolves, but the Fae as well. They had been contracted to obtain her."

The King ran a hand through his black hair that stopped just above his neck—one unruly strand curled over his forehead. "I asked about Malcolm's boy—an Alpha—not anyone else."

Sebastian's nostrils flared, his upper lip snarling. I could only sink into him, knowing that he too felt the hatred that was consuming my soul—a darkness so damning, I feared what would become of me if I let it spread.

"He attempted to violate your daughter in the worst way imaginable," Sebastian gritted through clenched teeth. There was a pause in the room as the Summit avoided looking our way. I glanced up at the King, angry that I was such a coward for feeling ashamed and tarnished. It didn't matter if he looked at me any different—I shouldn't have cared, but all I saw was the flash of silver in his eyes as they fell on me, trailing over my body as if he could see any evidence of the claims being made under the coat of dried blood on my skin.

"That wee ol' lass killed Logan?" he asked, the sternness in his features unreadable.

The Summit nodded. "With the help of the Lunas, she killed him and a few of his Pack members."

"Aye," the King murmured. "Were ye meeting today to place punishment?"

Everyone looked around the room for an answer but they all seemed stuck, as if scared to tell him the truth.

"Yes," I croaked. "I was supposed to receive sentencing for my crimes...until last night's massacre."

His eyes narrowed as he observed me. "And ye think it was me, aye?"

"They were your men. What do you think?"

"I didnae order this atrocity, but ye have my word I will find out who did."

A renowned sense of confidence enveloped me and I took a step toward him. "Your word means nothing to me."

"Miss Grey!" one of the Alphas scolded. I snarled in his direction, flashing my silver eyes. The Alphas gasped, taken aback by my brashness. Lunas weren't allowed to establish dominance—but I wasn't like most Lunas.

"Mackenzie," Jonah warned. "Don't take such liberties."

"Yer lack of respect for our laws in unacceptable," the King said. "Where are my guards?" he asked the Summit.

Everyone turned to the door as Henry reentered the room.

"They're dead. The guards are all dead," he said as he walked in with blood on his hands.

King Alexander's eyes flashed again and I steeled myself for whatever wrath came my way.

"Seize them," he growled. The Summit encircled us, giving us no way out.

"Another silver cage?" I snarled. I didn't care anymore. If I was going down it would be in a blaze of fury avenging the deaths of my friends. If the King didn't lock me up, I was sure Charles Cadwell would.

The King paled. "What? Who put ye in a silver cage?"

I turned to The Summit. "You're looking at them."

The Alphas winced as I tattled on them. If I hadn't been locked up, I could have saved my friends.

"S-She killed an Alpha! Started a rebellion! We were following your laws, your highness," a Summit member exclaimed in their defense.

I rolled my eyes. Even the King knew he couldn't get out of that one. He couldn't say I should have gotten special treatment.

"And how long have ye all known she was my kin?" the King cornered them. Checkmate.

Jonah cleared his throat. "Over a year, sir. Our apologies," he said.

"Who are ye?"

"Jonah Caldwell, Beta of the Brooklyn Pack—son of the Alpha of the Northeast." His milk chocolate eyes shone against the splotches of crimson across his angelic face. If he smiled, I wouldn't have been able to see his dimple.

"And ye?" the King motioned to Bash.

"Sebastian Steel, Alpha of the Brooklyn Pack."

He nodded. "Ye both aided in the massacre of my guards—with a lone-wolf—regardless of yer titles?"

"Yes," both of them responded in unison, not missing a beat.

"Aye. The three of ye will be flown to Scotland to await a tribunal. Ye will pay for what ye have done."

Bash and Jonah's breath hitched as everyone's attention fell on me. I walked to the screen, no I stomped over to the King. I hadn't escaped one domineering Pack to be controlled by another.

"No," I objected. The room quieted. "We're even. You killed mine and I took out yours. An eye for an eye."

The Kings gaze narrowed. "If I say run, ye run. If I say jump, ye jump. Ye follow my laws and ye do as I say, lassie. Ye willnae leave this room unless I say so."

"You son of a bitch—"

"Mackenzie," Jonah scolded but I ignored him.

"By blood yer part of my Pack whether ye agree or nae, which means I give yer punishment!"

"*Part* of your blood," I corrected. "Don't forget I'm your illegitimate offspring. And I'm not in anyone's Pack—ever."

The King's face flamed crimson, his embarrassment evident. "Yet my Pack will be the one that decides yer fate. I'd fall in line if I were ye—if ye want to live."

"I want to find out who killed the Lunas. After that, you do what you want. I don't care anymore."

The King nodded and waved to an Alpha. "Escort them to the airport, I'll have a plane waiting."

My eyes bulged and alarm took over. Hands clutched at my arms and I slammed into someone's chest. I thrashed against their hold, Bash and Jonah doing the same but we were outnumbered—by Alphas no less.

"You do this and my human family won't stop until I'm found!" I shrieked. "You don't think I have a back-up plan in place? You're dead, all of you!" It was a bluff.

"Stop," the King ordered. "What are ye ranting about?"

"I have a messenger ready to deliver the truth about everything if I don't return. The truth about me, you, this whole shitshow. And it's all on video," I smirked. I didn't have shit, but the one rule all supernaturals lived by was to keep their secret from humans. Maintaining their existence hidden was top priority and blowing the lid was the perfect threat.

"What about a compromise?" Bash suggested and I whirled on him. I wasn't his to bargain with.

"Are you out of your—"

"Just listen," he demanded and turned to the King. "Give her time to get her affairs in order, to see her family and assure them she's okay. Let Jonah and I bury our dead. We may not return, so grant us this one opportunity and then we will do as you say," Bash said. His eyes pleaded with me to understand. I didn't know where he was going with this but I'd follow suit. This was the time to stay united.

I swallowed my complaint.

The King contemplated the suggestion and after a brief moment he nodded.

"Aye. Bury yer dead and get yer affairs in order. And donae think about running. I will be watching yer every move."

"Thank you," Jonah said as Bash nodded in appreciation. I didn't say shit.

Henry chose this moment to cut in as he tucked away his

phone. "Sir, Malcolm is being escorted out of the city. Where is he to be taken?"

The King's features hardened. "Feed him to the wolves," he growled.

"S-Sir?" Henry questioned in confusion. The other Alphas froze, not understanding either.

"All of the St. James family," the King said. "I want them gone and a list of his successors sent to me by morning."

"But your highness," one of the Alphas attempted to argue.

"Would ye like to join him, Wilson?"

"No," Wilson shook his head and his eyes fell to the carpet.

I didn't understand what was going on, but I was sure what would happen to the St. James family wasn't going to be good. I pitied them. Although the ones I'd met so far had been horrible people, I didn't want to assume their whole family was too.

"You can't punish all—"

"Henry," the King interrupted, ignoring my protest. The Alpha nodded and left the room once again to carry out the order.

"This is a warning to ye all. I am *the* Law. Make sure yer Packs hear it loud and clear, aye?"

The Alphas bowed—including Sebastian and Jonah.

Those hard gray eyes turned back to me. He straightened in his seat and adjusted the lapels of his blazer before he said, "I'll give ye two weeks."

He ended the Skype call and the screen went black.

It wasn't a suggestion, it was an order.

I was going to Scotland.

ABOUT THE AUTHOR

Karina Espinosa is the Urban Fantasy Author of the Mackenzie Grey novels and The Last Valkyrie series. An avid reader throughout her life, the world of Urban Fantasy easily became an obsession that turned into a passion for writing strong leading characters with authentic story arcs. When she isn't writing badass heroines, you can find this self-proclaimed nomad in her South Florida home binge watching the latest series on Netflix or traveling far and wide for the latest inspiration for her books.

For more information:
www.karinaespinosa.com

ALSO BY KARINA ESPINOSA

Mackenzie Grey: Origins Series

SHIFT

CAGED

ALPHA

OMEGA

Mackenzie Grey: Trials Series

From the Grave

Curse Breaker

Bound by Magic

The Last Valkyrie Trilogy

The Last Valkyrie

The Sword of Souls

The Rise of the Valkyries